Love and Squalor

JESSICA SCOTT ROMANO

*For those of us who still dare to hope for a better world –
and actually go out and do something about it.*

"Make it extremely squalid and moving," she suggested.
"Are you at all acquainted with squalor?"
I said not exactly, but that I was getting better acquainted with it,
in one form or another,
all the time.

-J.D. Salinger, "For Esmé – With Love and Squalor"

One

"Hey, White Girl!"

"Hey, DeAndre..." I said with a sigh. Marcus giggled as I locked the rusty door behind us and we stepped out into the small alley behind the YMCA building. I had been working there for six months, but everyone I met refused to learn my real name. I was twenty-six years old – hardly a "girl" anymore – and I was certainly not the only white person in the (admittedly predominately black) neighborhood, but something about me seemed to scream "STEREOTYPE!" to the locals.

"How the kids treatin' ya today?" asked DeAndre, rearranging his nest of old newspapers and ratty blankets. He was homeless, and had been for fifteen years, but every time I offered to help him carry his things to the shelter a few blocks away, he just laughed and said "white girls..." like I was a grown woman believing in fairy tales.

"The kids are treating me fine. It's the parents that are giving me trouble," I replied, and Marcus giggled again. He was a chubby little guy; just six years old and already almost as heavy as I was. He looked like a little Buddha statue, with squinted eyes and an enormous smile full of missing baby teeth, and his skin was as dark as crude oil. He hardly spoke a word – he just giggled, as if everything in the world was delightful, and I couldn't help but love him.

What I *didn't* love was his mother. In the past six months, she had come to pick him up from my after school care class twelve times. I had offered to walk him home once, when she had called to tell me she had company at her house and "just couldn't get away," and ever since then, regardless of how many notes I sent Marcus in the house with, or how many voicemails I left her saying otherwise, she seemed to think it had become an established routine.

So, once again, I was holding Marcus' plump little hand as we made our way to Woodlawn Avenue, the spooky, halogen-lit street in the center of what many of the borough's residents called "The Wasteland."

Although it was 7:00 p.m. and twilight was quickly fading to full, early October darkness, the area was buzzing with activity. There was a strange mixture of "day people" and "night people" milling around: tired-looking Indian men selling the last of the day's smelly fish from the trunks of their cars, scantily clad prostitutes taking their places near the gas station and Lowman's Hotel on 6th Street, and a junkie on every corner, each in various stages of dead-eyed euphoria.

To be honest, I didn't mind a little company as I traversed the minefield of ethnic and moral diversity. I had been living in Luthertown Heights for almost half a year, but I didn't think I would ever get used to the aggressiveness of the squalor. Everyone I saw seemed to be crying out for help in some way. Some, like DeAndre, were homeless. Others were destitute, and had turned to hooking and dealing to find money to live on. Some were addicted to drugs ranging from heroin to crystal meth to some combination of both (Luthertown Heights had more strains of drugs than I had names for), and yet still others were just weary, down-on-their-luck miners or fishermen or fruit vendors who had long ago given up on any dreams they might have once had for doing better.

It was depressing, to be frank. It was a cesspool of the forsaken, and my heart cried out for each and every one of them. There was no hope to be found in Luthertown Heights – except in the faces of the children.

Back in my hometown of Louisville, Kentucky, forty minutes away and twenty years into the future, I had been a sixth grade teacher at a private school. I had worked there for four years, right out of college... and had hated every single second of it. I had had so much love and knowledge and enthusiasm to share with my students, but they hadn't wanted any of it. Aside from six or seven boys and girls, they had been spoiled, pretentious, irredeemable little brats, all of them. They had cared more about lipstick and money and gossip and sticking their hands up girls' skirts than they had about learning anything. Humiliating each other was the one and only subject they were interested in, and they all excelled at it. By the time I left St. Regis Academy, I had seen twenty seven girls burst into tears in the middle of class, and intercepted fifty-six cruel, coldhearted text messages – several of which had referenced their "carrot-top virgin" teacher, and guessed at either a) how many cats I must own or b) whether my carpet matched my drapes.

After six hundred and eighty-two endless school days, I had had enough. I had seen an ad for the after school care teacher position at the Y in the local newspaper, and I had packed up my things, turned in my resignation letter, and left town, praying that I was headed for somewhere where I would be needed.

The position paid half of what my old job had, so I had had to take on a side job cleaning house for a woman named Carmella Jones on the weekends, but seeing the light and innocence in the eyes of Marcus and the other neighborhood kids made it all worth it. There, in the middle of that broken-down town, I was making a difference. My life finally had meaning.

"Hey, White Girl!" shouted a chorus of grizzled, grey-haired men standing around a barrel fire outside of a liquor store.

"Hey, fellas!" I called back, waving. "I stick out like a sore thumb here, Marcus," I whispered to my escort. "Maybe I should dye my hair…"

He giggled in response.

It wasn't far from the Y to Marcus' house, just three blocks. One day, he would be old enough to walk it himself, but the thought of that made me nervous.

"Well, here we are!" I said, as we came to a large, lopsided brick apartment complex at the corner of Woodlawn and 44th Street. "You got your key?"

Marcus dug in the front pocket of his puffy red coat and came out with a chipped silver key. He held it up and grinned, his crooked baby teeth shining in the street lamp above us.

"Great! Now you've got it from here. I'll see you tomorrow!" He giggled again and gave my hand a quick squeeze before letting go and running up the steps of the building. "Oh! And don't forget to bring your backpack to school tomorrow!" I called after him, knowing he'd probably forget it anyway.

He threw me a wave and went in the front door, slamming it behind him with a bang like a gunshot.

I put my now-empty hands in the pockets of my own long, brown coat and waited. We had an agreement – if everything was alright when he got inside, Marcus would give me a wave from his bedroom window on the second floor. If it wasn't, I'd wait two minutes, and then come in to check on him. On the twelve occasions that his mother had come to pick him up, she had been high as a kite and almost as thin, so I worried a bit every time I had to turn him back over to her. I had no idea what went on in that apartment, and I didn't have the authority to check. And even if I *did* check and find something off, there was no real police force in Luthertown Heights to report it to, only a satellite office of the police from the next town over, and they rarely had someone on staff with the training to deal with a real-life crisis that didn't involve computer coding or taking messages.

After about ninety seconds, a pudgy little face appeared in the third window from the left on the second floor of the apartment building, and I grinned as we waved goodnight to each other.

I sighed, feeling a bit wistful, and began my long trek home.

There were twelve blocks between Marcus' home and mine – twelve street corners to pass, seven intersections to skirt, hoping not to get hit by a cloud of noxious exhaust fumes from someone's broken down old Chevrolet Cavalier, twelve different roads all marked with numbers I could never memorize in an order that didn't make sense, and all lined with houses in varying shades of grey.

As night fell over 27th Street, three blocks from my apartment building on 7th, I couldn't help but to admit that there was a strange sort of beauty in the shadowy wasteland in spite of all its flaws. The street lamps cast a fiery orange glow on the pavement beneath them, all dancing to different pulsating rhythms, but no matter how much they might flicker, they never went out. Full dark never came to Luthertown Heights, not even at midnight. Not even in the dead of winter. That city would not be claimed by the darkness, no matter how thick and insistent it became.

There was graffiti on several of the storefronts in town, but my own neighborhood looked like a Renoir art gallery. Every building, every fire hydrant, every tree, brick, and roof shingle was the canvas for some unknown artist to express himself on. Most people grumbled about it to each other on their way home from work, but I secretly enjoyed it. It never ceased to amaze me when I found a new face in the sea of neon-bright caricatures on the side of the mechanic's garage next door to my apartment, and I couldn't help but smile at the rainbow of pain and humor and pure, unadulterated expression splattered across the concrete. It was another, stronger light in the darkness that haunted the Wasteland, and I loved basking in it.

"Ay, it's our White Girl!" whooped a loud, booming voice that carried the entire length of 7th Street.

I felt my stomach clench.

For the most part, I wasn't afraid of anyone in Luthertown Heights. Sure, there were some people I wouldn't like to meet in a dark alley, and I probably wouldn't intentionally seek out the company of one of the hookers or junkies on 6th or 2nd Street, but usually, I felt as if I could handle myself around any person I came across.

The Uewatsu, though, were another story.

There were seven gangs in Luthertown Heights: the Sixes, a crew of burly, black factory workers who all miraculously had six fingers on one hand for some reason; the Dirty Dozen, a white gang whose uniform was comprised of scraggly, crotch-length beards and Confederate flag bandanas; the Creepers, whose turf consisted pretty much exclusively of the run-down cemetery on 8th Street; the XXX Runners, made up of former prostitutes who (according to town scuttlebutt) spent their Friday nights chopping off the testicles of men who had wronged them; a small Mexican crew who called themselves *Los Caballos*; an offshoot of the Crips; and the Uewatsu, an exclusively Native American gang whose name meant "death" in Cherokee.

Due to some sort of shake-up in the gang community, the Uewatsu had lost their former territory near Luthertown Park on 19th Street, and now apparently owned the rights to the patch of sidewalk right outside my apartment building.

Every night for the past four and a half months, they had gathered there, staying up until dawn, plotting or planning or scheming or whatever gangs did, laughing at the tops of their lungs and shouting at passersby every time I was right on the verge of falling asleep.

I usually managed to make it home before they began their nightly vigil, but Darrel McCaid had drunk three juice boxes that day and ralphed all over my classroom set of foam blocks, so Marcus and I had been late leaving that evening.

"Hey... guys," I said, giving them an uncertain wave as I fell into my carefully practiced walking pace that was slow enough to make me appear casual and unthreatened, but also quick enough to discourage lengthy conversations.

There were seven of them there tonight, all wearing black, all bearing the tell-tale dreamcatcher tattoo on their bare, muscular arms (in spite of the forty degree weather), and all standing directly in front of the gate that led to my front yard.

"Long day at school, teach?" asked Lars, whose long, shiny black hair hung to his waist, and who, my landlord had told me, had once killed a man with a tree branch.

"Yeah, one of the kids lost his lunch."

"Where did he leave it?" asked the one they called Goon because, well, because of questions like that. He had short, messy hair and a blank expression that made me wonder just what (if anything), went on in that curly head of his. My landlord had told me that he and his twin brother, River, had once hung a man by his ankles above a pen full of starving Rottweilers just because he had called them something racist.

The entire gang laughed uproariously at Goon's idiocy, and I smiled, uncomfortable, as I tried to look past them to the gate.

Aside from Lars, Goon, and River, there was Strongbow, who allegedly shot enemies of the gang with arrows coated in acid, and the gang's arrogant leader, an enormous seven foot tall man-mountain suitably named Bear.

He smiled back at me in silence as I stopped a respectful distance away from them, hoping they would move.

"Goon is a moron," he said finally, in a smooth, sultry sort of voice that made my skin crawl. "Don't listen to him."

"Hey!" shouted Goon, offended.

"It's okay." I shrugged, still smiling politely.

I saw movement out of the corner of my eye as someone on the edge of the group shifted his feet.

My smile faltered as I caught sight of the tall, lean, muscular Uewatsu referred to only as Slipknot – the most fearful member of the tribe. He wore a length of frayed brown rope around his throat like a sick sort of turtleneck, and had a long, jagged purple scar under his left eye that looked like dripping blood. They said he'd been to jail four times, and that they kept letting him out because he kept killing his cellmates.

He was a Luthertown Heights legend, and it was said that he had killed twenty men to earn his nickname – strangling them all with a noose fashioned out of the same rope he wore around his neck.

He was watching me as I took another tentative step toward the gate, and I realized then that I had never heard him speak before. I had also never noticed how his bright, emerald green eyes seemed to glow with a mysterious inner light in the falling darkness.

"How are you tonight, White Girl?" Bear continued, uncrossing his arms and advancing on me. The rest of the group followed suit.

"And how bout 'dem *tittaays?*" Goon shouted, before erupting into shrill, hyena-like laughter that was soon drowned out by the (much lower-pitched) laughter of the rest of the gang.

"They're...uh...hangin' in there," I replied, feeling the color rush to my face.

"Maybe we should check and see," suggested River, uncrossing his arms too, and licking his lips.

I instinctively crossed my own arms over my chest, then quickly let them fall as they all howled with laughter again. I was thoroughly embarrassed now, and had lost any sense of stability I might have had. My only option was to get past them and get into my apartment building as quickly as possible... but without seeming like I was in a hurry to get away.

"Well, it was nice seeing you all," I said, with another stupid wave, as I made to skirt past them.

Bear cut me off at the last second, stepping over to block my path to the gate. Just as he was opening his mouth to say something else suggestive and unnerving, though, Slipknot appeared on my left and jerked his head at something up the road.

"Well I'll be damned..." Bear muttered, stepping away from the gate.

I looked back the way I had come, and saw a young man limping up the street.

I glanced back at Slipknot, feeling oddly grateful to him for clearing me an escape route, but he swung open the gate without meeting my eyes.

Once I was inside the small, weed-pocked front yard, he nodded at the apartment building and closed the gate behind me.

With sweaty palms, I walked up the sidewalk and opened the front door.

I didn't look back.

Two

I slept unusually well that night. The Uewatsu were uncharacteristically quiet, and I was able to get a full nine hours in without my dreams being interrupted by any loud, harsh barks of laughter or catcalling.

It was nice... but unnerving.

When I left the house at 9:00 a.m., I was half-expecting to see a pile of bodies stacked along the fenceline like sandbags around a foxhole, but the street was empty. The Uewatsu were gone and so, it seemed, were the rest of the neighbors who normally left for work at the same time I did.

Chalking it up to coincidence, I tucked the tail of my itchy red scarf down into the lapel of my jacket, and started walking.

By the time I got to the YMCA, the ominous feeling that had come over me had passed. The sun was shining and the birds were singing in the burnt-out letters of the neon sign on the front of the building, and everything was okay.

I helped Miss Combs, the Y's receptionist, do some filing for a few hours, then I ate lunch with Mr. Gibbs, the septuagenarian custodian, at noon. The kids started trickling in at around two thirty, and at three fifteen, I passed out their daily snacks and read to the younger students from a dog-eared book about a shy caterpillar who had turned into a rather sassy butterfly by the end of the story.

All in all, it was a fairly uneventful day... until around four thirty.

The Y's after school care program (or the ASC, as we called it), officially ran from 3:00 p.m. to 6:00 p.m. every weekday, and had begun as a way to keep the neighborhood kids out of trouble until their parents could pick them up after work. The woman who had run it before me – Miss Rachel, whom I had never met, and whose last name I didn't know – had organized it, and turned it into something more akin to an after school club, with arts and crafts, book projects, and even indoor sports in the gym next door to the classroom.

I had taken her idea and run with it, helping the kids with their homework and coming up with a different theme or activity for every afternoon, so that they would be as well-rounded and as friendly with each other as possible. With the exception of a few grouchy eighth graders, the kids all loved the program and hated to say goodbye at the end of the day (something I took great pride in).

That day, though, it seemed like *everyone* was grouchy. Or, at the very least, restless. The smaller children had fidgeted throughout the entire caterpillar story, and the bigger ones had been unusually quiet, speaking only to snap at each other while they did their homework at the tables in the back of the blocky concrete classroom.

"Did I miss something, guys?" I asked, as I took a seat at one of the small, lopsided tables where they were working. I had sat down amongst a group of particularly broody twelve-year-olds, pulling little Chyna Martin onto my lap as I did so. I had been fixing a loose braid in her long, wild, black hair when the tension had finally gotten the better of me.

"What do you mean?" Janelle Ritter replied, not looking up from her timestables.

"Everyone seems grumpy today. Do you guys know something I don't?"

"I'm not grumpy!" Chyna declared, wiggling around atop my red-checkered skirt as I tried to rein in her curls.

"I know *you're* not grumpy, Chyna. You're never grumpy," I said, smiling. "You and Marcus are like little Cheshire cats!"

"What's a chesser cat?"

"It's a cat who smiles all the time," answered Janelle, her eyes still locked on her paper.

"From *Alice in Wonderland*," added Patrice, her best friend. She was doing her math homework too, but she kept shooting nervous glances at Janelle, as if she wanted to say something, but needed her permission first.

"We'll watch it on Friday," I promised Chyna, who cheered. "Now, what's up with everyone today?"

"You didn't hear?" Patrice had apparently given up trying to get the go-ahead from Janelle.

"Hear what?"

"About the Sixes."

"The Sixes? The gang?"

"Yeah, who else? Anyways, they're mad as hell."

"Why?" Even as I asked, something way down in the pit of my stomach was telling me I already knew the answer.

"Someone killed their leader last night, Shorty Biggs."

"Patrice." There was a warning in Janelle's voice, but her eyes were still on her notebook. Apparently she didn't like her friend telling tales out of school, especially when she was telling them to someone who hadn't exactly been welcomed into the Luthertown Heights community yet.

"Everyone's saying it was the Uewatsu."

"Patrice."

"They say they found Shorty strung up in Luthertown Park this morning with one of his eyeballs hangin' out of its—"

"Patrice!"

Janelle had finally looked up. She was glaring daggers at Patrice, who was on too much of a roll to stop now. Her mocha-colored face was flushed with excitement as she reached the dramatic conclusion of her tale.

"They say Slipknot did it."

I tried not to look as shaken as I felt. I had heard terrible stories about Slipknot and his ruthless, coldblooded killing, but I couldn't help but think of how he had offered me an escape route the night before, and how those big, enigmatic green eyes had shone so bright in the early evening darkness. Had he known when he opened that gate for me that he was going to kill a man in just a few hours' time?

"Why?" I asked, my voice more like a croak than anything. Chyna, bored now that her pigtail was fixed, leapt off my lap to go play blocks with the other kids.

"To start a war," said Janelle quietly, in a voice much too old and much, much too world weary for a thirteen-year-old. "Everyone knows that the first step in war is to take out the king."

Three

The rest of the afternoon passed without incident. What I had interpreted as grumpiness in my charges had really been something closer to fear, but it seemed to fade as the hours wore on, thanks to the doubling of my efforts to give them all something lighter and more pleasant to focus on.

Around five o'clock, we put on a play: a staged production of the caterpillar book I had read them earlier, with Chyna playing the part of the shy caterpillar (with difficulty, as she was the most outspoken child in the group), and Patrice playing her grown-up butterfly self.

This had thrilled everyone to no end. They had all gotten to make butterfly wings out of construction paper and fly around the room, bumping into each other and laughing as they filled our makeshift sky with color. Even Janelle had lightened up considerably by the time the invisible curtain fell, and she gave me a cheerful wave as she left for the day, making me feel like I had really accomplished something.

Marcus was still wearing his butterfly wings taped to the back of his jacket as we stepped out the backdoor at six thirty, and I was laughing as he leapt up and down so they could flutter as I carried his Teenage Mutant Ninja Turtles bookbag.

"Be careful or you'll fly away!" I giggled, glancing up as I locked the back door.

The laughter fell from my face as a strange, bizarre feeling washed over me. I took a step back from the door, my skin prickling with goosebumps, as I stared into my own smiling brown eyes.

While I'd been inside all day, the town's overly prolific graffiti artist had struck again, painting his latest masterpiece on the rusted, sheet metal back door of the YMCA – the door I always left through after work. This time, though, the face in the painting was my own.

From an artistic standpoint, it was fantastic – it was like looking into a rather flattering mirror. My long, auburn hair hung down past my shoulders in loose waves, my brown coat (perfectly tailored in the drawing even if it wasn't in real life) accentuated the curves of my hips and my breasts, and the eyes – *my* eyes – sparkled with flecks of green and gold, making them seem so lifelike that I swore I could feel myself looking back at me. I hadn't known that so many shades of color and subtlety and meaning were possible with simple acrylic paints! The mystery artist had even included the little brown freckles that were sprayed across the bridge of my nose.

Someone had been studying me closely. Very closely. But I could not, for the life of me, recall the last time I had let anyone get near enough to really look at me.

There was a small gasp as Marcus caught sight of the mural, then he erupted with infectious, bubbly, little boy laughter that brought a wry smile back to my face.

"Did you do this?" I asked him, pointing at my life-sized, 2-D coat collar.

He laughed louder, as if someone were trying to tickle him to death, and I sighed.

"Well, there goes my one and only suspect..."

Apparently that was hilarious too, and it kept Marcus in stitches all the way to his front door. He hugged my legs in farewell, and when his face appeared in his window a minute later, it was still full of mirth.

His joyousness had alleviated a bit of my paranoia, and as I walked the twelve blocks back to my own house, I couldn't help but to be filled with an odd, flattered sort of embarrassment. Someone – someone whose art I had secretly been admiring for months – had thought *me* of all people intriguing enough to paint. There were faces painted all around town, on buildings, on fences, on the backs of park benches, but they had all been faces I didn't recognize, faces I didn't know. But now my face was among them.

My face was special.

A small, quiet smile stayed on that face as I passed mural after mural, looking for myself in the graffiti artist's other works. I saw a horse and a dog, and an enormous, angry black bear. I saw a little girl crying and an elderly woman with long, grey braids and a blank, lost expression, and I saw the face of a man with empty, flat green eyes standing outside of what looked to be a forest of dead trees, but I didn't see me.

I was just slowing down to take in a tiny, red-brown chipmunk spray-painted on a fence post at the corner of my street when a shout ended my tour of the Luthertown Heights Art Gallery.

Startled, I looked up to see twelve Uewatsu standing in front of my gate, all wearing tan, cowhide vests and all shifting around, just as restless as my kids had been that afternoon.

"Hey, White Girl!" one of them called, and I jumped a bit at the forcefulness in his voice. Usually they teased me and made inappropriate jokes about my butt or my "tittaays," but this didn't sound like a joke.

And no one was laughing.

"Huh... hey," I replied, not sure whether to approach or to stay where I was.

"You got a phone?"

"A phone?"

"A cell, a mobile device, a *phone*, bitch! You got one?"

I physically recoiled as his words hit me like hard, sharp stones. "I... well... not on me," I lied. I tried hard not to look down at my coat pocket and give myself away. I had a phone, sure. But if I lent it to them, I would probably never see it again, and I couldn't afford another one.

"You know the number for the police?"

It was Bear talking, his once-seductive voice harsh and mean now. He wasn't flirting anymore. He was fighting.

"Um... 9-1-1?"

A shiver ran through the group as all twelve men shifted and muttered something amongst themselves.

Bear stepped away from them, moving toward me. His bare arms glistened, slick with sweat or water or oil in the lamplight. I'd heard he was seven feet tall, but I would have guessed eight. He looked like a statue come to life, like an angry god stepping down from a shrine to tower over me with his long, loose hair blowing softly in the night wind, and his black eyes glinting dangerously.

I couldn't have moved if I wanted to. I was rooted to the spot, too terrified to run, even if I would have had some place to run to. So, I stared up at him in silence, my lips parted in awe at the stone-crafted beast, and waited for him to speak.

"Did you dial that number last night?" The pitch of his voice was so low that I could feel it vibrate within me; a mini-earthquake at the foot of a man-mountain.

"Last night?" I swallowed, but my mouth was dry. "No, why would I?"

"I dunno," he said, shrugging his broad shoulders. "But someone did. Now Goon's locked up."

Goon? Why Goon? From what I had heard, it was Slipknot who had murdered Shorty Biggs, not Goon.

"I...what did he do?"

There was a collective hiss from the group, and a few grumbles of outrage.

Bear let out a short bark of laughter. "What did he do? She is asking me what he did!" he cried at his comrades, two of whom thumped their hands against their bare chests in a primitive, savage sort of threat.

"I... sorry, I didn't mean—"

As quick as lightning, Bears enormous hand shot out and grabbed me by the chin. His thick, rough fingers squeezed my cheeks, tightening around my jaws like a vice as he leaned in close.

"He didn't do anything, White Girl," he told me, his black eyes hidden by shadows now. "But the same can't be said for me and rest of my brothers if we find out you have been ratting on us. You understand?"

I tried to nod, but my brain seemed to have lost control of my spinal cord. My legs quivered beneath me as I made a pathetic little squeaking sound in reply, and he shoved me away, satisfied.

He stepped to the side, and I looked toward my apartment, my eyes blurry with unshed tears, and saw that the other gang members had parted themselves like the Red Sea, leaving my path to the gate clear and unobstructed.

"Go on," Bear said, as his voice took on that smooth, sinisterly seductive quality again. "Unless you wanna stay here and whip out those tittaays for daddy and the boys."

That kickstarted my brain. Moving with the short, jerky motions of a newly functional robot, I walked unsteadily toward the gate, massaging my chin and trying my damndest not to shed those fear-inflicted tears in my eyes and let them know how badly they had shaken me.

I had almost made it there, feeling the stares of the silent Uewatsu on me with every step I took, when another familiar figure stepped out of formation and over to the gate.

My already pounding heart thudded madly against my ribcage as Slipknot, the noose-wielding murderer, put his hand on the swinging gate and pushed it open for me. His eyes were like two orbs of emerald fire, burning with some inner light, some inner passion, some inner turmoil or strangled emotion that I couldn't even begin to fathom the depths of. I found it hard to breathe as I passed him, and even harder to look away.

One I was safely inside the yard, he closed the gate behind me once more. As I stepped up onto the porch, Bear shouted, "Remember what we talked about, White Girl. It would be a shame to lose those pretty tits of yours."

I squeezed my eyes shut as a shudder of revulsion passed though me. Then I unlocked the door and headed up to my apartment.

That night, I didn't sleep at all.

Four

The next day was Friday, but I couldn't swear to it, because I spent the whole day as a zombie, staggering, heavy-footed, around the Y, giving one-syllable answers to homework questions and trying not to fall asleep at my desk.

The Uewatsu had been dead silent again the night before, but I had heard every gust of wind that had rustled the tree branches outside, every word my neighbors had uttered from the first floor to the fifth, every tick of every clock, every bang of my heart, all magnified a thousand times in my head.

Luthertown Heights was a scary place to live, but I had never been afraid of it until that night. There was a storm brewing, and I was getting caught in it, whether I wanted to or not. For reasons I couldn't even guess at, Bear blamed me for Goon's arrest, and there was nothing I could do to convince him otherwise.

I had lain awake until dawn, wondering just what they would do to me if Bear came up with some sort of proof that I really was the rat. By the time I left for work, I had already been stabbed, hung, raped, shot with arrows, and seen my breasts cut off and put in a jar on Bear's mantle, so there was nothing left to scare me as I set out into the grey, drizzly morning and headed into the heart of the lonely city.

By the time I got *off* work, though, my fear had returned tenfold. For some reason, Marcus' mother had actually decided to pick him up from ASC that day... most likely to show off her now boyfriend, Eddie. He had been as broad as a barn door, with a head like a square and no less than seven gold caps on his teeth, but she had seemed happy with him, and Marcus didn't seem to mind holding his hand instead of mine when they all left together at six.

I had been happy for Marcus then, but now, an hour later, I felt lonesome for his pudgy little hand as I stepped out into the alley. Dark fell quickly in autumn, and it looked like midnight in the sky already with the flickering orange halogen lamps working hard to beat back the black shadows that crept up to smother their light. Though the evening air was mild, I pulled my coat more tightly around me and tucked my chin into my scarf.

As I glanced down at DeAndre's newspaper nest, I noticed that he wasn't in it. With a mixture of curiosity and melancholy, I wondered, not for the first time, where he went when he wasn't there.

My footsteps were loud on the pavement, and I paused for a moment to look back at my portrait on the rusted back door. Unlike the real me, that girl was still smiling, still calm, still sweet and sure of herself. She seemed content – happy, even – and it was painful to realize how far my spirits had fallen since yesterday.

I was just reaching out to touch my painted twin's freckled face, as if to steal some of her levity, when I heard a rustling sound behind me.

Clutching my hand to my lapel, I whirled around and found myself staring into the same bright, fiery emerald eyes that had bidden me goodnight the evening before.

Slipknot's chest was barely a foot away from mine. He was staring down at me, his dark, wild curls billowing in the wind and his caramel-colored face expressionless.

I stumbled backward and felt my shoulder hit the door, colliding with my painted self.

My own wide eyes took in his leather jacket, the tight, ripped black t-shirt he wore under it, and the thick, weathered rope wrapped five times around his neck. I thought about all the people he had supposedly killed with that rope, and I had to resist the urge to scream.

"I have come to walk you home."

I blinked stupidly at him. His voice was rough and hoarse, as if he had been screaming, but as far as I knew, he had never uttered a sound before that night.

"I...uh...what?"

"Come on." He turned around and started walking toward the street.

"I... wait, I don't understand."

He stopped, looking impatient. Then a thought struck me that chilled me right down to the marrow of my bones. "Oh, no... Did... Did Bear send you?"

"Bear does not send me anywhere," he replied, his raspy voice hard. "Where I go, I go by choice."

I took a moment to let that sink in. "So... you *chose* to come here?"

He didn't respond.

"You chose to come and walk me home? Why?" My confusion was beginning to make me angry. The Uewatsu had no right to do this to me. It was one thing to stand guard at my house, blocking my entrance with lewd pick-up lines and threats, but to track me to my workplace to harass me? This was too much! There were children there, children who thought of the YMCA as a safe haven, as a refuge from the crime that ran rampant in the streets, and I wouldn't stand for anyone taking that away from them.

"Luthertown Heights is not a safe place."

"Yeah, because of people like you and Bear and the Uewatsu killing everybo—"

"Exactly."

I was stunned into silence. With that one hoarse, raspy word, he had said everything. He had confirmed my greatest fears.

"The Uewatsu are out on a run. If you come with me now, I can guarantee that you will make it to your home safely."

I stared at him, following the line of the curved purple scar that ran down his left cheek. He had probably gotten that while killing someone.

"I... How... Why should I trust you?" It came out as a whisper. I hadn't really meant to say it at all. This was crazy. The Uewatsu were murderers, and I was on their list. I should not have been wasting time asking questions, I should have been running away.

"You should not trust me," he answered, in that painful, gravelly voice. "No one should."

Then, without another word, he walked away.

I gaped after him for about five seconds, watching the back of his curly haired head as he moved soundlessly in the direction of Woodlawn Avenue.

Then I cursed under my breath, because I knew I was going to follow him.

Five

"So... do you... uh... work around here?"

We had been walking in silence, side by side, for six blocks, and the curiosity was killing me. Why was he doing this? Why was he escorting me home like a gentleman after a date? Was he luring me into a trap?

It didn't seem like it... but that was the only explanation that even remotely made sense.

My head barely came to his shoulder, I noticed. He wasn't as tall as Bear, but he still cleared six feet, I was sure of it.

"No."

There was a quarter-sized, cowhide-wrapped dreamcatcher dangling from his left earlobe. The small, ruffled brown feathers hanging from its strings fluttered in the wind, as if they were still attached to the bird they had been plucked from. There were three round, turquoise beads accenting the piece – two in the intricate threaded webbing in at the center of the circle, and one near the base of the second of the three strings that hung from it. I wondered at their placement, because it seemed so random, but I had more important questions to ask.

"Have you been to the new fruit stand on 18th Street? I hear they sell fresh bananas."

He didn't dignify that one with a response, and I didn't blame him.

Embarrassed, I watched my feet as I walked, counting the new scuffs in the faux leather of my calf-high boots.

"So... uh..." I tried again two blocks later, "You said the Uewatsu are out on a run? What does that mean?"

"Nothing that concerns you, White Girl."

My gaze snapped up to his face. I narrowed my eyes at his lamp-lit profile. A dozen people called me that on any given day, but when he said it, it stung.

"I have a name."

"Everyone does."

I twisted my lips, oddly annoyed. He was having a very strange effect on me, and I didn't like it. "Okay, in that case, what's yours?"

"You know what they call me." He was still staring straight ahead, as solemn as a man at a funeral, but something in his face seemed to tighten, as if he were bracing himself for something.

"I know what they *call* you, but that's not your name."

He glanced at me, a flash of green in the orange-tinted wasteland. Just as quickly, though, he faced forward again, making me wonder if I had just imagined the whole thing.

He didn't say anything else until we arrived at the gate to my yard. Just as he had said, the gang was gone, and my stomach churned a bit at the thought of what they might be doing out there in the night.

Just like he had for the past two nights, Slipknot flipped up the latch on the gate and swung it open. It creaked quietly in the silent evening air, and I hesitated before crossing the threshold.

I looked up at him, fidgeting with the buttons on my jacket front.

He raised an eyebrow.

"I don't really know how to ask this, but..." I glanced at the run-down apartment building, full of potential for lurking tribes-men, then back to his face.

"There is no one in there," he said, reading my mind.

I exhaled, unaware that I had been holding my breath. "Thanks. And thank you for... keeping me company, I guess."

He nodded toward the building, and I stepped inside the yard. He swung the gate shut.

As he turned to go, I couldn't resist asking him one last question, one last time. "Hey, why did you do this?"

He stopped, with his back to me.

"Why did you walk me home, I mean?"

He was still for a moment, his body tense beneath the wrinkles of his faded, brown leather jacket.

Then he simply walked away.

Six

That night I slept well and deeply, troubled only by a few short dreams featuring enigmatic, disembodied green eyes and giant dreamcatchers.

I woke up late, though, and had to run the entire six blocks to Miss Carmella's. The streets, as was becoming the norm lately, were fairly empty, and completely free of gangbangers (helpful or otherwise), so I made it to her house safe and sound and completely out of breath.

"You are *late*, White Girl," Miss Carmella groused as I entered the house using the key hidden under a rock near the front walk.

"Sorry," I wheezed, flinging my sweaty scarf over a hook near the door and whipping off my coat so I could roll up the sleeves of my mint green sweater. "I overslept."

"Humph," was her reply.

I wiped my shoes on the welcome mat inside the kitchen, and made my way into the living room to say hello.

The sight of Miss Carmella sitting on her sunken couch was something I should have been used to by now, but it never failed to take me by surprise. Carmella Washington was seventy-three years old, with a squashed drugstore wig full of silver-grey ringlets and a flowery purple smock that she wore in lieu of any other article of clothing. She was around five foot nine, with a round, pinched face... and about six hundred pounds of excess body fat.

Six hundred and ten, if you listened to the tales of her youth, in which she reportedly met Martin Luther King, Jr. in a size zero dress that "just hung right off" of her ninety pound frame.

Things had apparently gone downhill after that day. She had been married four times and had gained one hundred and fifty pounds for each husband she had buried (some of the neighbors swore that she ate them), until she ended up alone, filling an entire three-person couch all by herself. She was too big to move and too mean for anyone to want to keep her company; her thirty-three-year-old son came by once or twice a week to change her smock, and I came by every Saturday at noon to clean her house for two hundred dollars from her pension fund.

She had a fridge at her right hand and a catheter tube under her smock, and she was, for all intents and purposes, a self-sustaining life form who lived on soap opera reruns and the local TV news.

As I gave up on a nice greeting and got straight to work running the vacuum, I wondered – not for the first time – what she did when she had to go "number two."

Some mysteries, though, were better left unsolved.

Even though Miss Carmella was a bit of a miser, I always put my heart and soul into cleaning her house. It was a modest, two-story Cape Cod-style home with three bedrooms and a bathroom no one ever used, but for some reason I found that the more rooms there were to clean, the better. There was a strange sort of peace in the scrape of my dust rag and the dull drone of the old, rattling vacuum, and I always left in the evening feeling as if I had just completed a particularly cathartic therapy session.

That day was especially zen for me, because for the first time in days, I was able to completely put Bear and the rest of the troubling neighborhood out of my mind. I had put in my earbuds, turned on my pawn shop MP3 player, and was singing along quietly to an old 80s song as I scrubbed the dust-shrouded bathtub when I heard a shout from the living room.

Certain that it was the massive, inevitable coronary I'd been dreading since the moment I'd taken the job, I threw down my sponge and ran to see what was wrong.

"Hold on, Miss Carmella, I'll call..."

My voice trailed off as I caught sight of the television set she was watching. It was the afternoon news, and a chill ran through me as I saw the bodies of no less than five Uewatsu lying face-up in the grass at Luthertown Park on 19th Street. There was black war paint streaked across their cheeks, and it mixed with the blood that ran from their empty eye sockets.

My legs grew so weak that I just sank to the floor where I was. I wasn't sure of the identity of the three members furthest from the camera, but I recognized the long, dark hair of Lars, and the choppy curls of Goon's twin brother, River.

"...no suspect in custody," the carefully accentless voice of the news reporter was saying as the grisly photo disappeared, "but several Luthertown Heights residents told our reporters that it was the work of another local gang, the Sixes."

"Six bodies for the six fingered man," said one of the old drunkards I recognized from the barrel fire outside of the liquor store. "An eye for an eye. They startin' a war."

Six bodies. Six. I had only seen five in the photo.

My mind immediately went to Slipknot, the coldblooded killer, my gentleman escort. Was he the sixth body?

"They done stepped in it now," said Miss Carmella, with a long, slow shake of her head. "Them crazy indjuns.."

"I...uh... I have to go," I said, getting to my feet. I suddenly felt sick to my stomach. Every blink of my eyes brought back those pale, eyeless faces – the faces I'd seen outside my house every night for the past four months – the faces I would now never un-see.

"Be careful out there, White Girl," Miss Carmella called, when I rushed out the door two minutes later, "there's a war goin' on!"

Seven

I didn't see the Uewatsu for the rest of the weekend. Not a single one of them...and especially not the one I seemed to be growing increasingly more worried about.

I didn't see much of anyone else, either. When I went to work on Monday, Luthertown Heights was a ghost town. Even the hungover hookers had holed up somewhere, out of the line of possible fire. Janelle had been right: there was a war on, and no one wanted to get caught in the middle of it.

No one but me, apparently.

Armed with a can of mace and three hours' worth of YouTube-based knowledge of Krav Maga, I had left my apartment at the usual time that morning, and had strolled as leisurely as I could to the YMCA – the only thing that could make me brush aside any and all concerns for my own safety.

As I had expected, attendance went way up that day, as frightened parents scrambled to find a way to keep their kids off the streets after school while they were still at work. My "class" went from seventeen children to twenty eight, and this, more than anything, convinced me that I had been right to take the risk.

Those kids needed someone to watch over them, and I was that someone, in spades.

"Welcome to the ASC, everybody!" I called cheerfully from the front of the classroom at three that afternoon. "I see we have some new faces here! I won't embarrass you by putting you on the spot and having your introduce yourself, but I *will* come around and say hi to you all individually in a bit, if that's okay."

The new kids were, for the most part, older than my usual ones, around fourteen or fifteen, and they were all huddled in the back corner, looking shifty and out of place.

"Tell 'em what day it is! Tell 'em what day it is!" urged little Chyna Martin. She was sitting on the floor at my feet, along with Marcus and most of the other four- to eight-year-olds.

I smiled. "I was just getting to that. Today is Monday, so it's what we here at the ASC like to call – "

"MUSIC MONDAY!" the kids on the floor all screamed in unison, their little voices shrill with excitement.

"Music Monday," I repeated, laughing.

"What the hell is dat?" demanded an angry voice from the back.

I glanced up, my smile still in place, to see a young man in a black hooded sweatshirt and baggy pants glaring at me as if I were a glob of chewing gum stuck to the bottom of his new Nikes.

"Every day we have a different theme. On Mondays, the theme is always –"

"MUSIC!" chimed the chorus at my feet.

"—music. There's a big box of musical instruments over there in the corner. Everyone who wants one can take one out and play it, as long as they remember to share. If you don't want to *play* music, you can grab one of the portable cd players in there and listen to it with headphones instead. Then, at the end of the day, I'll pick someone at random and they can play a song for us on their instrument or through the speakers on my desk. It's pretty fun."

"It's pretty *whack* if you ask me."

I bit my lip to keep from laughing. I hadn't been aware that the Fresh Prince of Bel Air was in my class. "Well, if you don't want to do any of that stuff, you can have some snacks and work on your homework instead. It's up to you."

"Ain't nothin' up to me," he shot back, surprising me with his ferocity. I was starting to get the feeling that me and my "whackness" weren't really the source of all that adolescent angst. "If it was upta me, I wouldn't even *be* here right now wit all these kindergarten *babies!*"

A few of the younger children frowned, apparently taking offense to that.

"Why don't you come up here and we can talk about it at my desk, while everyone gets their instruments?"

There was a collective "ooooo" from the peanut gallery, and I tried not to laugh again.

"Why don't *you* suck my dick, bitch?"

The kids were too stunned to "ooooo" at that. Their eyes were like saucers, and the room went silent as everyone waited to see my reaction.

I didn't have one. I worked at a free daycare in an inner city YMCA. This was not the first time my authority had been questioned.

"What's your name?" I asked, as everyone's eyes crossed the room from me to him and back again.

"Lamont Carter."

"Okay, Lamont. You can't use language like that in here."

"Says who, bitch?"

"Says me."

The other new teens looked impressed, but Lamont wasn't finished yet. "Well, *I* say that I can say whateva the muthafuckin' hell I wanna say, you cracker-ass piece of shit cu—"

"Alright!" I called over his harsh, angry voice, cutting him off. "Lamont, let's you and I go have a chat outside, okay? Everyone else go ahead and start playing. I'm looking forward to hearing what you all come up with!"

For a few seconds, no one moved. Then, slowly, haltingly, the kids got up from the bare, stained blue carpet and headed for the half-sized refrigerator box in the back full of secondhand tubas, tambourines, flutes, bongos, and slide-whistles I had bought from a pawn shop five months ago (along with my own MP3 player).

Lamont stayed where he was for a long time, staring defiantly at me, his brown eyes full of hate. Then, when he saw that I wasn't backing down either, he walked slowly up to join me at the front of the room.

"Janelle, keep an eye on things while I'm gone, please. I'll be right back," I called, as we headed for the door. Janelle waved in acknowledgement from a table in the middle of the room. Her expression was grave.

"Alright, Lamont, this way." I opened the door to the alley, and we stepped out into the crisp, afternoon air. I pushed the door to, wedging a rock between it and the jamb to keep us from being locked out, and so that I could keep an ear out for the other kids.

"So, what's going on?" I asked, crossing my arms against the cold. I was wearing a thick, blue turtleneck sweater dress over leggings, but the chilly wind was blowing right through the fabric.

Lamont seemed fine in his heavy hoodie and saggy jeans, and I envied boys and their weather-ready clothing. "Whatchu mean, what's goin' on? What's goin' on with you?"

"What's going on with me is that there's something going on with you. You can't say things like that in a room full of kids."

"And why not? It hurt your feelin's, White Girl?"

He stood up tall, meeting me at my five foot seven height, and puffed himself up like a frog trying to scare away a bird.

I was not impressed.

"My feelings aren't the problem. Yours are. What are you so angry about? Did you have a bad day at school today or something?"

He let out a humorless chuckle. "Yeah, cuz school's dat important."

"Well, what then? You're mad because you had to come to ASC?"

"No, man, I don't give a shit about yo fuckin' ASC!" He was shouting into my face at full volume, and I had to work hard to keep my face blank.

"Then what is it?"

"What the fuck do you care? You ain't no counsellor! You ain't nothin' but a glorified babysitter, bitch! You don't know me!"

That stung a little more than I would have liked, but I didn't let it show. "Well, I'd like to. Tell me abo—"

My words were cut off as he shoved me backward by my shoulders, slamming me into the concrete wall and knocking the wind out of me.

"SHUT UP!" he screamed, shoving me again, "SHUT UP!"

"Take it easy, Lamont," I said shakily.

"NO, *YOU* TAKE IT FUCKIN' EASY!"

He shoved me one more time and I hissed as my right shoulder scraped against a rusty nail head jutting out from the side of the building.

"Is there a problem here?"

I had closed my eyes for a second to rethink my mediation strategy, but they flew open at the sound of Slipknot's voice.

Once again he had crept into the alleyway without a sound, and was now standing two inches behind Lamont, his fiery green eyes aglow.

"Jesus!" Lamont croaked, stumbling backwards into me in an effort to get away from the rope-necked specter. "You're... you're..."

"I know who I am," Slipknot interrupted, his face as expressionless as ever, his voice deadly calm and raspy.

"I... I wasn't doin' nothin', I swear!"

"That is not what it looked like to me." He pointed to my

shoulder, and I was startled to see that there was a crimson stain running down the sleeve of my sweater.

Lamont blanched. "Oh, God. No, see, I..." Then, some of his bravado returned and he stood up taller. "My dad's in the Sixes," he said, puffing out his chest with pride.

"Congratulations."

"And I'm gonna be in the Sixes too, once he quits makin' me go to this whack-ass ASC."

"Good for you. What does that have to do with pushing women around in alleyways?"

Lamont swallowed. He looked at Slipknot, then at me. "You with this guy?" he asked incredulously. "You know what he is, right? A killer."

"Well, that sounds like what you want to be too," I replied coolly, brushing myself off and crossing my arms again. "Why don't you go inside now and do your homework."

"Bitch, I ain't no ki—"

"You heard what she said." Slipknot's voice was so calm and cool and threatening that even I got goosebumps that time.

Lamont's Adam's apple jerked against his collar as he swallowed hard again. Then, with one last fearful glance at Slipknot, he went back inside.

"You shouldn't have done that," I said quietly, when Slipknot and I were alone.

He didn't answer. He took a slow, cautious step closer to me and pointed at my shoulder again. "You should not let them see that."

I glanced down at the blood and winced. It stung like hell; thank God they'd made me get a tetanus shot before they hired me. "I don't think I have many options," I replied.

"Here." Before I realized what he was doing, Slipknot had taken off his leather jacket and wrapped it around me. It smelled like a freshly cut cedar tree, warm from the sun.

"Oh, wait, I can't –"

"Blood is a sign of weakness," he said, placing his hands on my shoulders for the briefest of seconds. "You are not weak."

Then, once again, he walked away without another word.

Eight

No one but Janelle and Lamont seemed to notice the jacket when I returned to the classroom. Lamont looked broody and nervous, casting me sidelong glances for the next three hours, and Janelle just looked disappointed. Whether I had intended to or not, I had chosen a side in the war that was brewing, and the ASC was supposed to be neutral territory.

Knowing this, I could have changed into my own coat once I got back inside. But there was something oddly thrilling to me about wearing the jacket of a known gang member and possible murderer. Who knew what secrets, what clues, what evidence that jacket held, and I was in full possession of all of them. Maybe I'd find a bloody bandana in the pocket that would prove Slipknot's role in Shorty Biggs' death. Maybe I'd save the city and stop the war with that worn, leather coat alone.

Or maybe I'd only make things worse.

If word got out that Slipknot really, truly *did* kill Biggs, then the Sixes would find a way to kill *him* too.

At the very least, Slipknot would be sent to prison, where he probably belonged. That idea, though, like the instruments my students were playing with tuneless gusto, struck a sour chord with me. In my mind, Slipknot was a wild, majestic creature, like a falcon, untamed by the laws of any man, and the thought of those piecing green eyes staring out through the bars of a jail cell made me feel sick to my stomach.

I decided not to check the pockets.

That night, after a rousing rendition of "Twinkle Twinkle Little Star" by Chyna on a dented kazoo, everyone went home, including Marcus. His mother's new boyfriend must have had a fatherly gene, because he accompanied her to Marcus' pickup again that night, and left holding Marcus' hand.

I followed them out the back door, a bit sad to see them head off into the evening as one big, happy family. I locked the door behind me and was just folding Slipknot's jacket over my arm when he came around the corner and into the alley.

"Oh!" I said. He never ceased to startle me. "Um... hi."

He gave me a curt nod in reply.

"I wasn't... expecting to see you there."

Silence.

He was wearing only a pair of thin jeans and a black t-shirt, both pocked with rips and tears that gave a glimpse of the copper-colored skin beneath. His neck was bound with rope, as always, and the lean, hard muscles in his bare arms flexed as he put his hands in his pockets.

"I...uh...I can't really wear this...here," I said, holding out his jacket, even though he was too far away to take it from me. "There's a little blood on the inner lining, but I think a bit of peroxide will get it out."

He didn't move to take it and my arm was beginning to get tired from holding it out. I lowered my arm and hugged the jacket to my chest for support as I took a deep breath. He was just a person. I could talk to him. There was nothing to be afraid of.

"I wanted to thank you, though," I tried again, my voice stronger and more sure this time. "Both for today and the other day."

Finally, a movement. He nodded his head in acknowledgement, and took a few steps forward, ending up just a few inches away from me again. The stuttering in my chest that followed was worrisome.

"Here," I said softly, pressing his jacket into his hand.

That time he took it.

His eyes never left mine as he put it on. He didn't check the lining, and he didn't seem to feel the need to make sure I hadn't damaged it in any other way either.

"I didn't put my hands in the pockets."

His expression didn't change, in spite of my awkward, unnecessary confession. I felt like he was hypnotizing me with the green fire that danced in his eyes.

I needed to leave before I said anything else stupid.

"Well, anyway, I've gotta go!"

"Don't." He put a hand on my wrist, and I froze.

"Wha...um...what?"

"You cannot go home now."

I swallowed hard and finally broke free of his stare. "I'm pretty sure I can." I shook his hand off my wrist, but he caught it again.

His rough-skinned grip was gentle on my sleeve, but his touch still scared the daylights out of me. I felt like a rabbit in a trap. What did he want from me?

"The Uewatsu are there. You should not cross them. Not tonight."

My eyes darted back to his. "Why? What's happened?"

"Six of us are dead." I expected to see sadness in his face, but it was as stoic as ever. "The ones who are living are looking for someone to vent their frustrations on."

My stomach fell. "Me."

That time his silence spoke volumes.

"I...uh...well, what am I supposed to do, then?" I raised a hand to touch my hair, and noticed my fingers were trembling. "I have to go home sometime!"

"You will, later tonight. Until then you will stay with me."

A high-pitched (mildly hysterical) laugh escaped me. "You? I don't even know you! How do I know that you don't have some plan to... to 'vent' on me too?"

He didn't reply, and my madness only grew.

"I've heard things about you, you know. I've heard what you do to people with that...that...well, *that.*" I pointed at the fraying rope around his neck, unable to say the word out loud for reasons I couldn't explain. "How do I know you won't strangle me too?"

The tightness I had seen in his face three nights ago returned. "I will not hurt you," he said.

"Why should I believe that?"

He studied my face for a long, long time, taking in my wide, frightened brown eyes, my pinprick freckles, and my surely pale, white skin. Then he said the one word that changed everything.

"Please."

Nine

"So..." We had been walking for twenty minutes, and Slipknot hadn't said a word. The awkwardness was really starting to get to me, but I couldn't think of anything "normal" to say to him. "About Lamont today..."

"You cannot let your guard down like that again," he replied, with a quickness that surprised me.

Offended, I shot him a glare. "I didn't 'let my guard down.' I knew there was a potential that he would get... rough. That's why I asked him to come outside."

"So your other students would not detect any signs of weakness in you. Good." He nodded in approval.

"What? No." I shook my head, not sure why everything he said sounded like it came straight out of volume one of "The Law of the Jungle." "It wasn't like that. I just didn't want him to scare anyone. Well, any more than he already had."

"But you allowed him the chance to scare you?"

I stopped walking. "No, I did not allow him to scare me. I wasn't scared!"

"Just like you were not scared of my brothers the other night at your apartment?"

He had stopped walking too, and was piercing me with that disconcerting green gaze again.

I glanced down at my boots as I felt the color rush to my cheeks. "I wasn't scared," I said, my voice too small to carry any real meaning.

Slipknot was quiet for a moment. When he spoke again, his voice was hoarse and inflectionless, as always. "If that was not the reason you brought that boy out into the alley, what was?"

I sighed and scuffed my heel against a patch of weeds growing up through a crack in the sidewalk. We had wandered along the northern edge of town, in the opposite direction of my apartment, and were now standing outside what had once been a waterpark for children. A dilapidated tunnel slide loomed, tall and crooked, in the distance, slanting down into a shallow, empty concrete basin that had once been a pool. Graffiti covered the slide, and I tried to make out the shapes and words and faces in it as I squinted in the lamplight.

"I thought I could get through to him better if we were one-on-one, instead of shouting at each other across a crowded room."

"What exactly did you want to get through to him?"

There was a bird near the apex of the slide. A bluebird, with enormous, lushly lashed brown eyes and little music notes coming out from its orange beak.

"Just that he could talk to me if he wanted to. That I'm here for him." I shrugged, sure that it sounded stupid, even if it meant everything in life to me. "I just wanted to reach him somehow. I want to reach all those kids."

"You cannot reach people who do not want to be reached."

I looked back to find him watching me. There was something different in his expression now, something careful, something cautious, something almost curious.

"I don't think that's necessarily true." I tiled my head to the side, considering him. "I think, deep down, everyone wants to be reached."

"Some would say that that is naïve."

"What do *you* say?"

The scar beneath his eye wasn't as bad as I thought. From a distance, it had looked harsh and jagged and mean, but up close, it looked almost as artful as the graffiti I adored as it snaked down the stubbled skin of his tawny cheek. He had another scar too, a small, crescent-shaped white one near the curve of his chin, a few inches below his lower lip.

He didn't say anything. Instead, he turned and began to walk toward the abandoned water park.

"Hey, I don't think we're supposed to go in there!" I called, as he squeezed through a gap in the wrought-iron gates.

He paid me no mind, and kept walking. After a few seconds of indecision (*like every goody-goody sidekick in any movie ever made*, I thought), I sighed again and followed him through the gap.

The already-still night seemed frighteningly lifeless as we crept toward the mammoth tube slide. It was as if every other creature on Earth had suddenly gone extinct, and we were the only things left alive. The darkness was thicker there too; it ran rampant over the place without the city's army of orange streetlamps to keep it at bay. The only light came from the bright white moon, shining down into the basin of the empty pool.

The silence weighed heavy on my chest, and I was almost glad for the deafening clatter I made when I tripped over a discarded beer can and sent it skipping like a stone into the concrete pit.

"Sorry," I whispered, wincing, but Slipknot made no sign that he had heard anything. He followed the can to the pool and sat down on the edge, dangling his long legs over the three-foot drop to watch it spin.

Once more, I hesitated, but once more, I followed his lead.

I perched on the rim of the concrete cavity, tucking my own legs beneath me. Then I gasped.

The bottom of the empty pool was covered in art. Not graffiti. Art. It looked like a painted scene from the fabled Garden of Eden.

Green grass spread out at the feet of a crowd of people – white people, black people, yellow people, brown people, red people – and full, leafy trees reached up toward a blue, cloudless sky full of more birds than I could count. There were flowers everywhere, tulips on the ground, daisies tucked behind the ears of the women with long, flowing hair, orchids on great, thick vines that snaked up the trees, and there was a whole flock of squirrels, dogs, and chipmunks that danced around their human counterparts, sharing in their apparent harmony. And hanging above it all was a huge, yellow-orange orb the same shade as those streetlamps that gave me such comfort, sending rays of sunshine down on all who stood below.

"Oh my God, do you see this?" I hissed to Slipknot, forgetting who I was speaking to in the throes of my absurd state of rapture, "It's *beautiful!* I've never seen anything like it!"

"Not in Luthertown Heights, you mean."

"No, not anywhere! This is gorgeous! It's so full of light and hope and... and... just joy! Oh, I wish I had a camera..."

What I *really* wished I'd had, though, was a tissue, or a better grip on myself. I had a lump in my throat the size of a walnut, and it was all I could do to keep from crying. The painting had affected me strangely, and on a deep, profound level. After all I had seen lately, after all I had heard and thought and witnessed, to see that vision of love and life in the middle of all that city's pain was like finding a piece of Heaven on the rocky shores of Hell.

"It is just graffiti..."

"It is not!" I sniffed. I felt simultaneously moved and devastated, and I couldn't explain why. I felt as if I had just found the meaning of life, but couldn't figure out how to distill it into something I could understand, something I could use, something I could carry with me.

I felt a tear slip past my defenses and slide down my cheek, and I hastily wiped it away. Just like that, the spell was broken. My awkward embarrassment returned tenfold, and I laughed nervously. "Sorry. I don't know why I'm so sensitive lately."

Silence met my apology, and I fidgeted with my hands, wishing I could leave, but not knowing where to go.

If anyone should have been feeling sensitive, though, it was Slipknot. Six of his "brothers" had just died, and that had to be killing him.

"I...uh... I saw the story on the news about the Uewatsu," I said quietly, shuddering as the memory of River's pale, eyeless face flashed before my eyes. "I was sorry to hear that."

"You were sorry? Why?"

I tilted my head again to look at his profile. He had a strong jaw: chiseled, statuesque. It was tight again, but almost imperceptibly so.

"Because they...well, because they died," I finished lamely. "It must be hard for you."

"I am not one of your students." He sounded as if he were resisting the urge to roll his eyes. "Do not try to reach me."

I felt a small grin creep across my face. "Oh, so you're one of the ones who doesn't want to be reached?"

He didn't answer, and my fledgling smile fell. I looked down at my hands as they lay in my lap. "When they said that six Uewatsu died, they only showed a picture of five." My voice was quiet, hesitant. I wished I could stop talking, but I couldn't seem to bring myself to shut up. "I was worried that maybe... well, no, I *thought* that maybe... that maybe you were..."

"That I was number six?"

It was my turn to answer with silence. I picked at the hem of my dress, feeling his eyes on me.

"Would that have mattered to you?"

I wanted to say that I didn't know, but the answer had been growing clearer with every passing moment.

So I decided to change the subject. "Why are you doing all this for me?" I asked, looking back up at him. "Walking me home, watching out for me at the Y, warning me about the others? Why are you trying so hard to keep me safe?"

"Maybe it is in my instincts to protect the White Girl."

It was the closest thing to a joke that he had ever uttered, but I didn't laugh. "God, I wish people would stop calling me that... I have a name."

"Everyone has a name."

I smiled slightly, against my will. "We covered that already."

I thought I saw a ghost of a grin cross his face in return, then his hand darted out and grabbed me by the shoulder – hard.

"Ouch!" I squeaked, trying to pry his fingers away from the wound I hadn't had a chance to treat yet. "What are you –"

He covered my mouth with his hand and pulled me to my feet. He looked like a wild animal; his pupils were dilated like a cat's as he searched the still night for danger.

I stopped trying to talk and held my breath, listening. At first, all I heard was the thundering of my own heart.

Then I heard the snap of a twig.

"Go," Slipknot whispered to me, shoving me back the way we had come. "Run home. Now. Don't look back."

"But what about—"

"Go!" He pushed me so forcefully that I almost fell down, and I had no choice but to obey his order. Clutching the collar of my coat, I ran back toward the wrought-iron gates, suddenly on the verge of tears once more, and suddenly certain that I would never see Slipknot again.

Ten

There was a murder at the waterpark that night.

The victim was a man named Cooper Katz, the new leader of the Sixes. His body had been found strung up in a tree, dangling over that empty pool I'd so loved.

I would never go there again.

When I had gotten home, my calves burning and my throat tearing with each wheezing breath, the sidewalk had been empty. There had been no Uewatsu at my gate. I had no doubt that they had been there before, though, just as I had no doubt that they were the ones who had shown up at the waterpark to interrupt our conversation, and to hang Cooper Katz.

What I *wasn't* sure of, though, was Slipknot's involvement. The hanging thing seemed like his calling card, but there had been no murder, no hate, no malice in his eyes when I left him.

For a week now, he had been watching me, protecting me, betraying his gang to keep me safe from his own "brothers" and anyone else who threatened to harm me, but why? Why me? If he was the cruel, vicious murderer everyone said he was, then why was he trying so hard to save the life of some redheaded white girl he didn't even know?

These thoughts and others weighed heavy on my mind as I walked to work the next day. I felt confused and discouraged, and I would have spent the entire day down in the dumps if it hadn't been for the unexpected gift that met me upon my arrival.

I felt the silly grin spreading across my face before I even fully processed what I was seeing. My 2-D twin was still smiling kindly at me from the back door of my classroom, but she had changed. There were a few more freckles on her face now, a few more glints of gold in her brown eyes, and a bit more of a rosy blush in her cheeks. There was a flower tucked behind her left ear now too, a pink and white orchid, just like the ones that had been growing on the trees in the painted pool the night before.

It was clear to me now that the same artist was responsible for both pieces, but that didn't matter. What mattered was the word painted above me, curving over my head in a delicate arc of thick, pink-accented white letters the same colors of the orchid. It was more than a word, though, it was a name.

My name.

"Annabelle," I whispered, moved almost to tears once more as I beamed up at the love letter written just for me.

"Who da hell's Annabelle?" griped DeAndre, as he returned to his newspaper nest for the first time in a week. He seemed more bad-tempered than usual, but I barely spared him a glance.

"It's me." I put my hands over my swollen heart and let out a laugh – the first real, true laugh I had laughed in what felt like forty years. "It's me, I'm Annabelle. Annabelle Fitzpatrick."

"Whatever you say, White Girl..."

Eleven

Over the next three days, Luthertown Heights' residents began cautiously emerging from their self-preserving cocoons. The fruit vendors reappeared on the corners, the hookers reappeared on the streets, and the old men came back to huddle around their barrel in front of the liquor store.

"Hey, White Girl!" they called whenever I passed, and I said "hey" right back. It didn't matter what anyone called me anymore, because somehow, somewhere in the depths of that godforsaken city, somebody knew my name. My *real* name. Someone, after six months, had cared enough to learn it, even if I wasn't sure exactly who that someone was.

I had my suspicions, obviously, but my top (and only…) suspect had been MIA for almost a week. I had seen neither cowhide nor curly hair of him or any of the other Uewatsu tribesmen since Monday, but I couldn't say that I really missed them (well, maybe one…just a little).

Life was pretty good to me that week. It seemed as if the impending war had been halted: there had been no more murders, no more harassment outside my apartment, and no more uncomfortable confrontations in my classroom with students who didn't want to be there. I had gotten through *Looney Toons* Tuesday (the day when I let the class watch cartoons on the YMCA's old, rabbit-eared television, complete with ancient VCR), Weenie Roast Wednesday (when I brought hot dogs and soda for everyone, and they spent the afternoon giggling at the word "weiner"), and Thoroughbred Thursday (when we all ran foot races in the gym adjacent to my classroom), all without so much as a bad hair day. Things were good for the first time in a long time, and it had all started with that magical painting outside my classroom door.

I should have known, though, that magic never lasts.

On Friday (Funny Costume Friday, to be precise), Marcus' mom had called to ask me to bring Marcus home after ASC let out, as she had an "err...um...prior engagement." Judging by the pauses between her slurred words and the dull, sluggish sound of her voice, that "er...um...prior engagement" had something to do with getting wasted.

So, I had agreed to walk Marcus home. I had actually missed his company, so I was glad to do it. He was a much better walking companion than Slipknot – he may have been just as quiet, but at least he laughed at my jokes.

"So, what's been going on with you, lately, Mr. Jones?" I asked, as we strolled beneath the sunset, swinging our clasped hands between us.

His response, as always, was a giggle. His round face was still shining with little boy joy after our costume party that afternoon. He had made a crown and a multicolored cape out of two dozen sheets of construction paper and what looked like three yards of Scotch tape, and had won our weekly costume contest by a landslide. He was still wearing it now; he was the perfect cross between prince and pauper in his crooked king's hat and stole, and everyone we passed called out a friendly word to praise him on it.

My oh-so-tender heart swelled again as I realized that, in his small, innocent, unassuming little way, he was bringing the community together. His fans might have been thieves, tramps, and junkies every other minute of their lives, but in that moment, they were all nice, kindly people, smiling at a little boy in a home-made costume.

"Nice cape, lil' man!" called one of the transgender prostitutes that worked the corner of 5th and 2nd.

Marcus beamed and waved his thanks, standing straight and tall with pride.

"You really did a great job on that." I squeezed his hand, unable to keep from smiling too. "Have you ever considered a career in fashion?"

He laughed again.

As we neared his house, I grew a bit more serious, as I always did when I had to turn him back over to his mother. "So, how do you like your mom's new boyfriend? Is he nice?"

He gave me a huge nod, his chin almost touching his chest, and I felt a rush of relief. Good. Maybe he would stick around a while then, and provide Marcus with some stability.

"Does he make your mom happy?"

He nodded again.

"Good, I'm glad."

We arrived at his front gate and stopped. As always, I squeezed his hand, preparing to say goodnight, but before I could speak, he took a step back. Frowning slightly, I watched as he took off his construction paper crown and held it out to me.

"You're giving this to me?" I asked, touched.

He nodded again. I reached out, but he shook his head, and gestured for me to lean down. Biting back a smile, I did as the king commanded, and he placed the crown atop my loose, wavy red hair. I was about to stand back up straight when he suddenly darted in and threw his chubby little arms around my neck.

I laughed as I hugged him back, and to my surprise, he kissed me on the cheek before he scampered away, into his building.

I guess he missed me, I thought, touching the paper crown on my head and trying, for the umpteenth time lately, not to cry.

He appeared in his window sixty seconds later, safe and sound and smiling, and I walked home, feeling every bit like a princess.

. . .

I remember being so happy on that long walk home. I remember reveling in every moment of the silly, childish giddiness that I felt while I wore that goofy paper hat and got cheered by the people I passed. I felt like Sally Field at the Oscars – people liked me! They really liked me! There, in that tough, violent, hard-scrabble community, there were people that cared about me, people who liked seeing me around, people who made me feel happy to be among them. I felt like the luckiest girl in the world.

But luck is a lot like magic – bound to run out.

I hadn't seen the Uewatsu anywhere for over a week, but that night I found them milling around on the sidewalk in front of my building. In spite of having lost six members over the weekend, it looked as if there were more of them than ever, all tall and lean and muscular and dark, and all stamped with the trademark dream-catcher tattoo on their right biceps. It was fifty degrees but they were all shirtless, save for their matching tanned, cowhide vests, and they all seemed to be waiting for something.

As I got closer, I could see a strange hunger in their dark eyes; they were like wolves starving for the flesh of a freshly killed lamb.

And I had a strong feeling that that lamb was me.

I looked for Slipknot's face in the crowd, wondering why he hadn't warned me about them this time, but he wasn't there. Bear wasn't there either, and the group looked listless and unfocused without him.

I stopped about five hundred yards away. They hadn't seen me yet. I'd just turn around and go somewhere else for a while. Maybe that quiet diner on 8th. Maybe Miss Carmella's.

But I knew already that it was too late. I had stepped into a trap, and it was about to swing shut.

"Going somewhere, White Girl?"

I jumped as Bear's smooth, slow, seductive voice spoke directly into my ear. He, like Slipknot, moved like a shadow. I hadn't heard him come up behind me; I hadn't registered a single footstep, a single rustle, a single breath of air. It was as if he had materialized from nowhere.

I tried to turn around, but he wrapped his long, coppery arms around my waist from behind, almost like a lover. He pressed his lips to my ear as he spoke again. "Uh uh uh, you're not going anywhere. Not until we're done with you."

"Help..." It came out like a whisper at first, then louder, like the squeak of a mouse stuck on a strip of glue. *"HELP!"*

That caught the attention of his cronies, and they all turned toward the sound, their hungry eyes flashing with sick anticipation in the glow of the orange streetlamps.

Bear laughed into my neck, making the hairs at the nape stand on end. "Oh, White Girl...how sad...you think you have friends here."

If this were a movie, that would have been the part where my knight in shining armor appeared with his sword drawn to rescue me.

Instead, Bear ran his rough, hot tongue along my jawline, and I screamed bloody murder.

"You taste good enough to eat," he told me, ignoring my desperate, ear-splitting shrieks as I struggled against his grip. "Too bad I have to share..."

I could see the rest of the wolves advancing on me, slow, steady, starving for their scrap of meat. I looked to the windows of the houses that lined the street. Didn't anyone see me? Didn't anyone hear?

I fought frantically to free myself, but Bear was too strong. He laughed again, a sick, arrogant sound. "What's the matter, baby? We only wanna see those pretty white titties of yours..."

His right hand moved to my left breast and I snapped. Bending my knee up high to my chest, I brought my foot down hard to kick Bear in the crotch. He let go with a curse, and I fell to the ground on all fours. I tried to scramble as quick as I could to my feet, but the rest of the pack was on me in seconds, clawing at me with their hands, tugging at my hair, pulling my clothes, dragging me across the pavement as they blocked out the lamplight with their hard, sweaty bodies.

I screamed again from beneath the squirming pile and a fist collided with my jaw, making me see stars. Another hit me in the eye, the neck, the stomach, and a hand closed over my mouth as another pair ripped open my coat, sending the buttons flying.

I was crying now, sobbing, trying to push them away, but I was powerless to stop them. There were thirteen of them and only one of me, and they were going to split me like a rotisserie chicken between them.

I yelped in pain as sharp fingers squeezed my breasts, my thighs, my stomach, preparing me for the main event I didn't dare imagine.

Bear's face, livid with pain now, found its way through the crowd and appeared before mine. He was on his hands and knees, crouching over me, and the wolves moved away, making room for their alpha.

I thought of begging for my life then. I thought of spitting in his face. But every inch of my body was paralyzed with terror, and I could only watch as he pulled a knife from his pocket.

There was a click as he flicked out the blade and I whimpered as he held it up for me to see. He turned it around in his hand for a moment, relishing the power it gave him. Then, suddenly, he thrust it downward and I screamed, knowing it was over, knowing I was dead.

But I wasn't.

As he split my sweater from the seam at the collar, through the lining of my bra, and all the way to the hem at the end, though, I wished I was.

The air was cold against my skin as he ripped away the flaps of clothing, exposing my breasts and stomach. The pack growled and moaned excitedly, and a satisfied smile stretched across Bear's face.

"Finally," he breathed, his voice thick and hoarse with lust. "Now we can all see those nice, pretty white titties you been hidin'."

"Bear!"

There was a collective jerk as the entire pack jumped and turned toward the sound of footsteps.

Bear sat up, frowning, and I closed my eyes, squeezing out two hot, thick trails of tears that slid down my burning cheeks. "What is it, brother?" he asked, sounding breathless and worried.

"The Sixes," said the voice. I knew that voice. I squeezed my eyes shut tighter, hating that voice with all of my might. "The Sixes are at the waterpark. They say you would not dare to meet them there again."

"What? I thought we took care of them when we took out Coo—"

"That is why they said it. They want a fight. They think that they can beat us now because they have a few new recruits."

I opened my eyes again, just in time to see a malicious smile twist Bear's lips. "We'll see about that."

Without sparing me a second glance, he got to his feet. "Take care of this, would you, brother?" he said, slapping Slipknot on the shoulder. Then he took off, gesturing for the rest of the wolves to follow him as I lay there, bare and shaking on the ground.

Twelve

"I did not know they were here," Slipknot said in a whoosh of air as soon as the Uewatsu were gone. His knees banged against the ground like drums as he knelt down next to me, and somewhere deep in the recesses of my scattered mind I noticed that he was no longer a shadow. He was real, and he was frightened. "I thought they would be at our other meeting spot until midnight."

He rested his hand on my shoulder and I flinched at his touch. I gathered my tattered shirt together, holding it over my chest with my shaking fingers as I sat up. "Don't touch me," I warned, my words choppy as I hissed them through chattering teeth, "Don't you *ever* touch me."

"I am sorry, this is my fault, I thought that they—"

"You're damn right it's your fault!" I shouted, shoving him away with my free hand. I got to my feet, tears stinging my eyes, and I let out a wretched sob as I caught sight of the crown Marcus had given me lying, trampled and torn, on the ground near where I had been pinned.

I thought about picking it up, but I knew I would never be able to look at it again without being reminded of that terrible, awful night.

"Let me take you to a hospital—"

"No! Leave me alone!" I shoved Slipknot away again, and stumbled toward the gate.

"Please, let me—"

He made to touch my shoulder again and I whirled on him, catching his wrist with lightning-fast reflexes I would have killed for just a few minutes earlier.

"This is *your* fault," I said, my chest pressed against his as I glared up into his eyes through the veil of tears in mine. "*You* did this! You set me up! You made me believe I was safe, that you were looking out for me, but the one time I really needed you? Where were you? Not here!"

I had never been so furious in all of my life. A small, rational part of me know it wasn't Slipknot's fault, not really, but I was suffocating – my very *soul* was dying – and I needed someone else to feel it too. The girl I was before was gone, ripped apart like my sweater, scattered across the ground like the buttons from my coat and that rumpled, tattered paper crown. I would never get her back. I would never see her again. I would never, ever feel safe.

Slipknot's once expressionless face was pinched with guilt and shame, and his fiery green eyes were full of a pain whose depths seemed to rival my own. Instead of comforting me, though, this only served to hurt me even more.

I let out another sob and collapsed into his chest. I could feel the scratch of the rope around his throat against my forehead as I wept into his t-shirt, and I felt his arms wrap haltingly, hesitantly around me.

His touch, though, reminded me too much of Bear's unwelcome grip on my waist and I leapt back as if he had scalded me.

He looked confused by my shifting moods, but he didn't back away.

"Wh... where were you?" I asked again, scrubbing at my cheeks. It was a futile gesture, though. I could wipe away the tears, but they wouldn't stop coming.

"I came as soon as I could," was his response. Evasive, as always.

"Why do you hang out with those... those scumbags anyway?" I demanded, really, truly needing to know. "Why do you associate with those creeps? Why are you a part of that... that gang? Why are you a part of *them*?"

He was silent.

"Do you want to be like them?" I persisted, getting angrier and angrier. "*Are* you like them? Do you go around killing people and raping girls in the—" I interrupted myself with a sob and gave up.

He reached out a hand and grazed my swollen cheek with his fingertip. "I am *not* like them."

"No, you're worse." I shook my head, reeling from yet another surge of emotions I was too distressed to process. "You're worse because you know they do these things and you don't stop them. You just let them do it. You're disgusting." I stumbled backward through the gate to my apartment complex. "I don't ever want to see you again," I whispered, unable to meet those fiery green eyes, unable to stop feeling his tender touch on my burning skin. "Never again."

He swung the gate shut and stood there, staring after me, long after I had gone inside.

Thirteen

I took one look at myself in my bathroom mirror and broke down completely. Half of my face was swollen and bruised, and the other half was as pale and white as a sheet. My hair was matted and mussed, and there were scratches and scrapes covering my entire body, glowing red against my milky grey skin. My eyes were wide and haunted; whatever traces of light and kindness they had once held was gone, replaced by something that reminded me of a frightened ferret I had once seen in a cage at a pet store.

Wracked with sobs, I turned on the water as hot as I could stand, and I stumbled under the showerhead. The water felt good against my stinging skin, and the soap felt even better. I got a visceral sort of thrill as I scrubbed as hard and as roughly as I could, because that time *I* was in control of the pain.

I scrubbed and I scratched and I scraped until my skin was raw, but it wasn't enough. I could still feel Bear's arms around me, could still feel the blade of his knife. I could still feel the grabbing hands of his deranged wolf pack, and I could still feel the loss of my crown.

Worst of all, though, I could feel the stares of my neighbors, watching from behind their ragged curtains as a woman got beaten, nearly raped, and left for dead. I had been a fool to think that there was any light in the darkness that was Luthertown Heights. I had been a fool to think that anyone cared.

The water ran cold as I curled up in the corner of my bathtub, hugging my knees to my chest, too broken to cry anymore.

Fourteen

I spent the entire weekend in bed, wallowing in self-pity and disillusionment. Then on Monday I woke up, bright and early, and ventured out into the cold, hard-hearted world once more. Luthertown Heights might have abandoned me, but I would not abandon its children. I had decided, as I had hidden beneath my bedsheets, counting my bruises, that the next generation would be a better one, a kinder one. They wouldn't take part in gangs, they wouldn't hurt people just to feel strong. They would be forthright and compassionate and decent, moral human beings. I would make sure of it. I would lead them by example. I might have been a broken shell of the woman I had once been, but I would glue myself back together and keep moving forward, keep helping, keep hoping, keep being there.

That's not to say that it was easy to face the city that had scarred me so badly. I hated myself for the fear I felt as soon as I stepped out my front door. I jumped at every noise I heard on the way to the Y, and I carried my can of mace, open and ready to fire, clenched in my hand the whole way. I had seen Bear's face in every shadow, heard the wolves' hungry growls in the voice of every person I passed. But I had made it.

The students gasped at the green-purple bruises on my chin, and the swollen patch around my right eye. Janelle had screamed out loud when she saw me. Chyna had burst into tears. Even Marcus had lost his smile as they all gathered on the carpet in front of my desk to hear what the theme of the day was.

"Alright, guys," I said, my mouth a bit dry, as I limped around the desk to stand before them. My right knee was still swollen from where it had hit the ground when I fell, but I ignored the pain. "Today is Monday, as you all know, so it's—"

"What happened to your face?"

I didn't have to look up to know that the question came from Lamont. I could recognize the contempt in his voice, just as he could sense the weakness in mine.

The other kids were completely silent – a rarity, to say the least. There was concern written on every one of their smooth, sweet young faces, as they waited to hear my answer.

I had known someone would ask and I had prepared my answer, thoughtfully and thoroughly, over that soul-sucking weekend.

"I was attacked," I said, standing up straight and tall and unashamed.

A collective shiver passed through the group. Even Lamont looked surprised. He hadn't been expecting the truth. He had been expecting the carefully constructed lies that all adults tell to keep kids safe. But I was not that kind of adult. If they didn't know what really happened, they couldn't stop it from happening to someone else in the future. Ignorance wouldn't save Luthertown Heights. Honesty and compassion would.

"How many of you know what a gang is?"

Hesitantly, the older kids raised their hands. I was surprised (and a bit disappointed) to see that Marcus did too.

"Patrice, can you tell the little kids what it is?"

Her face was pale beneath her shock of thick, bushy brown

hair. She swallowed hard, glanced at Janelle, then spoke. "It's... like a group of guys that all get together to do things."

"Like what kind of things?"

"I don't know." She shrugged. "Bad things. Drugs. Sex. Guns. Robbin' stores, stuff like that."

"Right." I nodded, giving her an encouraging smile. "That was a great answer, Patrice, thank you. Gangs are groups of people who are united for some purpose, or have something in common. If that was as far as it went, that wouldn't be such a bad thing. But, unfortunately, the type of gang I'm talking about takes it further than that. Like Patrice told us, they do bad things, they hurt people, and it isn't right."

"Is that who hurt you?" asked Janelle from the back. She looked as if she were on the verge of tears. "A gang?"

"Which crew was it that hit 'chu?" Lamont asked as a follow up. He didn't sound so macho and full of contempt now. He sounded afraid.

"That, I won't tell you," I replied with a sigh. "There is already enough 'choosing sides' in this town, I'm not going to make it any easier. That's why I'm telling you guys this: You have to make decisions for yourself, you have to do what *you* know is right. You can't just go along with something because you wear the same bandanna as someone else, or because you feel pressured into it. This town isn't full of gangs, it's full of *people*, individual people who know right from wrong, and who can make up their own minds. We have to remember that!"

My eyes had gone a bit misty, but I could see the older kids in the back of the room nodding solemnly. I hadn't given them an order, I had offered them a choice – something kids like Lamont may not have felt they had before.

"Does...uh...does anyone have any questions?" I asked, when the weight of their silent stares grew too heavy.

Slowly, haltingly, Chyna's small hand reached up.

"Chyna, yes, go ahead. What do you want to know?"

She looked around, a bit embarrassed. Then, with a chagrinned little smile, she asked, "So... is today still Music Monday? 'Cuz it's my turn to play with the flute."

The entire class roared with laughter, but no one was more delighted than I was. "Okay, okay, you're right," I said between chuckles, "enough of the serious stuff. Go ahead and grab your instruments. But I'd better not hear anyone playing any sad songs!"

The crowd cheered and headed for the music box, and I went back around to sit down behind my desk, content.

As I was watching Clyde Richards struggle with a bent zil on the class tambourine, Lamont walked up to me.

He approached me as if he were being pushed against his will, and I sat back in my chair, surveying him. His hands were clasped behind him, making him look like a repentant child awaiting a scolding, and he had taken down his hood, revealing a surprisingly open, innocent face with a tight buzz cut and the beginning wisps of a black mustache. His skin was the color of dark chocolate, and it glistened with perspiration in the overhead lights.

"Uh... ma'am?"

"Yes, Lamont?"

"Can I... uh..." I wasn't used to this hesitance from him. All of his bluster was gone, having been replaced by a worried, nervous look. "Listen," he tried again, "I know you didn't wanna tell 'dem kids who did that to your face. But I just want... I just *need* you to tell *me*."

I frowned, leaning forward. "Why is that?"

He sighed and looked at the window, then he ran his hand down his face in frustration. "I just need to know, okay?"

I studied him some more. "You need to know if it was the Sixes, your dad's gang," I said, when the realization finally came to me, "the gang you want to join."

"I never said – !" He cut himself off and growled, rubbing his hands on his stubbly scalp. "Yes, okay. Alright?" He said, trying to control the anger rising up in him. "I need to know if it was them."

"Why?"

"Because... because... God dammit, White Girl, just tell me!"

The other kids were watching us nervously now, clearly afraid that Lamont was going to give me another injury to add to my collection. I gave them a reassuring smile, then I turned it to Lamont. "No."

"No? What do you mean, 'no?' Why da hell not?"

"Because of what I said before, Lamont. You have to make up your own mind about people. I can't give you the answers. You have to decide for yourself if you think the Sixes are capable of something like this, and if you agree with it. You said you wanted more control over your life, right? Let this decision be your first step towards that."

He stared at me for a long time, his face crumpled in anger. Then, slowly, it smoothed out, and I knew he had made up his mind.

"Okay," he said, nodding. He was standing taller too, as if a weight had just been lifted from his skinny shoulders. "Okay, I get you. You're aiight, White Lady," he finished, giving me a bright, white smile before he turned away. "You aiight."

I bit my lip. I had been promoted from "White Girl" to "White Lady" in the span of just three minutes. I should not have felt so flattered.

Fifteen

Marcus' mother and her boyfriend were perfectly punctual (and seemingly sober) when they came to pick up Marcus that evening. Again, I was glad, but I was uneasy as well as I locked the door behind me, and stepped into the alley.

"Hey 'dere! Hey, White Girl!"

I jumped at the sound of DeAndre's voice. He had been missing again; I didn't know where he had been for the past week or so. But he was back now, apparently with a vengeance.

"'Bout time you came out here!"

"Hey, DeAndre," I said. I took a quick glance at my likeness on the back of the door, and was glad to see that her face, at least, was still open and freckled and free of dark bruises. "I haven't had a chance to say hi since you've been back! How ar—"

"You know damn well how I am, you little white bitch!"

I flinched at the anger in his voice. He had never spoken to me like that before. "I... excuse me?"

I stared into his heavily shadowed face, taking in everything from his wrinkled forehead to his salt and pepper beard, but could find no answers there.

"You been hangin' 'round them damn injuns, haven't ya?"

I felt the blood rush to my green-tinged face. "What are you talking about?"

"I seen dat one with the rope 'round his neck hangin' round here, walkin' ya home like he thinks he's a human bein'. Why you think I was gone? They animals, all of 'em. Shitty savages."

"I haven't been 'hanging around' anyone," I said coolly, crossing my arms. I was ashamed to admit how close his description had come to reflecting my own at the moment. I cringed at the memory of them circling me like wild dogs, but I snapped myself back to the present before I could lose focus.

"Oh, so them animals ain't the ones who did you?"

I recoiled as if he had slapped me. Insulted, I snapped back, "Nobody 'did' me, DeAndre."

"Oh, really?" He stood up, kicking aside some of his crumpled newspaper blankets. "'Cuz that ain't how I heard it."

"How did you hear it?"

"I head you let 'em all do you so that fool with the rope around his neck could call you his girl. That's the Uewatsu way."

I clenched my fists. "Where did you hear that? That's a lie!"

He shook his head in a gesture of overdramatized disappointment. "You lyin' to yourself. An' you lyin' to them kids. You act like you're such a sweet, innocent lady, offerin' to help me get off the streets, tryin' to keep them kids safe, but that ain't you. You ain't nothin' but a tramp. You just a common street bitch who spreads her legs for every copper-skinned son of a –"

A crack echoed through the alley as my hand collided with his face. I had never slapped anyone in my life, but I'd done it with gusto, sending spittle flying from his mouth, along with a grunt of pain. It felt good for a moment: raw and powerful and primitive. Then that moment passed.

"Oh my God, DeAndre, I'm so sorry!" I covered my own mouth in horror as I took a few steps back. "I didn't mean to—"

"See? Just like them other corner bitches," he said through clenched teeth. I could see the imprint of my hand glowing dark on his wizened cheek. "You ain't nothin' but a disappointment, just like the rest of us. You think you better, but you ain't. You belong in Luthertown Heights."

I dropped my hands. I opened my mouth to speak, but I couldn't find any words. DeAndre sat back down in his nest of papers, and I just went home, with a few new cracks in my shell.

Sixteen

I was still in a foul mood the next day when the kids began trickling in for ASC. I hadn't gotten much sleep because the Uewatsu had begun howling and catcalling at my window around 3:00 a.m. I had already been awake anyway, though, thinking about what DeAndre had said, and what I had done.

"Hi!" Chyna waved as she bounced into the room, carrying a stuffed white cat. It looked like half of its fur had been loved off, and almost against my will, I felt a little better. "Is it still Show and Tell Tuesday?"

"You bet," I replied from behind the desk, giving her my best fake smile.

She squeezed her cat to her chest with glee, and danced over to her spot on the carpet. A few of the other students waved hello when they entered, carrying lumpy, oddly shaped bags full of their greatest treasures, and I took a deep breath, feeling a bit more at peace now that I was back amongst their hopeful, youthful energy.

I was just standing up to greet everyone when Lamont hurled open the door with a bang. He headed straight for my desk and slammed his fist down on it, enraged.

"You *BITCH!*" he screamed at me, his voice hoarse and

broken, and I pulled back, alarmed. His face was covered in scabs and cuts and dark, black bruises, and his lower lip was swollen and oozing. His eyes were bloodshot, and tears stood in them as he glared at me with a hatred that shook me to my very core.

"Lamont! What – "

"You lyin' whore bitch!" He came around the desk, trapping me between the chair and the wall. "You did this to me!"

I blinked at him for a few seconds, uncomprehending. "I did what?"

"Come on, don't act like you don't see it!" He shoved my chair out of the way and stepped closer, pinning me to the wall. My mind flashed back to that night on the concrete outside my house, to Bear's face leering down at me, to my arms pinned to the ground.

"LOOK AT ME!" he roared when I closed my eyes, and he pushed me, hard, against the blackboard.

Without thinking, I pushed him back, just as hard, so that I could breathe. "Don't touch me," I muttered under my breath. I could hear one of the little girls crying from across the room.

"I'll touch you wherever I want to bi – "

Before he could finish, I grabbed his wrist and pulled his arm behind his back, like I'd seen a Krav Maga instructor do in a video on YouTube. In control now, I pushed him toward the back door to the soundtrack of my student's gasps and whimpering, and I shoved him out into the alleyway.

He tripped over his own big sneakers and fell to his knees as I kicked the rock into place and pulled the door to.

"You have no right to touch me like that, Lamont! Not in my classroom, not anywhere! I will not allow...I won't...I..." I trailed off, stupefied, as I glanced up from Lamont's crouching body to the new piece of art on the abandoned factory building across the alley. I found myself staring into the face of a beautiful, majestic grey wolf, whose eyes were like mine. It was incredible, almost mystical, full of strength and power and stoicism, but that wasn't what the artist wanted me to see.

Above the wolf, in the center of a blue-painted sky, was a cloud of words, all scrawled in black spray paint. It was a Cherokee saying, one I had heard before, but it had never spoken to me like it did at that moment.

"There are two wolves inside us all," it read, "One is Evil. It is anger, jealousy, rage, fear, arrogance, and self-pity. The other is Good. It is joy, peace, kindness, compassion, faith, and hope. Every moment of every day, they fight, each trying to gain control. In the end, one will be stronger. Which wolf will win? THE ONE YOU FEED."

"Bitch..." Lamont let out a choking sob on the ground, and I realized that I had been wrong – again. Violence didn't stop violence. Cruelty didn't stop cruelty. Compassion did. I was a compassionate person – that was the wolf I had to feed.

"Lamont, I'm so sorry," I said, dropping to my bruised knees beside him. Tears were in my eyes too as I put my arm across his shoulders. To my complete and utter shock, he didn't try to shake it off.

"You lied to me," he moaned, sitting back on his heels as tears began to stream down his blood-crusted face.

"What do you mean?"

"You said I could decide. You said I could choose my own life! But I can't..."

I frowned, rubbing his back as his face crumpled in misery. "Lamont... what happened? Who did this to you?"

He let out a sick, squelching sniffle and sobbed harder. His shoulders shook as I tightened my grip on them, and he said, "My pops. I told him I don't wanna be in the Sixes. I told him I wanna do somethin' else with my life. I told him I... I told him I... that I, well, that I wanna go to college and play basketball."

"Well that's great! That's a great dream, Lamont! I've seen you carrying your basketball around, I bet you're really good at it!"

"My P.E. teacher says I'm the best center he's ever seen." He sniffled, with a touch of pride. Then his expression darkened once more. "But Pops won't allow it. He says he's already got my whole future all planned out. He says the Sixes are goin' to war, and they need recruits. But I don't wanna go! I don't wanna be like them! I don't wanna hurt teacher ladies and do drugs all day! You know drugs screw up your game, right?"

"You don't have to do it, then," I said firmly, taking his hands and pulling him to his feet. "We'll find some way to work it out, okay? I know a few social workers, I'm sure they would be glad to —"

The rest of my oath was drowned out by a loud, short burst of sound, impossibly loud, impossibly close.

A gunshot.

"Oh my God," I whispered, as Lamont's swollen eyes grew wide and frightened. My stomach twisted and my legs were numb as I threw open the door to my classroom and found the carpet covered in blood.

And Marcus lying facedown in the middle of it.

Seventeen

"Call an ambulance!" I shouted as I rushed to Marcus' side. There was a hole the size of a quarter in his back, just below his left shoulder blade. "Hang on, Marcus, I'm right here."

He mumbled something and I rolled him over onto his back. I let out a low gagging sound as I saw that there was another hole in his chest, at least twice the size of the one on the other side. It was gaping like the greedy mouth of a drowning man trying to suck in air as he fought to stay at the surface of the water. Thick, dark, red blood was pooling atop his sky blue polo, and I pressed my hands against the wound as hard as I could without crushing his fragile, six-year-old ribs.

"What happened?" I asked of the frightened faces around me. The entire class was huddled against the walls now, cowering against each other. I felt as if I were on a stage, performing a bizarre, heart-wrenching play in the round. "Who did this?"

"It was Bobby," replied Janelle. Her voice was shivering as she spoke. "He brought a gun for show and tell."

My wide eyes flew to little Bobby Richardson, a seven-year-old with green eyes and the enormous ears of a man four times his age. "Bobby?"

He was standing apart from the group, weeping silently.

"He said it was his uncle Tony's," Chyna answered for him, weeping as well. "He was sh-showin' it to me and then...bang."

Horrified, I looked back down at Marcus. His eyes were round and glazed as he stared back up at me, unseeing.

"Janelle, go get Miss Combs from the front desk. Tell her to call an ambulance." I ordered, my own voice shaking now too. "Lamont, get these kids out of here, please."

Lamont nodded obediently, no longer my enemy, and ushered the children out the front door and into the lobby after Janelle.

"I'm sorry," Bobby sobbed, trailing behind the others. "I'm so sorry..."

Lamont took his hand and led him out, closing the door behind them.

"Okay, Marcus, it's just you and me now," I whispered, trying to ignore the slick, slippery feeling of his blood soaking my hands. "How are you feeling, can you hear me?"

He made a garbled sound, and a stream of blood and spittle bubbled up from his mouth and slid down his pudgy black cheek.

"No, no, don't...don't do that," I begged him, trying to stave off tears. "Don't do this, you're going to be okay, alright? Just hang on, someone'll be here to help us soon."

He made another gargling noise and gave a shudder.

"No, no! Listen Marcus, you've got to hang on! Let's...let's think about something nice, okay? Do you... do you remember last Friday, when you gave me that crown?"

He nodded his head once, just slightly, and I let out a squelchy laugh. "Yeah! There you go! I loved that crown. I wore it all the way home. I felt like a princess."

"Queen..." he croaked. It was the first time I had ever heard him speak.

And the last.

I smiled. "Oh, so I'm a... Marcus? Marcus!" His body gave a mighty jerk and his brown eyes rolled back in his head as he began to convulse. "No! Marcus!" I tried to hold him still, but he kept shaking, kept shuddering, as blood and spittle continued to pour out of him and over me. "Marcus, no, please!"

Suddenly a pair of arms swooped in and lifted up Marcus, pulling my sweet, kind boy away from me. "Wait –"

"The ambulance will take too long," said Slipknot, his emerald eyes blazing in a face that was the color of plaster as he stood beside me, holding Marcus like an eighty-pound infant. "We will take him in my truck."

I answered with another gagging sob, and we ran out the back door into the alley.

"This way." Slipknot ran like the shadow he was – quick and soundless, slipping through the crowded street without touching any of the startled passersby. I chased after him, hopelessly slow and out of shape, and finally caught up to him at the side of a dented red pickup truck two blocks away.

"The door is unlocked." He was barely out of breath as he pointed at the passenger's door with the crook of his elbow, but I couldn't breathe at all as I yanked it open and climbed inside.

I briefly registered that I hadn't known he had a truck, but at that moment, I felt as if I didn't know anything about anything. He leaned into the cab and placed Marcus gently on my lap, and I began to cry in earnest, wishing I had some sort of medical degree, some sort of bandage, something, anything, that would stop the bleeding. I knew how to sew stitches, but this was beyond stitches. This was beyond anything I was capable of fixing, and it was torturing me.

"We will be at the hospital in five minutes," Slipknot told me, but Marcus was quiet and still now. I had a feeling that timing didn't matter anymore.

He slammed the door shut and ran around to the driver's side as I watched my tears drip down onto Marcus' slack face. That face had been so sweet just a few minutes ago, so full of life and joy and little boy laughter. For months, looking into that bright little face, hearing his pure, angelic laughter, feeling him squeeze my hand when we said goodbye after I walked him home had made my job worth doing, my life worth living.

I could see that face, smiling at me from his bedroom window, waving to let me know that everything was alright.

But nothing would ever be alright again.

"Please hurry," I whispered, as Slipknot revved the engine and sped off into the golden afternoon. I pressed my hand over the wound in Marcus' chest, and felt no heartbeat.

Eighteen

Half an hour later, I was sitting in a chair in the waiting room at St. Joseph's hospital, staring at my hands. I hadn't washed them. They were covered in sticky, red-black blood in various degrees of dryness, and my bleary eyes followed the trails of it up my forearms, then back down to my palms.

I was still staring at them, my mind too numb with pain to think, when a hand appeared out of nowhere to touch mine. It was a big hand, a rough one, scarred in places, and it was streaked with dried blood too. Slowly, gently, it ran a wet white cloth across my palm.

As if in a dream, I watched as the brackish sea of crimson was washed away to reveal a pale, white hand I barely recognized as my own. As the blood-soaked rag moved between my fingers, I looked dazedly up at the man it belonged to.

The first thing I noticed was his worry. I had never seen him worried before – he had always been solid, blank, expressionless. But now his eyes were aflame and his scruffy jaw was clenched so tight that I could have sworn I heard his teeth crackling in protest. He was cleaning my hands but he was watching my face, trying to read my thoughts.

"This is all my fault," I told him, so that he wouldn't have to guess. "I should never have come up with Show and Tell Tuesday. I should never have left the room. I was only gone for a minute! Why did I..." I finished with a growl and clenched my fists on my lap. He gently pried them back open.

"You could never have known," he said.

"Yes, I could have! And I should have!" I cried. "*I'm* the adult! *I'm* the teacher! *I'm* in charge! I should never have taken my eyes off of my class! But Lamont..."

He was cleaning my left hand now, just as gently as he had cleaned the right one. His eyes never left my face.

"You cannot hold back the wind," he said, his raspy voice full of solemnity and wisdom. "You cannot keep what is going to happen from happening. That is not your job."

"Then what *is* my job? To let sweet little boys get murdered in my classroom?" I was crying again. "To let little boys murder other little boys?"

I felt the rough skin of his palms as he pressed them to mine. "It was not murder," he said. "It was an accident."

I let out a deranged bark of laughter. "That's what they can put on Marcus' headstone, right?"

"Do not speak that way."

"Why not?" I was getting louder now, as my grief threatened to suffocate me. "It doesn't matter anymore, right? Marcus is dead. He's *dead*. He's not ever going to... to... walk home with me again. He's not ever going t-to *smile* again, or make construction paper crowns or butterfly wings." The sobs were winning out over my words as their full meaning hit me, punching me in the stomach so hard that I wanted to scream in agony. "He'll never laugh again. Not ever. He...he had the sweetest little laugh... so happy, so... so..." I clenched my hands around Slipknot's, needing something to hold onto, something to steady me, something to keep me from exploding into a thousand pieces of broken shell on the floor. I dropped my voice to a whisper, barely able to see him through the burning tears in my eyes, and said. "He'll never laugh again."

That time when I leaned into him, Slipknot didn't hesitate. He wrapped his arms around me firmly, tightly, and let me sob my heart out into the bloodstained collar of his black t-shirt.

"He is at peace now, Annabelle," he murmured into my ear, "more at peace than he could ever be here in this godforsaken wasteland."

I pulled back a bit and blinked rapidly, trying to see him as I wiped my nose on my hand. "You know my name," I whispered, as something small and long-buried stirred inside me.

He responded by raising his hand and cautiously, delicately touching it to my face. He skimmed it along my cheekbone, and let it rest amongst the tangles in my hair as those emerald eyes bored into my soul.

Before I could ask him how he knew, or why he was there with me in the first place, there was a loud bang as the doors of the waiting room were flung open.

I jumped, afraid it was another gunshot, and Slipknot whirled to his feet, ready for action.

"Where is she?" demanded the cruel, hard voice of a man that I only barely recognized as Marcus' mother's boyfriend, Eddie. His eyes were those of a coke fiend – wide and wild and full of crazed energy – as he scanned the room, looking for me.

"Where is who?" countered the nurse behind the desk, not alarmed by him in the slightest.

"That White Girl from the Y, the teacher! The one who killed my stepson!"

"I'm here," I said, rising to my feet. Slipknot shook his head at me, and tried to block me from view, but I ignored him. What had he just told me? You can't hold back the wind. It was time to accept my fate.

"There you are, bitch," he said, his voice rising dangerously. "*You're* the reason Marcus is dead."

"No, she is not," said Slipknot. His own hoarse voice was tight with anger.

"You keep outta this, you... you timbernigger! I'm talkin' to *her*!"

"Where's Miss Amy?" I asked, putting a steadying hand on Slipknot's already steady wrist. "Where's Marcus' mother?"

"Where do you think she is?" I was frightened to see a tear slip down his square face. "She's lyin' on the floor at home, high as a fuckin' kite, like always! She don't even know!"

Oh, God, I thought, feeling sick to my stomach, *she doesn't know her son is dead...* I squeezed Slipknot's wrist harder.

"I came as soon as Miss Combs called me. But when I got here, they told me I was too late. Marcus is dead. He's DEAD!"

On the final word, he whipped a gun out of his waistband, another gun, another killing machine. I hadn't seen the gun that killed Marcus, and, absurdly, I found myself wondering if they were the same model.

The nurse behind the desk was worried now. She hastily punched some buttons on her desk phone, dialing security. Everyone else in the room was agape, not with horror or fear, really, but something more like dead-eyed fascination. They had already seen too much for this to scare them.

And so had I.

I think some strange, dark part of me was hoping he would pull the trigger. Some part of me wanted to die. I would never be happy again, I would never live a day without guilt or shame or fear, so why not get it over with now? Why not just end it already?

It was this reckless dispassion that urged me to let go of Slipknot and step toward Eddie. Slipknot grabbed at my hand, but I waved him away.

"Go ahead," I said softly, crossing the room to stop three feet in front of the gun barrel. "If it'll make you feel better, go ahead. I deserve it. I didn't kill Marcus, but I might as well have."

Slipknot muttered something behind me, but I kept my gaze

locked on Eddie. He made a sputtering sound as more tears followed the first, and the gun shook in his hands.

"Just know, though, that killing me won't change anything. It won't stop the violence. It won't stop seven-year-old boys from bringing guns to school, and it won't stop them from growing up and killing other boys on the streets. If they grow up at all."

His lip was quivering as I stepped up to press my heart against the gun barrel. I could feel its cold steel through my shirt. "I loved Marcus too, Eddie," I whispered, my own cheeks growing wet once more. "And I think – no, I *know* – that he loved me back. Do you really want to kill someone that your stepson loved? Do you really want to make this world he loved so much into an even darker place?"

The gun was trembling harder than his lip now. His finger toyed with the trigger, touching, not touching; certain, uncertain. I felt like a lifetime passed as I waited to see which way the wind was going to blow.

Then, just like that, he dropped his arm and let the gun fall to the floor.

"I love that boy," he said, as the hospital's security guards swarmed him, "I loved him like he was my own son."

"He loved you too," I replied, "he told me so."

He squeezed his eyes shut as the tears rolled down his crumpled face, and the security guards dragged him away.

Nineteen

"You are an idiot," said Slipknot, as we left the hospital. "He would have killed you."

I answered with one of his trademark responses: silence.

I walked two more steps down the cracked sidewalk before he caught me by the wrist and spun me around to face him. "Don't tell me you *wanted* him to shoot you."

I didn't meet his eyes. "We should go."

"No." He squeezed my arm. "Not until you tell me that I am wrong."

"About what?"

"About wanting to throw your life away."

I sighed. "Just let it go, okay? What do you care, anyway?"

He took hold of my other arm to keep me from turning away. "Don't you ever give into that impulse." I had never heard his voice so hoarse before, or so forceful. "Promise me."

I frowned up at him. There was something different in his eyes now, something like panic. When I didn't answer, he shook me and said, "Promise me, Annabelle!"

"I promise!" I replied, frightened by his intensity. "I promise. It was just a fleeting thought. It's gone now."

"Do you swear?"

"Yes, I swear."

He stared at me for a long time, looking for lies in my steady gaze. Then, just like that, he dropped my arms and turned away, heading for his truck. "Come on," he said. "I will take you somewhere you can get cleaned up."

I frowned after him. "Like my apartment?"

"No," he said. "Like mine."

My mouth fell open in surprise.

"Are you coming?"

Too intrigued to protest, I hurried to catch up to him.

. . .

"The Uewatsu will be at your apartment until late tonight. I will take you home when they are gone."

"You won't be with them?"

"If everything goes according to Bear's plan, no."

Slipknot lived on the very outskirts of Luthertown Heights, on the top floor of a brown brick apartment building that listed so far to the left that I was sure it would fall over before we even got out of the truck. There were nine floors in total, each bearing at least one broken window, and no elevator. We reached the top floor via the fire escape on the outside of the building, and I was huffing and puffing like an asthmatic when I finally caught up to Slipknot at his door.

He hadn't spoken a word during the entire drive over, and that didn't seem likely to change as I watched him insert a key into the lock on the fire door, apparently his entrance of choice.

"What's Bear's plan?" I panted, as the key turned with a click, and he eased the door open.

He put his finger to his lips and tiptoed into the apartment alone, leaving me out on the fire escape. Baffled, I crossed my arms against the cold – I hadn't put on a jacket before our mad, futile dash to the hospital with Marcus – and waited for him to come back. I felt exposed in the open air, a hundred-plus feet above the ground, and my stomach began to churn with doubt.

I really had not thought this through. What if this was a trap? What if Slipknot was preparing me as a snack for his ravenous wolf brethren? What if this wasn't his apartment at all, but some sort of murder house? I might have wanted to die before, but not now, not like that!

I bit my lip and took a slow step toward the crosshatched metal staircase. Just as I was about to begin my descent, though, Slipknot opened the door.

"Where are you going?" he asked, looking down at the stairs.

"Uh... nowhere."

His green eyes scanned the neighboring rooftops, then he beckoned me inside.

"I always have to check when I get home," he said, bolting the fire door behind us (not only a classic horror movie motif, but a safety violation to boot). "Sometimes there are people here who shouldn't be."

"Like Bear?"

"Or worse."

He moved past me where I stood, frozen in the doorway. I heard another click, and the room was filled with light.

"What the..." my heart had flown up into my mouth.

Every wall of the one-room apartment was completely covered in graffiti. There were tall, majestic trees; lush, flower-pocked bushes and greenery; blue skies full of clouds and singing birds and jumbo jet airplanes. There were animals everywhere: squirrels, mice, rabbits, lions, tigers, cats, dogs, wolves, and people, people that I recognized from television or book jackets, or from the streets around the Y, all in glorious, perfect, living color.

"Is... is that John Wayne?" I asked stupidly, after a long moment of shameless, openmouthed gaping.

Slipknot didn't answer. He moved into the kitchen area to the left side of the one-room apartment, where there was a stove covered in sea anemone and a fridge painted the colors of the sky at sunset.

I took one tentative step into the room, squinting at the cowboy in the bottom right corner of the wall that faced me. Yep. That was John Wayne, alright. He was wearing his trademark white cowboy hat, complete with subtle sweat stains above the brim, and was sitting astride a magnificent brown and white stallion as he smiled at me. Next to him was Martin Luther King, Jr., wearing a brown suit the same color as his skin as he stood behind a podium. In a cartoon speech bubble above his head were the words "I have a dream." To his right was Katharine Hepburn, smiling brightly in a blue-grey pantsuit, and next to her was DeAndre, the homeless man who lived outside the Y. He was wearing a white lab coat and holding a college diploma. On *his* right side was Maya Angelou, Barak Obama, Alan Alda, Gandhi, and finally, another familiar face.

"You know Miss Carmella?" I asked, as I gaped at her perfectly reproduced likeness. She was still heavy in Slipknot's painting, but her curves were more shapely, her eyes were more bright – she had been painted with love. "I clean her house on Saturdays."

He didn't respond to that either.

"What is all this?" I asked, sweeping my arm across the crowd of faces.

"People I admire," he replied. He stepped out from behind a brown oak kitchen table (the only unpainted surface in sight), and handed me a glass of ice water.

"You admire DeAndre?"

"There is more to his story than you know."

I sipped my water thoughtfully. "Will you tell me?"

"About DeAndre? Not now." He took a long drag from his

own glass of water, and I winced. Every swallow came with a stuttering, clunking sound, as if the water was struggling to get past some sort of blockage in his throat. I recalled, then, his hoarse, raspy voice, and wondered if there was more to *his* story too.

"So you're the artist," I said, as he finished off his drink with a choking sound and a long, painful-sounding exhale. "You're the one who paints everything in town. You're the one who painted me."

He went back to the kitchen to put his glass in the sink.

"Why?" I asked him.

"Why what?"

Well, that was a loaded question. "Why don't you paint on canvas, for starters?"

"Can't afford it."

"Why don't you sign any of your work?"

"You think anyone would respect a gangbanger with an eye for color?" He raised an eyebrow at me as he turned back around, and I almost laughed. Instead, though, I asked the question I had been wanting to know for almost two weeks now.

"Why did you paint *me*?"

"The shower's in there," he said, not meeting my eyes as he pointed to a door hidden amongst the crowd. "I'll get you something to wear."

I made a sound somewhere between a chuckle and a sigh of resignation. "I hate that you do that. You never answer anything."

"It hurts me to talk." He went over to a chest of drawers (covered in painted azaleas) near John Wayne's horse and dug through a stack of black and gray clothes on the top.

"Is something wrong with your neck?" That never occurred to me before. I had always thought that the rope was a symbol of his aggression, a wordless threat, but maybe it was more than that. "Maybe if you loosen that –"

"Here." He shoved some clothes into my hands and pointed toward the bathroom again.

I opened my mouth to say something more, but he had already gone back to the kitchen.

I felt out of place as I stepped into Slipknot's tiny bathroom. It was barely eight feet square, with room for just a toilet, a sink, and a slender shower stall. The walls in here, too, had been graffitied, this time with an ocean of starfish and bubbles and sharks. I felt as if I had stepped into a work of art; I was afraid to touch anything.

Slowly, gingerly, I peeled off my clothes, trying not to look at the crusted blood on them as I dropped them to the floor. I turned on the faucet and waited until the water was warm before I stepped under it.

Just like the other day, I turned it up as hot as I could stand it, so hot that it scalded my skin. Being alone again in that tiny room had eliminated any distractions Slipknot could provide, and the day's events came crashing down on me like a tidal wave. It was all I could do not to drown in them.

All at once I could see Marcus' face again, glassy eyed and blank, as he stared up at me from my lap. He was dead before he reached the hospital. He might have been dead before we even got into the truck. I had cradled him to me, wanting him to blink those big brown eyes, wanting to pass my life force to him, wanting to love him back to life. But I couldn't.

The bullet had pierced both his lung and his heart. There was nothing anyone could have done. I had never felt so helpless in all my life. I felt even more powerless than I had been when the Uewatsu jumped me. Physical, flesh and blood threats could possibly be stopped. Intangible ones like death, though, could not.

As Slipknot had said, you can't hold back the wind.

All I could do then was cry, and that's what I did again now, under the scalding water, knowing it wouldn't change anything, but wishing like hell that it could.

After a few more stifled sobs, I washed my skin and hair, watching the blood run like diluted red paint down the drain.

Then I turned off the water, toweled myself off, and got out of the shower stall.

The air was icy against my overheated skin, and I immediately pulled on the clothes Slipknot had given me: a long-sleeved black sweatshirt that hung off my shoulder and down to my knees, and a pair of jeans with holes in the shins that fell right off then I tried to walk in them. I decided to just go without them for now (as I had already spent a surely suspicious amount of time in the bathroom), and wore the sweatshirt like a dress over my own faded pink panties as I stepped back out into the apartment.

"I was starting to think you had drowned," said Slipknot from the kitchen. Something smelled wonderful. He was frying something on the stove, and draining a large pot of pasta in the sink.

"I think I almost did. Did you know that your bathroom is underwater? I think a shark almost bit me."

"Do not mind him," he said, turning around with a skillet full of meatballs. "He is..." His green eyes fell to my bare legs. "...harmless."

I put one bare foot over the other, feeling self-conscious, and his eyes darted back to my face. He narrowed them, oblivious to the rush of color in his cheeks (that rivaled the one I felt in my own), and said, "You have been crying."

My stomach fell. For a fleeting moment, I had forgotten about the hell that was now my life, but he had dragged me right back down into it.

"That smells good," I said, pointing to his skillet and avoiding *his* question this time. "Spaghetti and meatballs?"

He kept staring at me for another few seconds, then nodded.

"You didn't have to go to all that trouble." I crossed the room cautiously to perch on the edge of one of three rough, wooden chairs at his table.

"It is no trouble. And you have to eat."

I pressed my lips together awkwardly, not sure what else to say. I traced a crack in the wooden tabletop, listening to the sizzling of the meatballs and wondering how I could feel so hungry and so nauseated at the same time.

"It's kind of strange, being in your apartment," I said, to take my mind off my stomach. He didn't respond, so I just kept on talking. "I never really thought about where you would live, or what your house would look like. But I guess we're sort of even now, since you know where I live."

He switched on a third burner, lighting a flame beneath another pot – this one a saucepan – into which he poured a can of seasoned tomato sauce. I had a feeling that he would let me ramble on forever, and I had an even stronger feeling that if he didn't stop me, I just might.

"I always loved that graffiti around town. It always made me happy. I never would've guessed that you were the one who painted it. Not that you can't paint happy things!" I amended hastily, blushing again. "You can be happy, obviously. I mean, I guess you can, I don't know you very well... what's that about anyway? How is it that you're always around, but I don't know anything about you? That's... can I have another cup of water, please?" *Anything to shut me up...* I thought, squeezing my eyes shut.

He filled another glass under the faucet and handed it to me. Oh, good, he *had* been listening.

I gulped the water down and put the empty glass back on the table. The cool drink seemed to have sobered me up a bit, and my voice was steadier now as I wondered, "Can I ask you something?"

"After dinner." He switched off the burner and stirred his pasta into the sauce, along with the meatballs.

He got two white plates down from a sky blue cabinet above the sink (complete with airy clouds and another singing Blue Jay), and put one in front of me. It was old and thin and chipped on one side, but for some reason I very much wished I could keep it. Perhaps as a souvenir of the time I visited the house of a gentle-manly gangbanger.

He piled the plate high with spaghetti and topped it with parmesan cheese shaken from a can, and sat down across from me to repeat the process on his side.

I waited for him to dig in, then I followed suit. The meatballs were delicious, with just the right amount of spice, and the sauce was light and sweet.

I watched Slipknot as he ate, listening to the garbled click of his esophagus each time he swallowed. He kept his eyes on his plate at all times, as if he were concentrating hard, and he seemed to be literally choking down each bite. It was painful to witness.

"Please stop that," he rasped, without looking up.

"Stop what?" I replied, as if I didn't know.

"I do not like people watching me eat. Or drink. Or talk."

"Then what's left?"

He looked up at me, unamused.

I quickly dropped my gaze to my own plate. "Sorry."

We ate the rest of our dinner in silence. As I came to my last meatball, a warm, drowsy sort of feeling began to wash over me. It had been a long, terrible day, and I hadn't realized until then how exhausted I was. Images of my cozy bed kept swimming through my mind, and I was fairly certain that if my host didn't take me home soon, I would fall asleep right there at his table.

I rested my chin on my hand as he gathered up the dirty dishes and deposited them in the sink. I was just considering letting my heavy eyelids fall shut when Slipknot said, "Okay. You can have three questions."

My chin nearly slipped off my hand. "What?"

"I said you can ask me three questions."

I was wide awake now as I gaped up at him again. "Really? And you'll actually answer them?"

"If I can." He sat back down across from me. He was sitting up very straight, as if he were uncomfortable, and his scarred hands were clasped in front of him.

I felt like I had just rubbed a magic lamp. I couldn't believe I was finally going to get some answers! But what should I ask? I had dozens of questions for him, hundreds, thousands! But I could only ask three...

"Can my first question be to ask for more questions?"

The corners of his mouth twitched slightly. "I am not a genie."

"Okay, okay." I grinned. "That one didn't count!"

He nodded and waved a hand, encouraging me to proceed.

"Okay, first question. What happened to your neck?"

His jaw tightened. "Bad choice. I cannot answer that one yet."

"Why not?" I asked, disappointed.

"Is that your second question?"

This was getting old in a hurry. I don't know why I had believed he would really tell me anything I didn't already know. I sat back in my chair and crossed my arms over my chest. "No, the second question is this: How do you know my name?"

He sat back too, mirroring me. "The Uewatsu claimed your apartment building as part of their territory. When you first moved in, I asked the landlord for your information."

I wasn't sure how I felt about that. "Why?"

He shrugged. "Next question."

This was infuriating. It was like trying to have a conversation with a Zoltar Machine. With an edge to my voice I asked, "How did you get there so fast when Marcus was shot today?"

His green eyes were aflame once more as he stared deeply into mine, trying to decide how much to tell me. "I was close by."

"Most people usually run *away* from gunfire, not towards it."

"That is not a question."

"I'm out of questions."

He stared at me for a moment, his face unreadable. "I heard the shot," he said slowly, as if he were saying it against his will.

"And you ran toward it."

"Yes."

"Why?"

"Because I thought it was you who had been hit."

I uncrossed my arms. "You thought I'd been shot, so you ran to save me?"

He stared back, eyes blazing, as he clenched his fists on the tabletop.

"Even after what I said to you the other night about never wanting to see you again?"

I had never seen eyes so green, or so full of intensity. I didn't know what he was holding back, but it looked as if it were about to burst out of him.

"Why?"

"You are out of questions."

I stared back at him, more intrigued than I had ever been in my life. Then I dropped my eyes to the table and sighed. "Oh well. One out of three's not bad I guess."

"I answered two."

"Let's call it one and a half." I found myself smiling wryly as I glanced back up at him. "Anyway, you win."

"I would not call it 'winning.'"

Silence fell between us, and my smile faded into a weary sort of guilt. "I'm sorry about that, by the way."

He raised an eyebrow.

"About what I said the other night," I clarified. "I shouldn't have said that to you, it wasn't your fault."

"Yes, it was," he replied, sitting up straight again. "But I will not let it happen again."

I frowned. "How could –"

Suddenly a loud bang interrupted me, making us both jump.

"Ey! Slipknot! Open up!"

My spaghetti-filled stomach clenched as Bear's voice shouted at us through the front door. Before I could say anything, Slipknot had scooped me up, out of my chair, and was running across the apartment with me in his arms. He flung open the door to the bathroom and deposited me gently inside, pressing a finger to his lips again, his fiery eyes wide with fear.

He closed the door between us, and I was plunged into darkness.

I tiptoed closer to the door and pressed my ear against it to listen. I wanted to turn on the light, but I wasn't sure if it would be visible around the doorframe. So, I closed my eyes as the suffocating blackness pressed in on me, and pretended I was at home in my bed, having a scary dream that would surely be over soon.

I heard the muffled sound of the door opening, and Slipknot's muffled voice.

"Bear. What is it? Has something gone wrong?"

"We need you," Bear replied. He sounded winded. "The Sixes, they were everywhere. They have doubled their numbers since last week! It was an ambush. They got Cairo and Leather Jim."

Leather Jim? I mouthed incredulously. This was a very strange dream indeed...

"Dammit." Slipknot's voice again. Deadpan as always.

"You're coming, right? We need you!"

"I... I am not sure that I..."

"Listen." I could tell that Bear's voice had moved. Perhaps he had stepped closer to Slipknot, because his voice was quieter now, and more desperate. "Your Elisi can go without your visit for one night, right? We need you, brother. We're dying."

Slipknot was clearly hesitating, and I squeezed my eyes shut tighter, repeating *say no, say no, say no, say no,* over and over again in my head.

"Alright. Just let me get changed." I fought the urge to ball my fist up and bang it against the door. "I will meet you on the street."

"You won't regret this, little brother." There was a smile in Bear's voice now, and something bordering on excitement. "I can always count on you. Bring your piece."

"Okay. Go now. I will be right down."

Muffled footsteps were followed by the closing of the door. I had just stepped away from my own when it flew open, and I found myself blinking up into the solemn face of Slipknot.

"You can't go," I said, without preamble.

"I have to." He took me by the hand and led me over to a queen-sized mattress on the floor in the corner beneath the apartment's one and only window. "Stay here and get some rest. I will be back to take you home in –"

"No!" I exclaimed, fighting his attempts to have me sit down on his bed. "No, you can't do this! You can't go!"

He didn't answer. He moved to the dresser and pulled off his jacket and his own blood-crusted shirt, revealing a tanned, sinewy back covered in scars.

This only frightened me more.

"After all that happened today, how can you go out there and… and…" my mind flashed back to all of the blood on my hands, to Marcus' lifeless face, and tears sprang to my eyes.

He turned back around to face me as he pulled on the signature leather vest of the Uewatsu.

That was what broke me.

"This is not who you are!" I cried, barely able to look at him as he outfitted himself in the uniform of my would-be rapists. It made me sick to think of him as one of them.

But that's what he was, wasn't it?

"I have to go."

"Wait!" I sprang across the room in one clumsy bound and grabbed ahold of the lapel of his vest. "Please don't do this," I begged him. Once more, my eyes were blurred with tears as his bored into me. "Please, don't go."

His voice was low and rough as he gently pried my hands off his clothing. "I have to."

"*Why?* Why are you doing this? How can you go out there and kill someone? Haven't enough people died in Luthertown Heights already?"

"They will die whether I am there or not." He opened the top drawer of the chest and pulled out a revolver. He tucked it into the back of his waistband, like all good gangbangers do, and I felt faint.

"Then... then all the more reason not to go!" I pressed on, blocking his path as he headed for the exit. "Stay here with me, and we'll... we'll have spaghetti and meatballs again, like normal people!"

He kept walking until my back was pressed against the fire door.

"STOP!" I shouted at him, holding out my hands. His chest pressed against them, and I could feel his heart thundering, betraying the calm, impassive facade he had so carefully constructed.

I thought he would pick me up again and move me aside, as if I weighed nothing, meant nothing. Instead, though, he raised his hands and softly wiped away the tears that I had been unable to contain.

"If I do not go, he will kill us both," he said to me. His raspy voice was quiet now, sincere. Apologetic.

"Isn't there anything I can do to change your mind?" I whispered. His hands were resting against my face, cupping it, holding it. His touch was so gentle, so kind – nothing like that of the so-called "brothers" he was going to meet.

"It is not my mind that has to change."

He leaned in close and pressed his lips against my forehead, ever so lightly. "I will be back soon, Annabelle Fitzpatrick." I shivered as his mouth moved against my skin.

Then, he reached around me to open the door, and disappeared into the night.

Twenty

I still felt shaken as I lay awake in Slipknot's bed, two hours later. After all we had seen that day, he had still gone out to kill the Sixes with his Uewatsu "brothers." Was he shooting someone right now, as I lay there waiting for him? Was he stabbing them with a knife like Bear's? Or maybe he was strangling them with the rope from around his own neck, like the sadist everyone said he was.

But it wasn't like that.

The more time I spent with him, the more I knew he wasn't a coldblooded killer. Killers didn't help take wounded boys to the hospital. They didn't make spaghetti and meatballs. They didn't kiss girls on the forehead and swear to them they would return.

And that kiss! Why had he done it? Why had he held my face and wiped my tears? Why did he follow me around, protecting me from rowdy students and his own fellow tribesmen?

And why had he been so frightened at the thought of me being shot at the Y?

I remembered his face; the color of taupe, with unbridled terror in his eyes. I had thought it was fear of the blood, or of being too late to save Marcus, but maybe it was fear of losing me.

But how can you lose someone you never had?

I rolled over on his pillow. It smelled like him – like warm cedar and the air at the beginning of spring.

I growled and rolled over again. No. I was not doing this. I could *not* fall for a gangster. It was idiotic.

But, as Slipknot himself had said, you can't hold back the wind.

Twenty-One

I fell asleep around 10:00 p.m. and dreamed of gory corpses and silver guns and glowing green eyes that followed me wherever I went. They were blinking down at me from a painting of Marcus when I heard a sound and bolted upright.

Instantly alert, I pulled the blankets up to my chest as I watched the silver handle of the fire door jiggle. I was too frightened to move, so I just watched as it shook a few more times before the door swung inward and something heavy fell to the floor with a dull thud.

I quickly tried to disentangle myself from the sheets, plunging into the cold apartment air as the night blew in through the open door.

Finally, I freed myself and ran over to kneel beside Slipknot's limp body. His face was turned to the side and a bleary eye blinked up at me. There was blood dripping from a cut on his bare right shoulder, slicing through the center of his tribal tattoo and pouring from a split in his earlobe where someone had ripped out the dreamcatcher earring he wore. The purple scar on his face stood out vividly against his clammy, pallid skin, and there was a bullet hole in his upper left leg that was bubbling with thick, partially congealed crimson goo.

"Oh my God, what happened to you?"

I hastily grabbed his torso and shoved him further inside, smearing the laminate floor with blood. I slammed the door shut and rolled him over so that I could see his whole face.

"Told you... I would be back..." he grunted.

I had to struggle to hold back a hysterical laugh.

There was a hole on the front of his thigh too- the wound was through and through. If the bullet hadn't hit a muscle or an artery, he would be okay.

It wasn't just a cut on his bicep, though: a three-inch long chunk of his arm was missing, as if another bullet had winged him there. It, too, was clotting, thank God. Unlike Marcus, I could save this one.

"Hold still, I'll get some towels!"

"Kitchen... under sink."

I raced off to find them. I grabbed a glass of water while I was there too, and a bottle of rubbing alcohol from beneath the sink.

"Bandages?" I called.

"Bathroom. Cabinet under the mirror." He sounded weak and groggy, so I ran faster.

When I returned to him, though, full of adrenaline and out of breath, he had dragged himself up into a sitting position, leaning against the wall beside the door.

"What are you doing? Lie back down."

"No, I can do it," he said, trying to take the rags and the bandages from my arms.

I turned out of his reach. "No way! Let me do it!"

"I know how to stitch myself up." He sounded almost drunk, slurring his words.

"I can see that." I nodded at the lumpy, jagged scars criss-crossing each other over his bare chest. "Here, try to drink this."

I handed him the glass of water, and he winced as he tried to grab it, clutching the divot in his arm.

"Stop. Here." I knelt between his open legs. I put the rim of the glass to his mouth and tipped some water in. Half of it spilled down his chin, but he didn't seem to notice. He was watching me strangely, with a look on his face I had never seen before.

"Sorry," I said, once he had taken a few painful sounding gulps. I put the cup down and dabbed his chest with a towel to try to sop up the water. Once it was damp, I used it to clear away the blood from his other wounds, starting with his torn earlobe.

"This is going to need a stitch or two..." I tutted, as the bright red blood kept gushing. "Ears have a lot of tiny blood vessels in them, that's why they bleed so much. It's hard to stop the bleeding once it starts."

"I can do it."

"*I* can do it," I insisted. "Unless you'd rather go to the hospital? That would be better... I'm not that good at stitches...they never look right..."

He raised his eyebrows. "You've sewn stitches before?"

"My mother was a nurse." I replied, blushing slightly. "She taught me first aid."

"Stitches are a little more than just 'first aid'..."

I chucked, relaxing slightly. "She taught me first *and* second aid, then. She used to let me practice on dolls. Then, one time when the attending physician was out of the room, she let me stitch up her friend Lori's finger at the hospital where she worked. She had cut it trying to slice an avocado."

I glanced up from his shoulder wound to find that his strange look had grown even stranger.

"What?" I asked, feeling self-conscious.

"Nothing. I just... I have never heard you speak like that before."

I blushed harder. "Like what?"

"Like the world is not ending. Like we are just two people having a conversation."

Maybe he really was drunk.

"See?" I placed a folded towel over the hole in his thigh. "That's what it can be like when people actually answer your questions."

He sighed and leaned his head back against the wall, but I could have sworn that I saw the corners of his mouth twitch again. "Fine, ask me something."

"Where's the thread you use for stitches?"

"That is what you are going with?"

I laughed a little as I got to my feet. "That one is unrelated."

"Sure..."

"Well?"

"On top of the refrigerator, in a little black box. The needle is in there too."

"Any buttons?" I asked, as I went to retrieve it.

"No buttons. Maybe a zipper, though."

I stopped and whirled back around. "You just made a joke!"

"I know," he rasped, with his face as deadpan as ever. "I really must be fading."

"Well, stay away from the light," I said, not liking that joke nearly as much as the first.

"Deal."

I got the sewing kit and knelt back down in front of him. He scanned my face for a moment, his green eyes a bit clearer than before, then he closed them.

"Okay, *now* I'll ask my question." I dabbed away some more blood from his earlobe.

He nodded his permission.

"What happened to you?"

To my surprise, that time he really answered me.

"Bear was right about it being an ambush," he said, his voice a low monotone, "but he was wrong about the Sixes. Their number had not doubled; the Creepers were with them, and some of the Crips. They lured the Uewatsu into a trap so they could take us out."

I knew I shouldn't have let you go... I thought to myself. But to him I said, "Why?"

"Because they know what Bear is up to. He wants to take over *all* of Luthertown Heights, and claim it for the Uewatsu."

"And they were trying to stop him?"

He nodded again.

"Geez..." This was a lot to take in. "So, what happened when you got there? How did you get hurt? Or, better yet, how did you get back here alive?"

His lips twitched. "One question at a time, please."

"Sorry." I leaned closer to swab his earlobe with some alcohol. He barely flinched.

"When we got there, to the waterpark, there were bodies everywhere. At least six of the Sixes, Crips, and Creepers were dead, and so were Benny and Cal from the Uewatsu. Someone had shot out one of the streetlights, so it was dark. We kept tripping over their bodies."

I had stopped prepping his ear and was simply kneeling in front of him, aghast at all of the terrible things that had gone on outside while I slept.

"Bullets and knives and arrows were flying everywhere. It was a war zone." His dark face clouded slightly, but his monotone never wavered. "I got hit the first time trying to pull Sonny up from a ditch he had fallen into. Half of his face had been blown off, but he was still breathing. I had just gotten him to his feet when one of the Sixes nicked my arm with a bullet, and I dropped him. Sonny told me to leave him there."

He paused for a long time, his expression unreadable, his eyes still closed.

"Did you?" I was afraid to know the answer.

"I had to, Bear was calling me. He wanted me to cover him as he went for the leader of the..." he trailed off and I frowned. That seemed like an odd place to stop the story...

Then I noticed that I was squeezing his hand as it rested atop his wounded thigh.

I quickly snatched it back.

"The leader of the Sixes," he went on, his voice a bit huskier than it had been before, "Clem Katz."

"But I thought he was already dead?"

"*Cooper* Katz is dead. Clem is his brother. *Was* his brother. And now Calvin Katz has taken over for him. Clem was hiding behind a tree, blocked by three of his men. Bear hacked through them with a machete."

I blanched. "How could you watch all this?"

"It is not the first war I have seen, unfortunately." His voice was tinged with a hint of sadness now. "Anyway, Bear got through to Katz, but before he hit him, Katz shot me in the thigh. I fell, and one of the Creepers came up and ripped the dreamcatcher from my ear as a trophy. Then the Sixes, the Creepers, and the Crips all scattered, and the Uewatsu followed suit."

"Wait, they didn't even stay to help you?"

For the first time, a smile crossed his pale face. It was a dark smile though, a humorless one. "Bear saw that I had been hit. He saw the blood, and he left me for dead. But it is not the first time I have seen *that* either."

"What? Are you kidding me?" I had skipped right over incredulous and gone straight to furious. "He just left you there? What about all that stuff about you being his 'brother?'"

"In the wild, it is every wolf for himself. You can run with the pack, but if you can't keep up, they will leave you behind."

"This...that...that's bullshit!" I stammered, clenching my fists. "You tried to help Sonny!"

"I told you before." He finally opened his eyes. "I am not like them."

"Then why did you go tonight? Why did you run with them? They're assholes!"

"They are all I have."

"That's not..." I stopped myself. What was I saying? That that wasn't true? That he has me?

Was I an idiot?

He was looking at me strangely again, and I busied myself with the needle and thread. "You didn't answer my last question," I pointed out quietly, my face burning.

"How did I get back here alive?"

I nodded that time.

"I walked."

My eyes snapped back to his face. "From the waterpark? That's halfway across town!"

He shrugged. "I had no other choice."

"You had a hole in your leg! How did you walk that far? And up all those flights of stairs? What are you, Superman or something?"

"Not Superman."

"Then what are you, then? Crazy?"

His eyes were full of emerald fire as he stared into mine. "Determined."

I felt a chill go through me.

"I promised you I would be back. I keep my promises."

For some reason, I blushed again. "Well... I'm glad you made it."

He watched me silently, as I threaded the needle with some black thread and took a deep breath.

"So...uh... I guess I'm going to sew you up now."

"Okay." He didn't brace himself or anything as I leaned forward, my stomach nearly touching his chest as I held the needle up to his earlobe. He didn't question my qualifications, he didn't tell me to be careful; he just sat there, patiently trusting a stranger with his life.

"Can I ask *you* a question now?" He winced only slightly as the silver needle pierced his skin.

In spite of the chilly apartment air, I was sweating profusely. It had been a long time since I had stitched so much as a quilt, and the feeling of the needle moving through the dangling flap of thick tissue was making me nauseous. I could *not* screw this up.

"Sure, I'm an open book." Yes! The first stitch was complete and no one had died. "Ask me anything."

"Why did you move to Luthertown Heights?"

I smiled slightly. "Because *I'm* crazy." Second stitch done. And he didn't look like Frankenstein or anything.

"No, really."

"Because I wanted to go somewhere where I could make a difference." I tied a knot in the thread and snipped off the end. "I used to work at once of those expensive private schools in the East End of Louisville, and the children there were awful to each other. They didn't appreciate anything, because they *had* everything. I wanted to go somewhere where kids didn't have the same opportunities, because I wanted to *give* them opportunities, and..." I was getting a bit too spirited and full of unbridled hope, so I trailed off, embarrassed. "Anyway, I wanted to help people, basically. And up until today, I thought maybe I was." I bit my lip as it threatened to tremble again, and avoided his gaze.

"Nothing has changed," said Slipknot. "You are still helping those children."

"Yeah, by letting them get shot to death in my classroom," I replied darkly. I looked up at the ceiling for a moment to blink back my tears, and I saw that it was painted black, and covered in stars and planets.

I don't know why, but that made me want to cry even more.

It wasn't fair. There was so much beauty in Luthertown Heights: in the smiles of the children, in Slipknot's art, but it was smothered by a smog of violence that would not lift.

"Hey." Slipknot put his hand on my wrist.

I let out an embarrassed laugh. "Sorry. Today is a hard day for me. It's the day I found out that I'm not the heroine of this story, and that I can't save everyone. Or anyone, really."

He lifted his left hand, and I jumped as his rough fingers grazed my cheek. He tucked a strand of my wild red hair behind my ear, giving me goosebumps. "I'm pretty sure you are saving me right now," he said quietly.

My eyes grew wide as I stared into his, knowing that he meant more than just the sum of the words he had said, but not knowing why. Then, after what felt like an eternity lost in the flames of those bright, jungle green eyes, he dropped his gaze – and his hand.

"I think the grey thread might be better for the leg," he said, tapping the box. "It is stronger."

"Uh... right. Gotcha." I picked up the grey thread and fed some of it through the needle. "Well," I said, still feeling his touch on my burning cheek, "here goes nothing."

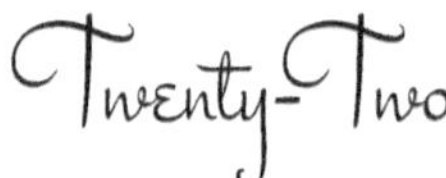

Once Slipknot was sufficiently sewn and bandaged, I helped him over to the bed, where he lay down heavily. He was exhausted, I could see it in his once-so-impassive face, but we were in a pickle.

"So...um... I guess I ought to get going..." I said, shuffling my feet at the head of the bed.

"Get going?" He looked alarmed. "Going where?"

"Home."

He shook his head so hard that I was afraid he would give himself rope burn. "No, you can't."

"What do you mean, 'I can't?'"

"It is too dangerous out there. And it is... what?" He checked a digital clock on the edge of the dresser. "It's 3:37 a.m. You are not going anywhere."

I crossed my arms. That was a bit unnerving. "So... what? I'm like a prisoner?" His jaw tightened, and I immediately regretted my choice of words. "I mean, *you* went out there..."

"Yeah, and look what it got me." He gestured at his bandages. He was completely shirtless now, and wearing a pair of boxer shorts. He was surely freezing, but I felt a bit flushed. I had been too focused on his wounds to notice before, but he had an impressive physique: dark, coppery skin that covered rows and rows of tight abdominal muscles and lean, sinewy legs; a taut stomach marred by several scars, but not an ounce of body fat, and a spray of dark hair across his hard pectorals that gave me an odd, primitive sort of urge to run my fingers through it.

I shook my head to clear out the fog. "Yeah, but as I remember it, I couldn't talk *you* out of leaving..."

He pressed his lips together.

In all honesty, leaving was the *last* thing I wanted to do. It was dark outside, and the city was running rampant with corpses and armed gangsters that would love nothing more than to add my "pretty white tittaays" to their trophy case along with Slipknot's earring. Add to that the fact that all I had to go home to was an empty apartment covered in construction paper pictures given to me by students I had failed miserably, and there was no good reason to leave at all. Ever.

Staying, though, could prove to be even more dangerous.

To remain in an apartment with a man I didn't know, overnight, in a room with only one bed, was just asking for trouble.

"Do you trust me?" Slipknot asked suddenly, as if he had been reading my mind.

"I...uh...what?"

"Do you trust me?" He repeated. He was piercing me with that green gaze again.

I squirmed under it. I wanted the answer to be "No! Of course not! You're a known murderer!" But that's not the answer my pounding heart was telling me to give. "I...well...I guess so." I shrugged. "Why?"

"Come here."

I did no such thing.

He was sliding over in the bed, toward a wall covered in forest trees, and he had thrown back the ratty comforter.

"I don't think—"

He sighed and pulled such an uncharacteristically exasperated expression that I almost burst out laughing. "Annabelle, I am not going to touch you," he said. In spite of the hint of annoyance in his voice, the use of my name hit me like a lightning bolt to the chest. He was the only one who ever used my name, and it never ceased to affect me.

"This is a big bed," he went on, as if he hadn't just revved up my heart to warp speed. "I will sleep here, and you will sleep there, and tomorrow we will figure out what to do about getting you home. Okay?"

I chewed my lip, uncertain. I shouldn't trust him, that much I knew. But I also knew from previous experience how warm and cozy that bed was, and the apartment air was so cold...

"Okay," I said finally, kneeling down to crawl onto my designated section of the mattress. "But no funny stuff."

"You know that I am not a funny guy."

I couldn't resist a giggle at his dry voice. "If you say so..."

He threw the cover up over me, and we lay on our sides, face to face, two feet apart. It was oddly intimate, and I wished he would turn off the light, so he couldn't see me blushing.

"Don't you take that off while you sleep?" I pointed at the fraying rope wrapped around his neck. I noticed I had lowered my voice to a murmur in light of our close proximity, and I cursed myself for making things seem even *more* intimate.

"Usually, yes," he murmured back. His gaze was roving across my face, as if he were trying to play connect-the-dots with my freckles.

"But not tonight?"

"Not tonight."

"Why not?"

His lips twitched. "Don't you ever run out of questions?"

"Would it upset you if I said no?" I giggled at my own joke, and his lips twitched even more. "Seriously, though," I said, growing somber, "isn't that uncomfortable? It looks itchy."

"It is," he confirmed. "But what is under it is worse."

"Why? What's under it?"

His eyes stopped their roaming and landed on mine. Something in my stomach flopped over as my heart sped up once again. "Sorry, you are out of questions."

Then, without breaking our gaze, he reached up to a switch on the wall, and turned off the lights.

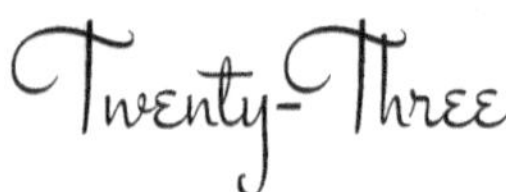# Twenty-Three

"No," I was saying, over and over, "no, no!"

They were after me, dozens of them, creatures that were half-man, half-wolf, chasing me through a dimly lit forest of painted trees. I was holding Marcus in my arms; he was dressed in a brown leather vest and wearing a construction paper crown, and he kept getting heavier and heavier each time my bare foot crashed to the ground.

"No. *No!*"

I stumbled and fell to my knees, sending Marcus rolling across a field of green-painted grass. "No! Stop!" I shouted, as he kept rolling, farther and farther away from me. "Marcus! Come back!"

I couldn't get up. The painted grass was melting, turning into a formless puddle around me. Some of the man-wolves leapt over me, gnashing their teeth as they went after Marcus, and the others grabbed me by the arms and stretched them wide.

I tried to scream as the wolves began to tear into Marcus' tender, little boy flesh, but no sound would come out.

One of the wolves turned into a man – Bear, the alpha. He was wearing a crown too, a sharp, golden one that dripped with blood.

He was holding the largest machete I had ever seen, and it glinted meanly in the dim light as he held it out to show me.

"You can try to run with wolves," he said, in Slipknot's voice, "but you will never be able to keep up."

Then he lifted the machete high into the air and brought it down. Finally, I screamed.

"Annabelle! Annabelle, hey!"

I was thrashing in the sheets, my body drenched in sweat and my face dripping with tears. Where was I?

Suddenly, the light clicked on and I saw the painted forest in front of me, and I shrieked again, covering my streaming eyes.

"Hey, Annabelle, listen, it was just a nightmare!"

There was that voice again. This time, though, it was full of concern. A hand touched my shoulder, and I jumped.

"Annabelle, it is me. You are okay, you are safe."

I sniffled as the dream finally began to lose its hold on me. Slowly, I lowered my arm and peeked out again.

Slipknot's face, as per usual now, was staring back at me. It was puffy with sleep and he seemed breathless, as if my nightmare had scared him, too. "Are you alright?"

I groaned and hid my eyes again. "Sorry..."

"No, do not be sorry," he said, reaching across my body to put a hesitant hand on my hip, over the blankets. "It was my fault."

I chanced another peek. "What makes you say that? You weren't even in the dream."

"I didn't hang up my dreamcatcher," he said, glancing up toward the ceiling. I followed his gaze and saw a big golden hook centered over the bed amongst the stars in Ursa Major. "I usually hang my dreamcatcher earring up there, but that Creeper took it."

"Do those things really work?" I sniffled again, distracted against my will.

"It depends on how many bad dreams they have to hold."

"Or how terrible the dream is..." I covered my eyes again.

"Do you want to tell me about it?"

"No, I want to curl up in a ball and die. You probably think I'm insane..."

"I do not think you are insane." I could still feel the heaviness of his hand on my hip. "After the day you had, I would have been surprised if you did *not* have nightmares."

"Yeah..." I muttered darkly. The wolves crossed back through my mind, and I shuddered involuntarily. Slipknot's hand grew heavier, more reassuring. I put down my arm for good and looked back up at him. A wry, humorless grin twisted my features. "Sorry I woke you up."

"I told you, do not be sorry." He moved the hand from my hip and brushed a mass of wet, messy hair out of my face so we could see each other better. "I am a light sleeper anyway."

"Well, after that, I don't think I'll ever sleep again..."

His lips twitched. "You would be surprised how often I have had that same thought. But the body needs rest. Sleep will always find you eventually."

"Not tonight..."

"The night is over." He nodded at the window at our feet. The sun was streaming in through the cracks in the vine-painted blinds, and I felt a rush of relief. "We survived."

"We survived..." I repeated, marveling over it. Imagine that. I had spent the night in the apartment – in the *bed* – of a notorious gangster, and I had lived to tell the tale. And my virtue was still intact to boot... even if he had technically violated his oath not to touch me.

I almost wished he would touch me again, though, as I turned my eyes back to him. His curly hair was tousled and messy, and it shone like dark honey in the morning light. I liked his face puffy, and the little speck of crust in the corner of his left eye. It made him seem more human, more approachable, more *real* somehow. The fright I had given him had passed as well, and his expression seemed more placid than usual. He seemed almost relaxed as he propped himself up on his elbow and watched me watching him. The fire in his eyes was still burning, but it had been dialed down to a low simmer for the time being.

"What are you looking at?" He asked. I couldn't tell if he was feeling curious or self-conscious.

"Your face," I replied simply. It was too early for caginess and being coy.

Touch of pink tinged his cheeks, and his lips moved slightly, as if he wanted to smile, but had forgotten how.

"Where did you get that scar?" I asked, reaching out to gently touch the raised purple line running down from his left eye.

His eyes grew wide as my finger touched his skin. The spark in his eyes reignited and his body tensed, but he didn't pull away.

"The questions are starting early today."

I chuckled and put my hand back under the covers. "Sorry, I'm just trying to get to know you." A look of confusion flitted across his face, and I frowned. "What's wrong?"

"Nothing," he said, shaking his head. "I have just never had anyone want to get to know me before."

"I know how you feel." I cast my eyes down as I poked at a thread on the underside of the red checkerboard quilt. "No one has asked me a single question about myself since I got to Luthertown Heights. Or before that, come to think of it... People don't even want to know my name."

"I know your name," he said, a bit too quickly. I glanced up to see that his cheeks were flushed again.

"I know." I smiled, wishing he knew just how much that meant to me. "When I saw it on the mural on my classroom door, I almost cried. And when you say it out loud..." I cut myself off as I felt my own cheeks burn. I wanted to pull the sheets up over my head, but instead I just laughed. "But I digress. You were going to tell me about your scar."

That strange look was back on his face. I still didn't know what it meant, but there was something in it that made me feel warm and tingly inside.

"My father gave it to me," he answered, mapping my freckles again as he spoke. "He said it would make me a man."

"What the hell does that mean?" I demanded, as a rush of emotions flooded me for reasons I couldn't even explain to myself.

His eyes focused on mine, and his voice was low and hoarse as he spoke. "My father was the founder of the Uewatsu. He had twenty-seven sons by sixteen different –"

"TWENTY-SEVEN SONS?!"

His lips twitched almost violently at my outburst. "Yes, twenty-seven sons, and four daughters. There used to be a Cherokee reservation not far from here. The settlers moved our ancestors there when they took over this land in the 1770s, and my father grew up there. He slept with every woman on the reservation that was over the age of fourteen."

I tried hard not to grimace.

"He said that he was sowing his seed to create an army. It was his dream to take over Luthertown Heights and to claim it for the Uewatsu. He said it was our 'birthright.' So he raised his sons like warriors. We each barely saw him alone, but as soon as we were old enough to walk, he started training us for battle. Each of us was taught a different combat skill. Strongbow had arrows, Bear had blades –"

"Wait a minute, wait a minute!" I gasped, sitting up. "You and Bear really are brothers? I thought he was just calling you that as like a gang thing!"

"We are half-brothers." He looked a bit ashamed. "All of us are. That is why we are in the gang."

"Wow..." My head was spinning. This was too much. Not only was he in the same gang as Bear, the creature I hated most in this world, but he was his *brother*? That couldn't be true... "Wait, you said everyone had a different combat skill..." I said slowly, trying to force myself back to the topic before my mind could rewind itself to my sexual assault. "What's yours? The rope?"

His jaw tightened. "Originally, no. I was the scout. I can see where the enemy is, I can anticipate where they will go next. I can find anyone or anything at any time, without anyone finding me."

"Wow..." I said again, impressed. "But what about the –"

He caught my hand as it reached out to touch the rope around his neck. "One story at a time, Annabelle," he said gently.

I blushed. "Right, sorry. Go on."

"I was the scout because I was good at it, but also because I refused to do anything else. I learned how to use the weapons, but I would not touch another human being with them. My mother died of Leukemia when I was fourteen, and life was too precious to me. I could not take it from anyone, not even one of my family's enemies.

"This made my father furious. One day, not long after my mother died, he caught me talking to Miss Carmella, the woman you clean house for. One of her husbands had just passed, and we had crossed paths in the cemetery. We had comforted each other. She gave me the first hug I had had in years. It made me cry.

"My father walked up at that moment to collect me for training. Carmella was afraid of him, but he let her walk out, unharmed. But when I tried to move past him myself, with my face covered in tears, he stood in front of the cemetery gate. He told me to stop crying that instant. He said to me, 'If you do not stop crying, I will cut those tears from your face.' But I could not stop. I asked him to let me go, and he said 'Not until I make you a man, son.' Then he pulled his hunting knife from its sheath on his belt and sliced open my cheek. He told me he was cutting off the flow of tears, permanently."

"Oh my God..." I whispered, horrified.

"'Warriors do not cry,' he said to me. 'Remember that if you want to be a part of our tribe. We are all you have.'" Slipknot took a shuddery breath. "That was the last time I ever shed a tear, fifteen years ago. In that respect, my father succeeded in making me a man."

"I'm so sorry," I said, moving closer to him. I touched his scar again, letting my fingers linger there this time, feeling the hot, smooth raised skin beneath them. A tear threatened to slip down my own cheek, but Slipknot brushed it away with his fingertips.

"Do not be sorry," he murmured back, resting his wet hand on top of mine. I thought he would brush that away too, but he held it there, pressing it to him, as if he never wanted me to let go.

I looked deep into his fiery eyes, wanting so much to know what other pain lay hidden within their depths, bottled up for over a decade. I wanted to erase that pain somehow, to make it all go away. To make him feel at peace. To make him feel loved.

"What is your name?" I whispered, suddenly feeling that nothing else in the world mattered more. "Your real name."

His entire face changed. Surprise lit up his eyes, followed by something much deeper, something much more meaningful. I had touched him, I could tell, and I knew then that I was not the only one who needed to hear their own name spoken out loud.

"Luca," he whispered back, his voice rough and broken. "My name is Luca."

After a long argument about hospitality versus injury, I was in the kitchen frying eggs for Luca as he sat at the table. He looked awkward there, as if he wasn't used to sitting down, or wasn't accustomed to having other people do things for him.

It was cute.

"Are you sure you do not want me to do that?" He asked me, for the umpteenth time.

I sighed. "Luca, I told you. I'm the nurse, and I put you on bedrest. Or...well, chair rest, I guess. Now just sit there and be patient! It's almost ready!"

I flipped one of the half-dozen eggs in the skillet and put a pinch of salt on the upper side. I could tell he was watching me, but I pretended not to notice.

"Say that again," he said quietly. "The first part."

I bit my lip to keep from smiling. There was magic in names, and I knew he felt it too.

"Luca, I told you," I repeated, as if it wasn't a strange request.

"You were right..." he mumbled, with something like awe in his voice. "To hear my own name, my *real* name, after all this time is very... strange."

"Strange good, or strange bad?" I turned to smile at him, and felt my stomach flutter at the look on his face.

"Strange beautiful. Say it again."

"Luca."

The intensity in his fiery eyes grew deeper. "Again."

I turned off the stove and took a step toward him. "Luca."

He laid his hand on the table, palm up, as if he were reaching for me. There was an odd electricity in the air between us, almost as if the name really was casting some sort of spell over us.

"One more time, please."

"SLIPKNOT!"

We both jumped violently as Bear's voice shouted through the fire door. When Luca didn't answer right away, he began to bang on it, hard, with his fists.

Luca got to his feet, staggering slightly on his wounded leg. I grabbed a hold of the t-shirt he had thrown on when we got out of bed, and I pulled him in close to me.

"Don't answer," I whispered, as my fluttering stomach turned to lead.

"SLIPKNOT! BROTHER! DO YOU HEAR ME?"

For the first time since I had met him, Luca looked conflicted. "I have to," he whispered to me, without moving.

"No, you don't!" I hissed back, grabbing his shirt with my other hand too. "If you answer it, he's just going to drag you into something else terrible!"

"But if I do *not* answer, he will just come back."

"BROTHER!"

I closed my eyes and let my head drop to Luca's chest in defeat. He was right. He would never go away unless Luca answered him. Maybe not even then.

"Go hide in the bathroom," Luca whispered in my ear, resting his cheek against mine. "I will get rid of him. I will not go anywhere this time."

"Do you promise?"

"I promise, Annabelle."

I took a deep breath and stepped back. Without looking at him, I hurried off to the bathroom, knowing that if I glanced back, I would never go.

"SLIPKNOT!"

"I am here, Bear, I am here," Luca called, sounding harassed. I closed the door to the bathroom and stood on the other side, listening. I could hear him limping across the laminate, and the thud as the fire door was pushed inward.

"Why the hell didn't you answer me?" came Bear's voice, vicious and mean.

"I was asleep. I took some pills for the pain in my –"

"No one gives a shit about your pain, little brother! We need you tonight."

My leaden stomach dropped.

"What is tonight?"

"Tonight we're taking out all those sons of bitches, just like Father wanted."

"What... what are you saying?"

"I am saying that we are going to trap the Sixes inside their headquarters tonight, and set the motherfucking building on fire. They will burn alive, every single one of them."

I put my hand over my mouth, horrified.

"Fireman Joe is already in. He says he can set it up to make it look like an accident. But we need you to be the lookout, and let us know when the Sixes are all inside.

"Why me?" Luca's voice was cold. "You can see my leg. I am no use to you tonight."

"You are our scout, brother! We need you."

"Please say no, please say no, please say no..." I whispered under my breath.

"I cannot go tonight," said Luca, and I felt faint with relief.

"Find someone else. I cannot walk that far, and I could not report back."

"Since when you do you say no to me, brother?"

I immediately tensed up again. I knew that voice. It was Bear's warning voice – smooth, powerful, subtly seductive. It was the last thing I had heard before he attacked me.

"Since I got shot in the leg and you left me in Sixes territory to die, *brother*." Luca's voice was hoarse, but just as powerful as Bear's, and twice as bitter.

Bear let out a bark of laughter. "Come on, little brother! You can't take that personally! You know the rules of the pack. You would have done the same thing if it had been me."

"You are wrong." I heard a shuffling of feet. "Please go. I cannot help you tonight. I cannot keep up with the pack."

There was a pause, and heavy footsteps moved toward the fire door.

"Alright, Slipknot, have it your way. But just know that I don't like this. Not one bit."

"Understood."

"Oh, and you know that redhead from 7th Street?" Bear added, as if it were an afterthought. "The white girl with the nice tits?"

Luca was silent.

"Rumor has it she disappeared. Some kid in her class got his guts blasted by some other kindergarten baby and no one has seen her since."

"Oh," said Luca.

I had a bad feeling about this...

"Someone said they saw you driving her and that kid to the hospital. That was awfully nice of you."

"The boy was bleeding out. I could not just leave him there."

"Sure, sure." There was a knowing smile in Bear's velvet voice. "But what *I'm* wondering is, what were *you* doing there to help him in the first place? You told me you were going to be scouting the waterpark."

Luca didn't answer.

"Anyway, if you see her, let me know." Bear was finally moving away now. From the landing, he added, with savage relish, "I'd love to get my hands on those titties again."

The door slammed, and the apartment was silent.

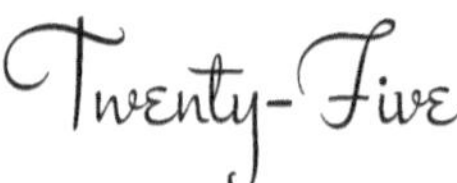

We ate our cold eggs without speaking. Luca and I were both brooding – him about his awful brother, I assumed, and me about how much I hated the violence in Luthertown Heights. There had to be something I could do to stop the Uewatsu from murdering all the Sixes, but what? If I warned the Sixes that the Uewatsu were coming, they would just strike first and kill *them*. Either way, it would be a bloodbath.

And either way, it would be on *my* conscience.

I knew too much now. I had been dragged into the gang war against my will, and now I was smack dab in the middle of it. I had sworn no allegiance to the Uewatsu, but I couldn't rat on them and risk their lives. Neither was I aligned with the Sixes, but if they burned to death that night, it would be because I didn't warn them.

"I will not let him hurt you, you know," said Luca softly from across the table.

I jumped. I had been so lost in my own thoughts that I had almost forgotten he was there.

"What?"

"Bear," he clarified. "I will not let him touch you again."

"I know," I said. And I did. I still had no clue why Luca had decided to appoint himself my guardian – me, of all people – but I no longer doubted that I could trust him.

My answer seemed to satisfy him. He visibly relaxed as he pushed around a scrap of rubbery egg white on his plate with his fork, and I felt that warm, affectionate feeling coming back.

"I don't want you to get into trouble over me, though..." I continued worriedly, remembering the threat underlying Bear's parting words.

He raised an eyebrow.

"Maybe I should go home now." My heart broke a bit as I said it, and a bit more when I stood up, knowing it was the right thing to do. In fact, it was overdue. I liked Luca's company, but I should have left a long time ago, or never come at all. My presence only put him in danger.

"Wait, no." Luca shook his head, alarmed once more.

"Luca, it's the only way I can be sure Bear doesn't think you and I are...are...conspiring or something."

"Conspiring?"

"Oh, you know what I mean." I sighed, miserable. "One of these times, he's going to come to your door and find out that I'm here. Then he'll kill you, and do lord knows what else to me."

"But I will not let him!"

I had begun to walk back toward the bedroom area to retrieve the clothes I had come in with when I heard his chair scrape across the floor as he staggered to his feet.

That only made things harder.

I had placed my folded, blood-caked jeans and sweater on top of the dresser next to Luca's clothes the night before, and it made me sad to think that I would never see such a pleasant, domestic sight in that apartment again. His big, black and grey t-shirts contrasted so strikingly with my bright green sweater and acid washed denims, but they looked nice together there, side by side.

They looked like home.

"I've been taking care of myself for a long time, Luca," I said, unable to look at him, but unable to look down at the copious bloodstains on the clothes I had just picked up either. "And besides…" I bit my lip. No, I couldn't finish that thought out loud.

"'Besides' what?" He had caught up to me, and was blocking my way to the bathroom now. He was out of breath from the effort of dragging his bad leg the short fifteen feet from the kitchen, and again, I wanted to reach up and loosen that rope from around his neck so he could get some more air.

"Never mind."

"No, tell me." His voice was stern, almost angry.

"Just let it go," I said, trying to move past him.

"Besides, I am just as dangerous as those other guys? Besides, I'm a killer too, so you should stay away from me? Besides, I will just turn you over to my brother so he can defile you?"

The fire in his eyes burned me and I took a step back. He was furious now, angrier than I had known he was capable of being. It was the first time I had ever really been afraid of him.

"Luca, no! Of course not!" I exclaimed, offended by his misinterpretation of my perception of him. "Why would you even think that?"

My genuine shock and confusion seemed to douse the fire raging within him, and he reached out to me with an apologetic hand. "I'm sorry." He grazed my arm with his fingers, then let them fall away.

"Do you really think that I could feel that way after all we've been through?" I demanded, not ready to forgive him yet, in spite of the sparks he had left burning on my skin. "After all the times you've helped me? After all the times you've put yourself in danger for me? You think I don't know better than to think those terrible things by now?"

He looked truly ashamed. His hand twitched at his side, as if he wanted to touch me again, but wasn't sure if he should.

"'Besides, I'm going to do something dangerous,' that's what I was going to say." I dropped my gaze to my bare, cold feet. "I didn't want to tell you because I know you'll try to stop me."

"Damn right." They were harsh words, but they came out in a soft rasp, like the sound of a tulle skirt skimming across a hardwood floor.

"I don't think you can, though," I said, looking thoughtfully back up at his face. Something was changing inside me; a plan was solidifying. I was convincing myself of something that had previously just been wishful thinking, and I knew now that I could not be dissuaded, not even by him. I would save the Sixes. I would save the Uewatsu. I would save everyone.

Or die trying.

"Then let me go with you." Luca took my hand.

I smiled, touched by the loyalty I still didn't understand. "No, you have to stay here and rest your leg."

"My leg is fine!" He was getting angry again, but this time, as he pierced me with his burning emerald eyes, I felt more exhilarated than afraid. "Annabelle, please. What can I say to make you stay?"

"Nothing. I'm sorry. I have to –"

I had turned toward the bathroom door once more, but he jerked me roughly back to him. I gasped as he took my face in his hands, burying his long, muscular fingers in my hair as he leaned down to meet me at eye level. "Annabelle, I am begging you," he said through gritted teeth, his nose just an inch from mine. "Do not go. Please. I *cannot* lose you."

I opened and closed my mouth, unable to make any words come out. His intensity was frightening, and his desperate devotion was baffling. "But *why?* Why does it matter to you what happens to me? You barely even know me!"

He was out of breath again, as if he had just run into the arms I was now resting against his chest. He seemed to be struggling against something within himself, some inner demon, or some inner truth, and I had no idea who was winning.

Then, suddenly, the strength seemed to leave him and he rested his damp forehead against mine. "Because you are the light in the darkness," he whispered to me. "Without you, the world is too dark to bear."

My hand found its way to his cheek of its own accord. My thumb skimmed across the stubble on his chin, my fingers felt their way up to the wild curls that framed his face. "But why?" I asked again, my heart almost too full to speak. He was so close to me, so warm, so strangely helpless in my arms. We were face to face, skin to skin, breathing the same air, and I never wanted it to stop, even if it was inconceivable to me that a man like him could ever care so much about a nobody like me.

"Do not ask me why." He moved so that his lips were touching my face, grazing my cheekbone as he spoke, giving me goosebumps as he slowly, haltingly, hesitantly wrapped his arms around my waist. "Just promise you will not leave me."

Promise you will not leave me.

The words struck me right in my pounding heart. Not the apartment, not the city, *me*. Do not leave *me*.

"Okay," I whispered back, closing my eyes and finally allowing myself to melt into his embrace. "I promise I won't leave you."

His arms tightened gratefully around me, but I wasn't finished.

"But only if you promise *me* the same thing."

He was silent for a long time as my arms slowly encircled his rough-roped neck and my fingers found their way into those soft, springy curls I had been so longing to touch. How long he hesitated, I don't know. But finally, after an eternity in his arms, he put his lips to my ear and swore me the same oath. "I promise not to leave you, Annabelle."

"Thank you," I whispered back, intoxicated by the smell of leather and spring that seemed to emanate from his skin. "Now can I use your phone?"

"What the hell was that?" he asked me, looking at me as if I were from another planet.

"I just evacuated all the Sixes from their headquarters. So, when the Uewatsu go to burn the building down tonight, they won't be there."

Luca swallowed hard. His eyes were the size of saucers, and my grin widened.

"But... but Katz will know he did not call the exterminator."

"Katz doesn't sleep at the headquarters. The leader of the Sixes stays in a different apartment building, and only goes to HQ if something's going on. Everyone knows that."

"But his men, they'll ask –"

"You think they'll question an order from their boss?" I made a "pffft" sound. "Please."

He blinked, trying to find another hole in my plan. "But... but... the Uewatsu will know it was a trick! They will trace the phone call."

"I blocked the number," I said, handing the phone back to him. "They'll probably smell a rat, but they won't be able to find it. They won't have any proof that you and I had anything to do with it whatsoever."

"And Angie Kinkaid? Who is she?"

"A hooker I met once at the market on 18th Street. She doesn't live on 6th, I'm not sure anyone does."

He looked completely flabberghasted.

"Any more questions?" I asked sweetly, leaning back on my elbows atop the mattress.

Then he did something I never could have predicted in a thousand years.

He laughed.

It burst out of him like phlegmy, rheumatic gunfire, choppy and grating and full of rust, but it was the most incredible thing I had ever heard. It sounded so strange, so out of place, like rock music in a dusty mausoleum, and it brought me back to an upright position so that I could watch as it spilled out of him like crumpled coins from a slot machine.

It changed everything about him: his once-stiff posture relaxed, his broad, solemn shoulders shook, and his face! His face was the best part. His green eyes, once so haunted and full of pain and intensity, now sparkled with mirth as he rocked forward, clutching his stomach. Those sad, hopeful little twitches at the corners of his mouth had finally won out too, and his lips were stretched wide to reveal al his square, blocky white teeth and a tongue that almost matched the pink-red color creeping into his copper cheeks.

I think that was the moment I fell in love with him.

His laugh soon turned into a cough, though, then into a rattling wheeze, and he settled down, wiping his eyes as he drew in a few deep, ragged breaths. "You are a genius," he croaked, once he had recovered. "How did you think of that?"

I shrugged, unable to stop grinning. "It just came to me. It was the only way I could think of to get everyone out without anyone getting hurt, and without breaking my promise to you."

"And that accent!" He chuckled again. "Where did that come from?"

"Oh, did you like that?" I teased, wishing he would keep smiling at me like that forever. "I studied linguistics in college. I can do any accent perfectly."

"Really?"

"You bet yo muthafuckin' ass I can," I replied, and he burst into laughter again.

It turned into a cough much more quickly this time, though, and I felt my own smile falter. "Do you want me to get you some water?"

"No," he said between wheezes. In spite of my worry, he was still grinning. "I will be alright in a minute. It is just my throat. I am not used to laughing. I am fine, really."

"Okay..."

I wanted to ask him about his throat again, but I knew if I

did, I would risk losing that smile for the foreseeable future. Still, though, I found myself worrying that there was something terrible hiding under that rope on his neck. Something like cancer or some other disease that was much more fatal in towns like Luthertown Heights than they were in other places these days.

"Hey, what is wrong?"

He must have noticed the stricken look on my face, because his smile finally started to fade. I missed it already...

"Nothing!" I said, too quickly, as I hopped up. "I'm just going to get you some water. And me. I'm thirsty too. Doing accents is hard work!"

"Okay." I didn't wait around to see if he was buying it, but I was pretty sure he wasn't. "There are ice cubes in the freezer if you would like some."

I filled up two glasses with ice water and sat back down next to him on the bed. I was sitting a bit closer this time, close enough for my bare knee to touch his pant leg, and he tensed slightly, as if he thought he should shy away, but didn't want to.

"I am sorry if I scared you just now," he said, taking his glass from my hand. Sweat was already beading on it, and I had to wipe my palm on the comforter to dry it. I had gone a bit overboard with the ice. "I know I sound like a...a monster or something."

"Oh, no!" I almost choked on my drink. "No, I think you sound wonderful!" His eyes widened and I blushed. "I mean... I love the sound of your laugh. It makes me – Crap! That's worse..." I groaned and covered my face with my hand.

He chuckled, though, and I felt a bit less mortified. "You should have heard it before." He sighed. "Back when I sounded like a real person."

"You *are* a real person," I said, setting down my glass on the floor by my feet. "And your laugh is beautiful. Up until a few minutes ago, I didn't know you even knew *how* to laugh!"

He grinned. He was rusty at it, I could tell, but each time he smiled, it seemed more natural. I could barely picture his face without it now. "I didn't. Not until you got here."

I blushed even harder. "Well, I'm glad to be of service! A laugh a day keeps the doctor..." I tried off. I had inadvertently triggered my worrying again.

"What is wrong, Annabelle?" Luca sat down his water without drinking any of it and turned his upper body to face me, taking special care that his knee never lost contact with mine.

"Nothing, I'm being stupid."

"Hey, come on." He reached out a hand and hesitantly touched mine. "You are not stupid. Tell me."

I looked down at his fingers, noticing the way his reddish-tan skin contrasted with mine, and I felt my ridiculous worry increase. "Your throat..." I said quietly, alarmed by how near I was to crying again. "It's not... it's not, like, cancer or anything, is it? My grandpa died of throat cancer when I was seven."

Luca was completely silent. I couldn't even hear him breathing as I waited for a reply, with my cheeks burning like hot coals beneath those freckles he seemed so fascinated by. Then, slowly, he raised his hand and lifted up my chin to that he could meet my eyes. "It is not cancer," he said, with that strange, unreadable look on his face. "It is just scar tissue."

I glanced at the rope coiled around his neck. "Does it hurt?"

His fingers skimmed across my jawline, and he touched a lock of my wayward red hair. "Sometimes. But it is not fatal."

I exhaled in relief. "Thank goodness." I wanted to smile at him, but there was that odd electricity between us again, and I didn't want to break the spell.

"You really were worried, though, weren't you?" He tilted his head to study my face, as if he had never seen anything like me before.

Surely my cheeks were just going to melt off.

"I... well... well, yes." I shrugged.

"Why?"

His question was sincere, just as sincere as mine had been when the situation was reversed. Unfortunately, though, I couldn't answer him yet either.

"Sorry, you're out of questions." I smiled as I took his hand out of my hair and held it in mine.

He seemed to be distracted by the feel of my fingers wrapped around his, because he didn't push any further. Instead, he studied our hands as they lay atop the mattress between us: white and tan, cream and toffee, my skin and his. As if he had never felt another human hand before, he slid his thumb across the back of mine, feeling its texture and giving me goosebumps as he marveled at it.

"You are so soft," he said, as if that small patch of skin between my thumb and forefinger was representative of me as a whole.

"Is... is that weird?" I let out a nervous chuckle. I was no good at these intimate things, and everything he did moved me on such a deep, profound level.

"No, it is nice," he said, his voice more hoarse than ever. "Everything I touch is hard. Everyone I *know* is hard. But not you."

"And not you," I said, watching his face as he continued to stroke my hand. I thought about how he had walked me home that night, how he had kept me safe, how he had tried to help me save Marcus, how he had let me lean on him, even though he hadn't been close to anyone in years. He wasn't hard like Bear and the other Uewatsu. He was soft inside. He felt things deeply, like me. He cared.

He let out a huff of laughter. "I am not soft. I am hard and jagged and broken."

That last part sounded much too familiar. I squeezed his hand, and he finally looked up at me. "Well, then we make a great pair, because I'm *soft* and broken."

"You are not broken," he said, his green eyes shining. "But if you are, I will fix you."

My heart stammered against my ribcage. Had he really just said that to me? "That's the sweetest thing I've ever heard," I told him honestly, so touched that I could barely get the words out.

He grinned wryly and put his palm against my cheek, without so much hesitation this time. "And to think, it came out of the mouth of a lowlife hood."

I laughed. Then, for reasons I couldn't explain, even to myself, I couldn't resist the urge to fling my arms around his neck and hug him at that very moment.

He tensed up as our chests pressed together, but then he wrapped his arms around me and held me tightly, fiercely, to him. I remembered then, about what he had said about how Miss Carmella's hug had made him cry, so I hugged him twice as hard, trying to put fifteen years' worth of missing affection into that one, heartfelt embrace.

"Please do not leave," he croaked into my ear for the second time that day. It sounded almost as if it were an internal thought that had escaped into the open air, a prayer he hadn't meant to speak aloud.

It was so unexpected, so sincere, that all I could think to whisper back was, "Never."

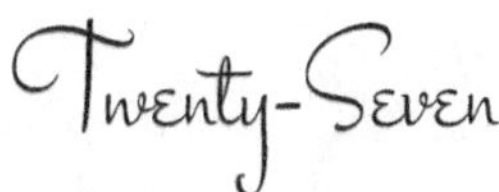

After a light lunch of fried bologna sandwiches and freshly brewed iced tea, Luca decided to give me a painting lesson. Balancing on one leg like a well-muscled flamingo, he extracted two rolls of white paper from the bottom of his dresser, and a dozen or so small bottles of tempera paint from the top one (which explained why his clothes were stacked on top of the dresser instead of inside it).

He carried these over to the bare spot in the middle of the one-room apartment, then went back for some brushes. I offered to help at least six times, but he insisted on doing it himself, claiming that the more he moved, the faster his leg would heal.

So, I toyed with the bottles of paint on the floor, noticing that they all contained a different color than what the label on the bottles said. The plastic containers themselves were fairly translucent, but behind a label that that read "Apple Red," I could see a thick, viscus liquid that was clearly "Royal Blue."

"This doesn't look like Primrose Yellow to me..." I said, holding up a bottle full of purple paint.

Luca grinned. He plopped down across from me on the floor, sweating slightly from all his exertion, and unrolled one of the papers into a three- by four-foot square. He put a bottle of paint on each of the corners nearest him, and gestured for me to do the same, so that our canvas would lay flat. "That is because you don't know my system," he grunted, straightening out his leg at a sixty degree angle at his side.

"And what is your system?"

"My system is to collect the empty paint bottles from the dumpster behind the grade school and the Y, and refill them with paint I steal from the craft store a little at a time."

I didn't know whether to laugh or feel sorry for him. "You know you could have just asked me for paint, right?" I replied, as he tossed me a brush. "I buy the paint for the ASC, I would've been happy to lend you some."

He raised an eyebrow at me, and I felt a swooping sensation in my stomach. "Before today you knew me only as 'Slipknot, notorious killer and right-hand man to the leader of the Uewatsu.' You cannot tell me that you would lend *that* man paint."

That time the sensation in my stomach was more of a lurch. I hadn't known he was Bear's right-hand man. And I had been beginning to forget the whole "notorious killer" thing too... "Sure I would." I shrugged. "If you'd told me what you wanted it for."

"For painting pictures of you on your classroom door?" He teased. He pulled a square of cardboard from his back pocket and unfolded it next to the paper. It looked like part of a cereal box that was covered in a mosaic of dried, multicolored paint.

"In that case, I would have given you extra."

He grinned, and started flipping open the tops of the squeeze bottles. "Okay," he exhaled, rubbing his hands together, "what is your favorite color?"

I instantly thought of his eyes, and blushed as I answered, "Green."

"Perfect," he said, grabbing a bottle labeled "White." He squirted some paint into a little pile on top of his messy paint card, and I felt myself growing a bit excited. Painting lessons from the artist who had painted my favorite works of Luthertown Heights art? It was like taking a master class from a celebrity.

"What are we painting?" I asked, already loving it, whatever it was. The green paint glistened appealingly in the fluorescent light directly above us, but it didn't come close to the bright, burning emerald color of Luca's eyes.

"That is up to you." As I watched him add some yellow and some white paint to his palate, I noticed how happy it seemed to make him, and how happy *that* made me.

"But you're the artist! The only things I ever paint are smiley faces and trees with leaves that look like clouds on the ASC kids' construction paper pictures." I felt a pang at the thought of Marcus' construction paper masterpieces, and felt my enthusiasm fade a bit. Maybe one day Luca could have been giving Marcus art lessons instead of me.

"Then I will start by teaching you how to paint a proper tree." He hadn't noticed my dip in cheerfulness, and I was grateful. There was no reason to bring *him* down with *my* guilty conscience. Especially not when he looked so joyful. "The secret is in the leaves."

"Oh, so the secret is not to just make a big blob of green?" I joked, as he motioned for me to dip my brush into the paint.

"In this case, no." He laughed. "If you want to make your fake tree look like a real tree, you have to sculpt each leaf individually, like this. See?"

He leaned forward over the paper and began to make an outline in the shape of an orange slice. He filled it in with green, then smiled up at me. "Now you make one."

"Already? I thought there would be more instructions."

He laughed again. "The instructions will come as we go along. Come on, make a leaf right here, next to mine."

I felt slightly nervous as I stretched my arm across the paper, having to elongate my entire body just to reach the top of our future tree. Biting my tongue in concentration, I held the brush firmly near the tip, like a pencil, and made a pointy-edged, wobbly oval next to his. "Oops, mine's bigger," I laughed, as I sat back on my feet.

"That is perfect!" he reassured me. "No two leaves are the same size and shape. The more difference there is between the leaves, the more lifelike our tree will be. Why don't you come over to my side and color it in?"

Blushing preemptively, I did as he said and sat down cross-legged at his side, pulling the hem of his sweatshirt over my knees as I bent over to fill in my leaf.

"There," I said proudly, sitting back up. "Now what?"

"Now for the details." He took another, much skinnier, pair of brushes from his back pocket, and handed one to me. He dipped his own into the edge of the pool of green paint on the palate, and mixed it with a light pull from the yellow. Then, he used his tie-dyed brush tip to draw a long, slightly curved line up the center of his leaf, following it up by adding a few smaller horizontal lines branching out on either side of it.

"Oh, wow!" I exclaimed, as that green oval turned into a leaf before my eyes.

"That is my favorite part," he admitted, in a tone that bordered on sheepish, "when something suddenly comes to life."

"You're amazing! How did you learn all this?"

He handed me his still-loaded brush and pointed at my leaf. "My mother was an artist," he said. "She used to make jewelry. She painted the beads herself, and when I was little, I use to always ask if I could help. One day, when I was around three years old, she gave me some paper to paint on instead. Hold the brush a little higher. It will make a thinner line."

"Ooops," I said again. I had just made what looked like a long, tie-dyed caterpillar in the middle of my leaf.

"No problem." He smiled, smudging the paint into the paper with his forefinger. As he rubbed it in, it began to look more like a sunspot on the leaf, and my mouth fell open in awe as my leaf came to life too. "Anyway, when she gave me the paper, it was like a whole world opened up for me. I painted pictures of everything I could think of: my toys, my mother, my house, my dog, Ernie. It was like I couldn't stop myself." He handed me back my original green brush, and we each started on a second leaf. "I wasn't that good at it at first, but when I got older, my mother taught me a few tricks, and started bringing home art books from the library. I was hoping to go to art school after I graduated high school, but... well, you know how it goes."

"How does it go?" My second leaf looked much more like a leaf than my first, and I was starting to really enjoy myself.

He sighed heavily. "Well, after my mother died, I lived with my Elisi, which means grandmother in Cherokee. She has Alzheimer's, and ended up going to live in the assisted living facility next door to this apartment building when I was sixteen. I didn't know how to take care of her, and my father was never around. I still try to go visit her every night. I live here to be close to her, even if she does not always know who I am, and gets scared when I come to see her."

I frowned. Bear had mentioned his Elisi the night before.

"Anyway," he went on. He was on his sixth leaf now, and I had stopped working entirely to listen to his story. "Then my father made me drop out of school to be in the gang full time. For a while, that was it for my art career. Go on, do some more." He nudged my painting arm encouragingly. "You are doing great."

"That's awful..." I said, referring to his story, not to my sloppy fifth leaf (which was also awful). "How did you get back into it again?"

"One of my half-brothers, Adam, asked me if I wanted to help him tag his ex-girlfriend's building one night, about a year later. I went along with it, and as soon as he put that paint can in my hand, I felt everything come back to me. He painted 'Lisa sux dix' – with 'x'es instead of 'cks'es – and I painted the top half of Van Gogh's starry night."

I laughed out loud. "That's amazing! Is it still there? You have to show me sometime."

He grinned. "Sure, anytime."

For the next few hours, we painted peacefully, sharing small-talk and swapping compliments as our first few little leaves grew into a beautiful, bushy Ash tree. By dinnertime, we had given it a thick brown trunk as well, and Luca was teaching me how to etch details into it with a black, felt-tipped pen he had stolen when the conversation came back around to me.

"Tell me something about yourself," he said, as he watched me make a graceful, swirling knothole in the middle of the trunk.

"Something like what?"

He shrugged, and his shoulder brushed against mine. We had grown closer over the course of the day, not just emotionally, but spatially as well. He had no problem now with his limbs touching mine, and he didn't even seem to notice that my right knee was laying over atop his wounded thigh. "Anything. Tell me about your family. Or your mother, the nurse."

I leaned back to inspect my work. "Hmm... well, I'm originally from Louisville," I said, handing him the pen for his turn. "My parents still live there. My brother too. He and my dad run a tire store, Fitzpatrick's Tires. It's the family business."

"And they are all okay with you living here in Luthertown Heights with hookers and thugs and criminals like me?"

"Not really." I sighed and leaned back on my hands, feeling the cool, slick floor beneath them. "That's why they don't talk to me anymore."

His hand skittered, and he made a long, thin slice in our tree trunk with his marker as he whipped around to look at me. "What?"

I shrugged. "They said I was an idiot for leaving my teaching job at St. Regis Academy. They said it was a stable job, and only stupid people leave stable jobs. But they never understood how it feels to want something *more* out of life. I love them, of course, and they're happy, I guess, but not one of them has ever actually *reached* for anything. They all just settled. My mom got offered an entry-level nursing job right out of high school, and she took it. She's still got that same job today. Same doctor's office, same desk, same everything. My grandpa passed on his tire store to my dad, and he was set for life. Same with my brother. But I didn't want something that was just handed to me. I didn't want something that was just 'good enough.' I didn't want to settle. I still don't. I want to make a difference in the world. I want to change something. I want someone to know I was here after I'm gone."

I didn't recall sitting up while I was talking, but as my speech came to a close, I noticed that my hands were clenched into fists on my lap, and my bruised spirit felt like a trapped bird, beating its wings against a cage of my own creation.

I forced a laugh and glanced at Luca, who was staring at my fists too, as if transfixed. "But, well, you know how that goes," I joked. I took the marker back from him and drew a few more notches in our incredibly lifelike tree trunk.

"So... your family... they are all alive, but they do not want anything to do with you because you wanted something different than what they had planned for you?"

"Basically, yeah," I replied, feeling a bit prickly now. It sounded even more pathetic when he said it. I hadn't thought about my family for months now – I had been training myself not to. I had blocked out the memory of my guilt and their betrayal by focusing that much harder on my kids in the ASC, but I couldn't do that anymore. That memory hurt even worse.

"That is another thing we have in common, then."

I didn't look up from a tiny snake I was drawing in our tree bark. "What is?"

"We both come from families full of idiots."

I slowly put down the pen and sat up. I tucked a strand of hair behind my ear. I liked being associated with him, even in sad, depressing ways, but I couldn't let his statement hang there between us without admitting one of my greatest doubts.

"But what if they're right and *I'm* the idiot, not them?" I asked quietly, reluctant to meet his eyes for fear of what truths I might find in them. "I mean, you yourself said that it was stupid of me to come to Luthertown Hei—"

"I never said it was stupid." His voice was firm, and his hand was on my knee.

"Well, it was kind of implied." I gave him a smile and a shrug, trying not to let him see how much I enjoyed his touch, even if I knew he was only doing it to make me listen.

"No, it wasn't. If I ever did anything that implied that you are anything other than brave, intelligent, and admirable, then I apologize."

I blushed (again), and almost looked away, but I was caught now, like a moth drawn in by the warm glow of his emerald eyes. "You think I'm admirable?" I asked, not believing that anyone could ever admire me: a simple girl whose main goal in life was to teach underprivileged kids how to do paper mâché.

A crooked smile stretched across his face as he brushed his thumb across my scabby right knee. "Why do you think I painted you? I told you that I only paint people that I admire."

I felt my heart skip a beat as he finally answered the question I had been asking myself for days, as well as the one that had been haunting me for years. *That's* why he had painted me. I had inspired him. He admired me.

I was important.

"What are you thinking?" he asked, when my pause went on for too long.

He was tilting his head to the side, smiling sweetly at me, and before I could stop myself, I blurted out the bravest, most idiotic, most honest thing I had ever said in my life.

"I'm thinking that I really want to kiss you right now."

His reaction was immediate, and would have been offensive if I hadn't been familiar with his history and his mannerisms. He was completely, totally, physically taken aback by my words. He jerked and sat up straight, almost as if I had slapped him, and his eyes were like two green headlights in his face, shining so bright that they were in danger of burning themselves out. His mouth fell open in shock or horror, I couldn't tell which, and he quickly withdrew his hand from my knee.

But he didn't leave.

Too terrified now to say anything else, I just sat there, waiting for him to say something. Before he could, though, there came a familiar banging on the fire escape door, and I barely suppressed a groan.

"Slipknot! Slipknot, answer the door!" Bear bellowed, and I grudgingly got to my feet and headed for my designated hiding place. I dragged my feet and slumped my shoulders, already feeling heavy with the weight of whatever new problem Bear was about to drop on us.

Out of the corner of my eye, I saw that Luca hadn't moved a muscle. He was gaping after me as I went into the bathroom and quietly pushed the door closed behind me.

Stupid, stupid, stupid, I thought, wishing I could bang my head on the door. I really *was* an idiot. You never tell a guy that you want to kiss him! Girls learn that in third grade! If he wants to kiss you, he will. And if *you* want to kiss *him*, you do it without discussing it beforehand! What was wrong with me?!

"SLIPKNOT!"

"What, Bear? What?" Luca shouted back. It was the loudest I had ever heard him speak, and it sounded as if it had cost him half the skin inside his throat to do it. "What do you want now?"

"Someone warned the Sixes! They're gone!"

"What are you talking about?" Luca sounded distracted; he wasn't even pretending to be interested. Who was being the idiot now?

"Their HQ is tented, they're spraying for fucking cockroaches!

We were going to hit them early, as a surprise, but – come on, would you open the door already?"

"No."

"No? What do you mean, no?"

"I mean I am sick of this shit, Bear!" Luca exploded, and I clutched the collar of my oversized sweatshirt in alarm. He was going too far. He was going to make Bear angry, and when Bear was angry... I shuddered as I stopped myself from finishing that thought. "You come over here at all hours of the day and night, telling me things I do not want to hear, and expecting me to feel sorry for you when your plans for a modern day Holocaust do not pan out! So no, *brother*, I am not letting you in."

Silence met his outburst, and I held my breath. Then a low, all-too-familiar laugh began to rumble through the door, and I felt a chill run up my spine.

"What? What is so funny?" Luca demanded.

"You have got a girl in there, don't you?" Bear asked, in that slick, greasy voice of his. "Who is it? Bernice? Sylvia? That chick from 5th Street with the big fat ass?"

"No one is here, Bear."

"Aw, come on. You don't have to lie to me, little brother. I'm happy for you! It is about time! Twenty nine's a little old to be a virgin..."

I heard a growl from the living room. Nope. This was not going to end well at all.

"Who is it, brother? Janet? Cherise? Bett – no!" I heard a smack, as if he had just hit himself in the forehead. "Oh my God, it's the white girl, isn't it? She's been there this whole time! *That's* where she disappeared to!"

"Do not be stupid. I would never bring her here."

"Oh, yeah, she's too good for this place, right? Too proper. Too fancy. Too *white-bread*, right? She probably only fucks doctors or lawyers or trust fund guys."

"She is not here, Bear." A growl had seeped into Luca's voice now. The beta was warning the alpha.

"Nah, she probably doesn't fuck those guys either..." Bear went on, reveling in his lewdness. "She's probably married to Jesus. That's what I was thinking that night when we held her down and I freed those nice, round, white –"

There was a much louder bang on the inside of the fire door and I jumped. "I TOLD YOU, *SHE IS NOT HERE!*" Luca roared through the slab of metal between them: a flimsy, two inch barrier that was separating Bear from a throttling, from the sound of it. "And I told you to get out of here. Go!"

"You also told me that you would let me know if you saw her again," Bear said. He was speaking through gritted teeth now. He was done playing games. "You know she's mine, Slipknot. I told you that the first time we saw her."

Luca said nothing, but I could hear his heavy breathing from across the room.

"You can't stay in there with her forever, little brother."

"I told you: She. Is. Not. Here."

"Alright, I will believe you." His voice was deadly calm now, and dangerous. "Of course I will, you are my brother. But *you* believe this, Slipknot. If I find out that you've been lying to me, I'll fuck that little bitch right there on your floor, and I'll make you watch. You hear me?"

Luca hesitated, then said gruffly. "I hear you."

"I will be back tomorrow afternoon to tell you the new plan," Bear said, moving away. "You had better let me in."

Luca growled in response, and I sank down onto the bathroom floor, covering my face with my hands.

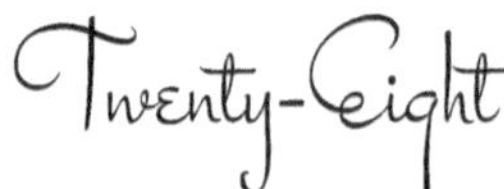

"Come on, Annabelle, come out of there."

"No." I sniffled, wiping my nose on the sleeve of the sweatshirt he had lent me. Bear had left ten minutes ago, but I still hadn't come out of the bathroom. The thought of what he was planning to do with me had given me flashbacks to the last time he had touched me, and I had had a panic attack at the mere thought of it.

He had been interrupted last time, but this time he would really do it; I could feel it in my gut. His cronies would pin me down right there on top of the beautiful tree Luca and I had just painted, and Bear would hold his knife to my throat and rape me while Luca watched, powerless to stop it.

"Annabelle, please..."

"No!" I shouted, trying to return my breathing to normal. "I don't want... I don't want you to see me like this."

I was still huddled in the corner closest to the door, with my knees pulled up to my chest and my arms wrapped around them. I had never had a panic attack before, and for a moment, I had been sure I would die of pure fear, cowering there on the bathroom floor. I hadn't been able to draw a single breath as I had recalled the feel of the cold night air on my bare breasts, and the rough, grabbing hands of the Uewatsu warriors.

Then the tears had started, and my breath had returned with choppy, hiccupping gulps, and now I felt drained and miserable, trapped by a future I could not escape.

The door was unlocked, but Luca wouldn't come in without my permission. *Like a vampire*, I thought darkly. *Like a vampire who runs with a pack of werewolves...*

"It does not matter what you look like," he murmured through the crack between the door and the jamb. "I just need to see you."

The sincerity in his voice made that stupid something in my stomach flop over, and I cursed myself for ever coming to Luca's apartment in the first place, because now I was trapped in more ways than one.

"Fine, just come in." I scrubbed angrily at my cheeks with my fist, and turned my face to the wall as I heard the door open, and Luca limp inside.

"Hey," he said softly.

"Hey." I sniffled again, unable to face him. I was embarrassed on so many levels, and scared on so many more. I couldn't handle looking into those fiery green eyes right now.

I heard him slide clumsily down onto the floor beside me, and I flinched when his knee brushed my side. For a long time, he just sat there, saying nothing, while I tried hard not to cry any more than I already had. Then, without a word, he snaked his arm behind me and gently tipped me over to lay against his chest. He stretched his bad leg out to my side, and wound one arm around my waist and rubbed my back with the other. He rested his chin on top of my hair, and I closed my eyes, engulfed by some strange sort of blissful agony as I inhaled the warm, autumn scent of him.

"I told you already that I will not let Bear hurt you," he murmured into my scalp. "I will not let *anyone* hurt you."

Two tears slid down my burning cheeks. I didn't answer. It

wasn't that I didn't believe him, because I did. It was more the fact that I had learned now that Fate didn't care what your intentions were: it was going to take what it wanted from you regardless.

"Tomorrow we will leave here. We will go someplace else. Someplace better. What do you say? I have been wanting to leave Luthertown Heights for a long time now anyway."

"What about your brothers?" I croaked, my voice thick and broken. "What about your family?"

"They are not my family anymore."

"Because of me..."

"Because of *me*," he said emphatically, squeezing me tighter. "I am like you. I want something more than this, something better. I just never realized that I could have it until now."

I made a low growling sound deep in my throat and mashed my clenched fists against my forehead. This was maddening. Everything he was saying sounded so perfect, so right, but it wasn't. It couldn't be. I had known Luca for less than a month – and I had only learned his name that morning! There was no way that I could trust that he was any different than the other wolves in his pack. He could say all these wonderful, heartfelt things, and he could make me feel important and special and safe, but that didn't change the fact that we barely knew each other.

And that he was an Uewatsu.

"Talk to me," he whispered, his lips moving against my messy hair.

"I can't. I'm confused..." I resisted the urge to growl again. I hated that I was always so vulnerable now. I was like a helpless, needy fawn, dependent on a big, strong, possibly homicidal fellow forest creature to take care of her. I despised myself. I should never have let it get to that point. I should have had the courage to fight off Bear. I should have had the foresight to save Marcus. Everything I had done in the past week had been wrong.

"Maybe I can help," Luca replied, seemingly unfazed by my desperate self-loathing. He was completely and utterly calm as he continued to rub my back, up and down, in long, slow, soothing strokes, in spite of the fact that I was as stiff as a board in his embrace.

"I feel like I shouldn't *let* you help me," I said, letting the words spill out into his t-shirt. "I feel like I trust you too much now, but I don't even know you."

"What do you want to know about me? I will tell you whatever you need to know. Ask me anything."

That time I really did growl again. Why was he being so nice to me? What had I done to earn this? Was it just pity now? Was that it?

"You never answered my questions before," I pointed out. My voice sounded harsh and almost vicious.

He was quiet for a moment, thinking it over. "That was because *I* wasn't ready to trust *you* yet."

"But you are now? What's changed?"

He paused again, and I finally snapped. I broke free of his embrace and sat up to glare at him. I could feel myself misplacing my anger again, but I couldn't stop it. "See? I knew it! You won't answer me. You're hiding things from me!"

"What am I hiding?" His expression had reverted back to his carefully practiced look of neutrality, and in that moment, I hated us both.

"Well, let's start with that!" I said, flinging a shaky hand at the rope wrapped around his throat. "How many people have you killed with that thing? The last rumor I heard was twenty. Oh, plus Shorty Biggs."

"Rumors are lies." The fire was burning in his eyes. A warning this time, perhaps?

If it was one, I didn't heed it.

"How many then? Ten? Twelve? Forty? Fifty?"

"None," he answered, his voice hard and raspy. "But not for lack of trying."

"Aha!" I shouted, pointing my finger in the air as if I were a detective who had just found the last clue she needed to solve a case. "So you *are* like your brothers, then!"

"Do you want to know the truth?" he asked me then, his eyes flashing dangerously. "Are you sure that that is what you really want?"

"That's what I've wanted this whole *time*, Luca!" I cried, almost ripping my hair out in frustration as I sat up onto my knees. "All I want is the truth! That's all I've ever wanted from you!"

"Alright, then that is what you will get." His voice was cold now, and his eyes were hard and empty as he reached up with his hands and found the knot at the back of his neck.

I knelt there in his lap, my anger leaving me as a heady mixture of curiosity and terror took its place, and I watched, transfixed, as he slowly unwrapped the length of brown rope that had been coiled around his neck since the first moment I had seen him. There were about six feet of it in all, layered in overlapping rows that rubbed the pale skin on his neck raw. I could see red splotches beneath his chin as he slowly revealed his Adam's apple, getting closer and closer to the end of the rope. As he pulled away the last coil of frayed nylon, I clapped my hands over my mouth as fresh tears sprang to my eyes.

"Oh my God, Luca," I whispered through my fingers, wishing to that same God that I could look away. It was awful; the sight of it hurt me in ways I never would have thought possible, and I realized what a fool I was.

"The only person I ever tried to kill with this rope was me," he said, his hoarse voice wavering slightly. His eyes were wide; he felt vulnerable, exposed, ashamed, even, with the cold air touching his bare skin, just as I had that night on the concrete road in front of my apartment. But this time it was I who was the monster. It was I who had forced him to reveal something he wasn't ready to share.

With a trembling hand, I reached out, haltingly, to touch my fingers to the long, thick concave purple scar that looped around his neck: the imprint of a hangman's noose. It was deep, unbelievably deep – like a trench dug into his tanned skin, and I didn't know how he could breathe at all, let alone talk or whisper or laugh with me. It looked like a horseshoe, with the curve lying in the hollow of his throat, and the ends going up toward his ears. I could even see the imprint of the braided rope in the scar, making it all too easy to picture the real thing there.

He cringed a bit as I traced the outline of his scar, then I snapped my hand back as if it had burned me. It hurt too much to touch it. It hurt too much to imagine the kind of pain he must have been in, the kind of torment he must have felt, to do such an unspeakable thing to himself.

"It is ugly, I know," he said roughly, picking up the rope from the floor. "That is why I didn't want to –"

I suddenly leaned forward and put both my hands on his face. "Promise me you'll never do that again," I begged him, trying hard not to crush his face as I tried to rein in my desperation.

He looked surprised by my intensity, but I didn't let up.

"Luca, promise me!"

"I promise, Annabelle, I promise."

I exhaled in relief and rested my head against his forehead, just as he had rested his against mine a few hours ago. "I'm so sorry," I whispered to him, meaning it with all of my heart, and for so many reasons.

I heard the rope fall to the floor as he put his arms back around me, where they belonged.

"That is why I was so adamant about you not being reckless with your own life after what you did at the hospital with Marcus' stepfather," he said, his words coming quick and fast, nothing like his usual speech pattern. "You scared me, Annabelle. You scared me then, and you scare me again every time that you try to leave this apartment without me. I am afraid that if you leave, I will never see you again. I am afraid that we could be more alike than we seem; that you could feel that same angst that I felt, that you could give in to your inner demons like I gave into mine and—"

"Shhh," I said softly, leaning back so that I could see his face. He was wearing himself out; he was talking a mile a minute, barely able to breathe, and each word seemed to bring him closer and closer to losing his raspy voice entirely. His eyes were wild and wet and darting from freckle to freckle as he stared hard at my face, as if he were desperately trying to memorize their placement before it was too late. "Luca, I already made you that promise, remember?" I stroked his cheek with my hand, and found them both to be trembling.

"Yes, but if Bear –"

I shushed him again, putting my finger against his slick lips. "A promise is a promise," I said firmly. "And this is about you, not me. What happened, Luca? Why would you want to..." I couldn't bring myself to say the words as I grazed the indentation in his neck. "Why would you do this to yourself?"

He stared at me for a long, long time. His vibrant, iridescent green eyes were full of agony, but there was something else in them too, something stronger.

Something like hope.

"Come with me," he said, letting me help him to his feet. Then he folded his hand around mine, and led me out of the painted sea and into the forest.

Twenty-Nine

"I hung it from there." Luca pointed up at a three-inch, golden hook above his mattress. He had told me before that he usually hung a dreamcatcher there, but apparently he had hung much bigger things, much more precious things, there too. It didn't look large enough to hold the weight of a man without being pulled out of the concrete ceiling, but I shuddered just the same at a vision of Luca hanging there beneath those painted stars.

"I had picked the mattress up and learned it against that wall, there," he continued, now pointing to the painted tree line adjacent to his bed, "and I dragged over one of the kitchen chairs..."

His voice was strange again, almost hollow somehow, and his eyes had glazed over, as if he were watching it all through a window into the past. We were sitting on his bed, he with his legs sprawled out across the comforter, me with mine folded beneath me as I sat beside him and squeezed the hand that had led me out of the bathroom, too afraid to let it go.

I wanted him to start at the beginning, to talk me through every single step of the thought process that had led him there, to that exact spot, with such dark intentions, but I forced myself to let him tell it his own way.

"I was not expecting it to hurt so much..." he mumbled, staring off into space. "When I kicked away the chair and I fell, the rope snapped taut, and I immediately felt it break my larynx."

I squeezed my eyes shut, wishing his descriptions were less vivid, and wishing they didn't affect me so profoundly.

"I thought that I would die then. But no, I just kept hanging there, for what felt like hours. After all I had been through, I could not live anymore, but I could not seem to die, either. It was agony."

"I could not breathe, but I was still thinking, thinking about all of the terrible things that I had seen and done and let happen. I wanted to die so badly! I wanted to erase all of those memories. But apparently it was not my time.

"The edges of my vision were just starting to go dark when Bear burst in here like he always does, and he found me. I had left the door unlocked that night, so that someone could find my body before it started to... well..." He cleared his throat, then started again. "Bear asked me what the hell I was thinking, then he pulled out his knife, and he cut the rope.

"I crashed down to the floor, and he kicked me in the stomach, telling me that I was an idiot, that suicide was for cowards. Then, as I was lying there, gasping like a beached carp, he leaned down and put his face next to mine. He said, 'Now you owe me your life, little brother.'"

"What an asshole..." I whispered. What kind of person says something like that to their brother? Luca obviously needed help and support, but he wasn't going to get it from his so-called family.

To my surprise, Luca's eyes cleared and he let out a small, sad laugh as they focused on me. "Yes, he is an asshole. But he was right. I owed him my life. I still do. That was nine years ago."

"But *why*, Luca? Why did you do it?"

A somber look came over him, and he cast his eyes downward. Speaking to our clasped hands, he said: "Because I was a monster. For years, my father had been grooming me to be a part of the

Uewatsu – a true part. I had tried to get out of it, I had tried to tell him I was not made for such things, but he would not listen.

"On my twentieth birthday, he decided that it was time to officially initiate me. The others had been initiated when they were sixteen, but I had managed to postpone it until then by making my father question my capacity as a warrior.

"That night, though, he decided that he had waited long enough. He, Bear, Goon, and River took me to Luthertown Park, where they had tied a woman to a tree. I recognized her, she was one of the prostitutes from 18th Street. I used to see her at Sal's fruit stand when I went to buy apples. She would always say hello to me and wave."

He took a deep, ragged breath and paused for a few moments to let his throat recover from the strain. I couldn't imagine how much it must be hurting him to talk this much all at once, but at the same time, I couldn't stop him. I needed to know what happened. I needed to know everything.

"My father said that she was someone that no one would miss. He said that she would make me a man, and then I would take her life. That would be my initiation."

I squeezed his hand so tightly that I was sure I heard a bone crack, but he didn't pull away.

"My other brothers had only had to steal a memento from a member of a rival gang to be initiated. But my father hated me for my weakness, and he wanted to 'make me strong,' like Bear, my oldest brother, and his most loyal son.

"So he told me to use her, and then kill her, and I would be a true Uewatsu. Goon and River untied her. She was crying. She had a rag in her mouth, but she was sobbing, begging me with her eyes to let her go. I will never forget those eyes. They were a grayish blue, like the Ohio River...

"Bear shoved her down onto her knees. He was enjoying every minute of it, the bastard. Then he gave me his knife, and my father told me to make him proud."

Luca paused again to catch his breath and rest his voice. There was anger in his face, and something like regret, and I realized then that I didn't want him to go on. I was afraid to know what he had done, and afraid of what it would feel like to find out that my instincts about him were wrong, and that he was more like the cretins who raised him than I wanted to believe.

"You don't... you don't have to tell me the rest right now if you... you know, if you don't –"

"No, you need to know," he said, with a small, sad smile. He stroked my cheek with his finger, then went on. "I could not touch her. I could not even look at her. I was repulsed by what my father and brothers wanted me to do. But I could not tell them that.

"So I just stood there, trying to find the courage to say something, and trying to think of a way to save the woman. But I waited too long.

"'What is the matter?' my father asked me, 'is she not pretty enough? We can get you another.' My brothers were all standing around us in a circle, waiting for me to do something. So I said to my father, 'I can't. We have to let her go. This is not right.' And the woman started to cry harder. 'Do not worry, son, we will get you a better one,' my father said, knowing that that was not what I wanted. 'But until we find one you like, you can watch Bear and learn.'"

Horrified, I looked at Luca's face. It was pale, and his eyes had fallen shut. His lip quivered, but as he had told me before, he had been trained not to cry.

"So Bear raped her there, on the ground. I tried to stop him, but Goon and River held me back, under my father's instructions. I shouted, begging them to leave her alone, but no one listened. They all took turns with her, even my father. Then when they were finished Bear slit her throat with the knife, and I had to stand there and watch her die.

"'That is what men do,' said my father. 'They take what they want. And until you can learn to do that for yourself, we are going to bring another girl here every night.

"That is when I decided to end my life," Luca said, his voice hoarse and barely audible now. "It was the only way to save those women. I had been contemplating it for a long time anyway, since my mother had passed. So I came back home, took out the rope, and hung myself. But in the end it wouldn't have mattered if I had died anyway. When Bear found me, he had been coming to tell me that our father was dead, taken out by the leader of the Sixes on his way home from the park."

"Jesus…" I breathed. Did the violence ever end? I felt sick to my stomach, not just over the thought of Luca's pain, but over the fact that an uncomfortably large part of me was glad that Luca's father was dead, so that he could never hurt anyone ever again.

"Bear had always liked me, so he let me into the Uewatsu without an initiation. He had the others call me Slipknot, and told them made-up stories about how I had strangled a woman with my rope. He made me his informant, his right-hand man, but he never made me kill anyone. But, he also never let me forget how good he was to me, and that I owed him my life."

He was quiet for a while then, and he turned his gaze to the hook in the ceiling. "For a long time, I wished I had died that night."

"And now?"

He lowered his eyes to meet mine. He caressed my cheek again with his fingers, letting them linger there as his thin lips pulled up into a fond, affectionate smile. "No. Not anymore."

"I'm glad," I said, and I meant it with all of my battered, aching heart.

"Me too."

"And yes," I said softly.

His eyes had fallen to my lips. Distracted, he asked, "'Yes,' what?"

"Yes, I'll run away with you."

His eyes darted back to mine. "Really?"

I nodded. Then I wrapped my arms around his neck and sank into him, soaking in the closeness, the warmth, and the bonfire scent of his skin. I had been right about him all along; I hadn't needed to be afraid of him or what he could do to me. All he wanted was the same thing that I wanted: to help someone, and to be accepted for who he really was.

"Then we will leave first thing in the morning," he murmured, his lips giving me goosebumps as they moved against my neck. "But first, would you come somewhere with me? There is someone I have to say goodbye to before we go."

With his arms wrapped around me and his soft, tender voice in my ear, I was powerless to say anything but yes.

Thirty

After a quick dinner (fish sticks and frozen French fries, which he spent most of the meal apologizing for), Luca and I headed down the fire escape. To my surprise, he had taken my hand as soon as we had stepped out onto the wrought iron landing, and he was holding it like a shy sixth grader on a first date: delicately, and with a palm that was warm against mine, but a bit soggy as well.

It was sweet, and in spite of all that had happened and everything he had just told me, I felt almost happy for the first time in a long time.

"Are you laughing at me?" he asked, grinning nervously as he huffed and puffed his way down the stairs. His leg had stiffened up since that morning. It had taken us nearly fifteen minutes to make it down to the third floor of the building, but I was in no hurry.

"No," I answered, beaming like an idiot in the twilit evening.

"Then why are you smiling?"

I really did laugh that time. "Don't ask," I told him.

"Come on." He let out a grunt as he stopped to massage his thigh. "Tell me."

"It's stupid, really."

"Annabelle..."

"Okay, okay." I sighed, leaning against the railing. "I was just feeling... I don't know... 'content.' That's all. This is nice, you and me."

His already flushed face grew darker in the waning light. "Oh," he said simply.

I took his hand again. "Come on, let's go. We're almost there."

He held my hand with a bit more confidence that time as we finally reached street level. The buildings around us were buzzing with activity as Luthertown Heights' commuting residents came home from work, greeting their families and preparing their evening meals. The chatter and the street sounds were pleasant for the time being: it was not yet the witching hour. I knew, though, as soon as full dark fell over the city, the werewolves and other monsters would emerge from their dens and begin once more to wreak their havoc upon the living.

That thought spooked me a bit, so I scooted closer to Luca as we made our way, slowly but surely, to a squatty, glass-front building to the right of his apartment complex. It looked squashed in comparison to the other buildings around it (all of which were at least five stories tall), as if something large had flattened it beneath its foot. The enormous, square front windows were almost entirely covered by huge, childish yellow bubble letters, spelling out the words "WANING MOON ELDER CARE." To my surprise, all of them were intact. With so much glass and so little brick visible, it was just begging for vandalism in a town like Luthertown Heights.

"Did you do that?" I teased Luca, pointing at the fat, chunky, foam pain lettering.

He raised an eyebrow and threw me a look that said, "please," and I laughed.

"You and I should paint something before we leave," I went on, as he opened the door for me. "Something really big. It'll be like leaving our mark on the city!"

"Sure," he replied. In spite of his exhaustion, he sounded enthused. "What should we paint?"

"Hmm... let me think about it for a while."

Waning Moon Elder Care looked a lot like Luca's apartment, sans his beautiful artwork. The entire operation seemed to take up only one large, square room with a big empty space in the middle. There were twenty to thirty beds lined up along the four walls, each with a small plastic night table beside it and a folding paper curtain for privacy. There were also several squashy purple armchairs scattered around, one of which Luca gestured to as he made his way toward a desk at the head of the room.

"Grab that one," he told me, "it is the most comfortable."

I did as he said and put my hands on the back of the chair quickly, as if someone were coming up behind me to steal it. I needn't have worried, though. Aside from Luca, me, and a bored-looking woman behind the front desk, the only other people in the room were tucked into the beds.

I felt a chill go up my spine as I looked around at all of the wrinkled, sickly faces poking up from beneath the plain white sheets. With the glass windows and the room's layout, it felt more like a zoo than a nursing home, and it gave me the creeps. How could anyone let their grandparents live here?

"Okay, I signed us in." I jumped as Luca appeared at my elbow. "My Elisi is over here, the second bed from the back."

I nodded and helped him push the chair toward the far corner of the room, where a wizened, weathered, copper-skinned woman lay, sleeping peacefully. With a jolt, I realized that I had seen that face before, amongst the random figures in Luca's paintings around town. She had had long, grey braids there, but in real life, her long, curly white hair flowed over the pillow and down the side of the bed like a waterfall. There was a spray of dark, brown-black freckles scattered across her nose as well.

Luca's nose.

"Elisi?" Luca said tentatively, putting a hand on her feeble, brittle-looking shoulder. "Elisi, it is your grandson. It is –"

Suddenly, the silent, antiseptic-scented air was rent by a loud, shrill screech. Luca's Elisi bolted upright in bed, her enormous, emerald green eyes bleary and wild, and she grabbed Luca's arm.

"Elisi, it is –"

She screamed again and I covered my ears. Her mouth was like a big, black "o," with no teeth in sight and a greyish tongue that vibrated in time with the sound waves passing over it.

She was glaring at Luca as she took a breath, and I felt like screaming myself when she let another one rip.

"ELISI, PLEASE!"

Luca's loud, commanding voice startled her into silence. The black hole closed and she slowly lay back down against her pillow.

"It is you again," she said quietly, her voice crackling from the strain she had just put on it.

"Yes, Elisi, it's me, L – "

"Why do you keep coming to this place? What do you want from me?"

Luca glanced apologetically at me, and I could see that his green eyes, so much like his grandmother's, were full of sorrow.

"I wanted to introduce you to someone," he said, hesitantly reaching out to put his hand at the small of my back. He guided me forward slightly, and I noticed that my own palm was soggy with sweat now as I held it out to her. "This is Annabelle."

"Nice to meet you," I said, smiling in spite of my apprehension.

"I am Immookalee, but I do not see what that has to do with you," she spat.

"Immookalee? That's a beautiful name!" I said sincerely, dropping my unshaken hand. "What does it mean?"

Immookalee just glared at me, but Luca answered, "It means 'waterfall' in Cherokee."

Like her hair, I thought, watching it cascade over the pillow and down nearly to the floor. For some reason, that thought enchanted me, and my anxiety died away.

"Your hair is so pretty," I told her. "I wish mine was that long!"

She made a spitting sound. "You know they say that girls with red hair are devils, right?" she asked Luca. "Is this your final trick, you fiend? To bring the devil to kill me?"

I was thunderstruck by the cruelty in her response, but Luca just sighed. "I am not a fiend," he said, without much conviction, "I am your grandson."

"No grandson of mine would look so repulsive!"

My mouth fell open as I looked Luca up and down. Sure, he had rewrapped his neck rope before we had gone out, but other than that, he looked perfectly respectable to me! Much moreso than I did; I was wearing another of his long, stretched-out sweatshirts full of rips and holes over my blood-speckled jeans and boots from the day before. I hadn't had a hairbrush with me, either, so I had just run my fingers through my curls to try to untangle them, and that had been the extent of my grooming. If anyone looked gruesome, it was me, not Luca.

In fact, as I looked at his sad eyes in the bluish florescent lights, and watched the way his own curly hair framed his scruffy, tawny face, I thought he looked more handsome than I had ever seen him.

Some of my thoughts must have shown on my face, because he frowned at me curiously, and I turned beet red.

"I cannot help that, Elisi, it is a scar," he said in a weary voice, as he turned back to her.

Oh! The scar... I barely noticed it anymore there, purple and raised beneath his eye, as I looked at his face.

"The mark of the devil is more like it," Immookalee muttered. "Did *she* give it to you?"

"Of course not!" Luca looked appalled. "It was – "

"I think your grandson looks very nice," I said hastily, cutting him off. It was a stupid thing to say, but I couldn't just let him stand there and be insulted.

I felt Luca's eyes on me again, but I couldn't meet his. My face was burning like a candle, and I wasn't sure what he would see in it now.

"That creature is *not* my grandson. He is a beast."

I opened my mouth to argue, but Luca spoke first. "Whatever I am to you, Elisi, I have come to say goodbye. Annabelle and I are going away tomorrow, and I will not be back here to see you anymore."

"Good!" Immookalee snapped.

Luca looked hurt. "Is that really how you feel about it?" he asked quietly, and I felt my heart break.

"Yes! Now get out of here! Good riddance to you and your devil both! Go! Go now!"

Luca put his hand on the small of my back again, and we turned around to leave. As we passed the squashy purple armchair, I felt another pang as I realized that we had never even had the chance to sit down on it.

Luca didn't look back as we crossed the empty room, and he didn't say another word until we were back outside in the cool October air.

"I'm sorry," he said, hobbling back toward his building. "I really wanted you to meet her. The *real* her. But this was one of her bad days. Her Alzheimer's makes her forget me. And when she forgets me, she hates me."

"Well, then we'll stay, and come back on one of her good days," I replied, slipping my hand into his. "We don't absolutely *have* to leave tomorrow. We just have to avoid Bear and –"

"There is no use. It is done. And there is no avoiding Bear. If it wasn't for this stupid leg wound, I would say that we should leave tonight."

I pursed my lips and watched my feet as we walked. Leaving town had seemed like such a good idea a few hours ago. It was the perfect solution: Luca and I would be safe, and I would be free of the hell that that town had put me through. It would be a brand new start for both of us. I hadn't realized until then, though, that Luca would be leaving something behind that he would miss.

"I should have just left," he said. "She will not remember I came by anyway. It just did not seem right to leave without saying goodbye."

"You did the right thing," I said firmly, wrapping my arm around his and leaning my head against his shoulder. "I'm sure that somewhere deep down inside, she appreciated it."

"I am not so sure... would you appreciate it if a stranger like me kept coming by and bothering you every night?"

I bit my lip as I grinned. "Isn't that how you and I met?"

He chuckled. "If I remember correctly, you did not appreciate it much either at first."

"Sure I did! You just made me... nervous."

"Because you were afraid of me."

"No," I replied. "Because I wasn't."

Luca seemed to be in a much better mood after that. As we scaled the nine flights of fire escape scaffolding, he told me more about his Elisi, and how she had been the original source of all the artistic talent in his family.

"Back when she still lived on the res, she used to make dream-catchers. Everyone in a thirty-mile radius had one of her dream-catchers. That is where my father got them all for the Uewatsu... even if he did not tell Elisi what he was using them for."

"And now yours is gone!" I fretted, looking at his bandaged ear as I helped him up the last flight of stairs.

"To be honest, it is my earlobe that I really miss," he teased, giving me a wry grin.

I laughed, and was just about to come up with a witty reply when we reached the ninth floor landing and Luca stopped cold.

The light was on in his apartment. It spilled out onto the wrought iron platform through the half-open door, bathing our feet in a butter-yellow glow that made my entire body seize up with fear.

I clutched Luca's arm, forgetting about his other assorted wounds. His brow was furrowed as he began to creep forward into the light. Just as he was reaching for the doorknob, there was a ripping sound inside, and I stifled a scream.

It was Bear, I was sure of it. Bear, like his grizzly namesake, was on the other side of that door, lying in wait for us like the predator he was. I had thought I had until tomorrow, but apparently Fate was not one to wait.

I would have been perfectly content to stand there frozen on the fire escape for the next few hours, but Luca had other plans.

Pushing me behind him, he pushed open the door and burst into the apartment. In his fury, he grew three feet at least, into a towering, snarling beast, and I felt goosebumps spring up across my skin as he transformed into an Uewatsu before my eyes.

"Who are you?" he growled, as I hurried in behind him. My heart was pounding so loudly in my ears that I could barely hear him. Did he just say "who are you?"

"Your worst nightmare, mothafucka," came an answering voice, and my pounding heart stopped beating.

I knew that voice.

My legs were trembling as I pushed past Luca to get a glimpse of the young man pointing a gun at his chest. "Lamont!"

I barely recognized my former student. The day before, his lip had been busted and his eye had been bruised, but today his face was a swollen, amorphous mass of cuts and dried blood. His eyes stared out through two slits above a clearly shattered nose, and his puffy lips made him look as if he were having an allergic reaction to something.

He was wearing the same clothes as the day before, standing there in the center of the room amidst the tattered remains of our painstakingly crafted tree painting, and he was holding a shiny silver pistol in his right hand. It shook as he held it out, as far away from his body as possible. I noticed that he had it tilted on its side, like a thug in a gangster movie.

"What...what the hell are you doin' here?" he asked me. His

bottom lip was quivering. His legs too. "You ain't supposed to be here."

"Neither are you!" I countered without thinking. I tried to step forward to take the gun from him, but Luca caught me around the middle and held me against his hip.

"Hey! Don't touch her!" Lamont shouted, lifting the gun a bit higher, but Luca didn't let go.

"Lamont, calm down," I said. "What is this? What's going on? What are you doing here?"

"I asked you first!" He sounded a bit hysterical, and in spite of the weapon in his hand, I knew that he wasn't doing this by choice.

"I'm here because Luca is my friend," I replied, trying to talk in calm, soothing tones. "He took care of me after what happened with Marcus yesterday. He's saved my life more than once. He's a good man, Lamont. Put the gun down."

I seemed to affect both men with my words. Lamont's gun wavered, and Luca's arm tightened around my waist as if my declaration had startled him.

"That... that can't be right," stuttered Lamont. "My pops says that he and all his brothers are like dirty wild dogs. He says they're more animal than human."

"That's not true."

"He says they don't deserve to live!" He raised his gun again, and I quickly moved in front of Luca, shielding him.

"Lamont, please! Don't you remember what I told you?" I asked, ignoring Luca's attempts to push me aside. "We all make our own choices, remember? We can't judge people based on what group they hang out with or what gang they – "

"WELL I AIN'T *GOT* NO CHOICE, MAN!"

His words were so loud that it felt as if he had smacked me with them. Tears began to leak out from the slits in his face, and I took a tentative step toward him.

"Just tell me what's going on," I said softly. "Just talk to me. I can help you. You don't have to do anything you don't want to do."

"Maybe I *do* wanna do it! You don't know me, bitch!"

"Do you, then?" I asked him. The rest of the world was falling away as I closed the gap between us. It was only Lamont and me now, Lamont and me and my belief that he would do the right thing.

Just as I had at the hospital, I stepped in front of the gun. It was shaking violently in Lamont's hand as I guided the muzzle to rest against my heart.

"Annabelle..." I heard Luca mutter from a distance, but I shushed him.

Locking eyes with Lamont, I asked again, "Do you? Do you really want to kill someone?"

"N...not *you!*" He sniffled, his swollen eyes darting desperately between Luca and me.

"Well, if you want to kill Luca, you have to kill me too. That's the deal."

"Annabelle!"

Because when you kill one person, Lamont, you're not just ending *their* life, you're destroying lots of other lives that are connected to theirs, you see?"

He shook his head jerkily, uncomprehending.

"If you hurt Luca, you'll also be hurting me. If you hurt me, you'll be hurting Luca. And yourself, too, if I'm right."

His panicked eyes were locked on mine.

"No matter which one of us, or how many of us you kill, you'll always have that on your conscience. Is that what you want, Lamont? To be a killer for the rest of your life?"

Several tense seconds passed. Then, slowly, he shook his head no.

"Exactly!" I exclaimed, with a rush of jubilation. "You're not a killer, Lamont, you're a basketball player! You're not a gangbanger, you're a teenaged boy with his whole life ahead of him! You don't have to do this!"

"But if I don't, they'll kill me." He sniffled once more, and a dribble of red-tinged snot ran down from his ruined nose.

"Who?"

"My pops. My uncle. The Sixes. This is my initiation. I have to take out an Uewatsu in order to join the gang. If I don't, I'm dead."

"Okay…" I said slowly, trying to think, "Okay, we can fix this. Let me just –"

"Here."

I jumped as Luca hobbled up beside me and dangled something shiny in front of Lamont's face.

Lamont looked both startled and suspicious, but when he realized what he was looking at, he slowly lowered his gun to his side. "Keys?"

"To my truck," said Luca. His raspy voice was curt, but his attempt to create a treaty was clear. "The red one parked at the curb. Take the truck back to your headquarters. Tell them you shot me when I came in the front door, just like you had planned to. Or better yet, just drive out of town and don't look back."

"But… but I…"

"Give me the gun."

Before Lamont could argue, he had taken it from him and aimed it at the front door. Lamont and I both jumped as he fired it, leaving a large, smoking hole in the floor, and sending the crushed bullet skittering out onto the fire escape. He fired again, shooting out into the night, then handed the gun back to Lamont.

"On the first shot, you missed," he told him. "Now go, while it still smells like gunpowder."

"But… but… why?" Lamont asked, gaping at Luca in wonder as he held the butt of the smoldering weapon pinched between his thumb and forefinger.

"Because someone tried to initiate me once too."

Lamont turned his swollen eyes to me, and I smiled, in spite of the tears that had sprung to mine. "Go," I told him. "But be safe!"

He looked at me a moment longer, then he suddenly sprang forward and threw his arms around my neck. "I will never forget this, Miss Annabelle," he sobbed into my ear.

Then he ran off into the night, as either a free man or a card-carrying member of the Sixes.

Luca looked visibly shaken as he shut the fire door and leaned against it. "I was not expecting that." His voice was hoarse, and his face was pale beneath his purple scar.

"You saved his life," I said, still in a state of total shock. "I can't believe you did that!"

He closed his eyes and rested his head against the door, as if he were having second thoughts. "I told him why. Even if I did not really do it for him."

"You did it for me." It wasn't a question. I knew who he had done it for. I walked slowly toward him, but stopped when he spoke again.

"Yes, but I should not have."

My swollen heart, so full of affection and warmth for him, sank. "What?"

"You lied to me," he said, opening his eyes. "You promised me that you would never do something like that again. It was the hospital all over again."

"No, it wasn't. This was completely different!"

"Oh, sure!" I had never heard him use sarcasm before. It didn't suit him. His face twisted in anger as he mocked me. "Sure, it was completely different from the last time you stepped in front of a loaded gun and dared someone to shoot you."

"This *was* different!" I insisted. "Lamont was never going to shoot me!"

"Oh, yes? And how do you know that? Are you a psychic now as well as an idiot?"

I flinched as if he had slapped me.

The anger immediately drained from his face as I took a step back, shaking my head.

"No, Annabelle, I'm sorry, I –"

"I am *not* an idiot," I said quietly, blinking back tears. "I knew what I was doing."

"I know, listen, I –"

"Forget it," I interrupted, crossing my arms over my chest as he reached out for me. "Can I go to bed now, or do we have to leave?"

Luca's expression was pained. The corners of his blazing eyes were pinched with regret, and his mouth opened and shut wordlessly several times before he spoke. "We... we can still stay here tonight, I think. We will leave in the morning."

"Okay."

I closed myself up in the bathroom for a while after that – not crying this time, but clenching my fists on the rim of the ceramic sink as I glared into the bruised face in the mirror hanging over it. What had happened to me being brave? That's what Luca had told me before, wasn't it? That I was brave? That he admired me? Now I was just an idiot again – the one thing he had said I never was – doing dangerous, reckless things and making him feel like he had to save me.

As I stared into my own troubled brown eyes, though, I knew in my heart that even if I had the chance to do it again, I would have still done anything I could to save Luca. Or Lamont. Caring about people wasn't idiotic. It was a strength. Perhaps the greatest one I had. I was proud of it, I was proud of what I had done. If

Luca couldn't see the value in it, then maybe he wasn't the person I thought he was.

I waited a few minutes longer, drawing things out by washing my face and raking my fingers through my tangled hair again. Then I opened the bathroom door, planning to give Luca the silent treatment for the rest of the night, and perhaps the rest of the foreseeable future.

That proved impossible, though, when I saw what was waiting for me outside.

"Luca, what...?" I felt the corners of my lips – which I had purposely, determinedly, set into a deep frown – begin to pull up as if on strings as I looked out at the expanse of floor before me. I had only been in the bathroom for fifteen minutes, twenty, tops, but in that time, Luca had covered every inch of the slick, brown laminate with painted flowers.

There were dozens of them, hundreds, maybe! All in different colors, different sizes, different shapes and species. There was a spray of white baby's breath near my right shoe, and an entire garden of multicolored daisies a few feet beyond that. There were purple irises, deep orange marigolds, dark, midnight blue delphiniums... there was even a patch of bright, sun-yellow daffodils near the front door. And in the middle of it all, surrounded by a swirling vine of pale pink orchids (my favorite!) were the words "I'M SORRY," written in fat, bold, black letters.

Not sure whether to cry or laugh, I looked up at Luca as he stood there in the same place I had left him, right in front of the fire door. He was looking bashful now, with his hands in his pockets and his head lowered as he watched me, waiting for my reaction.

"You... how did you do all this while I was in the bathroom?" I said incredulously, going with the first coherent thought that came to my mind.

Luca shrugged. "Graffiti artists learn to work fast. And I was highly motivated."

I bit my lip as that thing in my stomach flopped over one last time and exploded into a swarm of butterflies that threatened to burst out of my chest.

"I am so sorry, Anabelle," Luca told me, taking a step forward onto one of my daffodils. I noticed that there was a smear of pink paint across his chin, and I was hit with an insane urge to try to kiss it off of him. "I should never have said that, not even in anger. You are not an idiot. You are the bravest, smartest, kindest person I know."

I took a step forward too, hating to crush the baby's breath beneath my boots.

"I am just so afraid of losing you," he went on, taking another step. "But Annabelle, I swear to God, if you ever look at me again like you looked at me when I said that, I will die on the spot."

"Don't say that!"

"But it is true!" He was getting closer now, just out of reach of the arms that were so desperate to hold him. "I *never* want to hurt you. I never want to make you cry. I never want anything or anyone else to either. Can you... do you think you could... could you forgive me?"

I took one look into his pleading, pained, smoldering emerald eyes, and answered him the only way I knew how.

In one fluid motion, I closed the space between us and threw those desperate arms around his neck, pulling him close, pulling him down to my level as I pressed my lips to his.

He hesitated for a moment as his entire body tensed up. Then he coiled his long, lean arms around me and kissed me back. His movements were slow, delicate, careful, as if he were afraid that he would hurt me, or worse – make me pull away.

He needn't have worried, though. I wasn't going anywhere.

For the second time that night, the rest of the world fell away as I lost myself in Luca's kiss. It was so sweet, so tender, so full of reined-in passion that I found myself praying that it would never end. The warm, smoky scent of him enveloped me, and his breath became my own as I leaned into him and he held me close, cupping my face with one hand as he pressed me to his chest with the other.

It was beautiful, it was wonderful, it was bliss personified, until he pulled back a few moments later to rest his forehead against mine.

My throat was too constricted and I was too flushed to speak, so I just lowered my hands to his chest, feeling the rapid thump of his heart through his t-shirt.

"So... does that mean that you forgive me?" he asked, his voice hoarse and husky for a different reason now.

"Was that not clear?" A mischievous grin spread across my face as I caressed his nose with mine. "Maybe I should repeat myself..."

"That might help clarify things, yes," he replied. My eyes were already closed, but I could hear the smile in his voice, and I could feel it as it pressed against mine seconds later.

Thirty-Three

"Can I tell you something?" Luca murmured into my ear a little while later.

In spite of our increasingly passionate kisses, we had gone to bed before we could get *too* lost in each other. Although our purity remained intact for the time being, Luca had lifted his ban on touching in bed, and was currently snuggled up behind me, nuzzling his scruffy face into my neck as he pressed his taut abdominal muscles against my back.

"Of course," I replied, enjoying the warm, tingling sensation that spread through my entire body at the sound of his low, breathy voice. He had his left arm around me, and I was holding his hand in both of mine as I pressed it to the fluttering heart in my chest.

"That was my first kiss," he said, sounding more amorous than embarrassed. "Well, the first one was, anyway."

"Really?" I turned my head to look at him. Would he ever stop finding new ways to move me?

"Is that strange to you?"

"No! Well, I mean it's strange to me that no other girl tried to kiss you before I did, but it's not strange in any other way. It makes it even more special."

I could feel his grin as he brushed his lips across the nape of my neck, making the little hairs there stand on end.

"I should have known..."

"You should have known what?" It was getting very hard to think through the haze he was creating in my brain.

"That it would not matter to you how 'experienced' I am. That is why I did not want to kiss you before. Or hold you. Or even touch you, at first. I have been alone for so long, trying to keep my distance from people. I did not want to get close to anyone. I did not feel like I deserved to. So now I am not accustomed to... human contact."

"Well, you'd better get used to it," I said, as I turned over in his arms to nestle my head into the hollow of his bare, scarred neck.

"Yes, ma'am." He kissed me on the forehead, and enveloped me with both arms.

As we drifted off to sleep, all wrapped up in each other, I couldn't help but think about how much had happened in the span of just a few days. Luca was once nothing but a silent (if admittedly intriguing) shadow, but now he had morphed into the most solid, most real, most essential thing in my life.

For six months and most of the rest of my life, I had felt different and lonesome – a nameless person with a face everyone I met would soon forget. As I lay there in Luca's arms, though, I finally knew what it felt like to be understood, to be cared for, to have a name.

In his arms, I had finally found where I belonged.

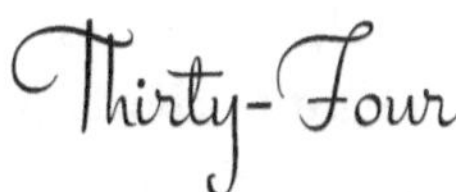

"I wish we could take it with us." I pouted, trying to memorize the pattern of the flowers Luca had painted on the floor.

We had woken up early, at the exact moment the pale sun had decided to kiss the sky good morning. We had packed two scuffed, cowhide satchels with some of Luca's clothes and food and paints, and at 6:30 a.m., we were on our way out the door.

"I will paint you new ones when we find a place." Luca smiled, kissing me on the top of the head on his way to grab his leather jacket from the bed.

"It won't be the same..."

My eyes traveled sadly from the love note on the floor to the beautiful green forest on the side wall, to the wall of faces (famous and otherwise), to the sunset on the fridge next to the front door Luca never used, and finally, to the stars and planets spread out across the black ceiling. It was all so beautiful, so perfect. How could I just leave knowing I would never get to see it again? And, worse yet, how could I let Luca leave his masterpieces behind?

"I took some photos with my phone while you were in the bathroom," Luca told me, limping over to drape his jacket across my shoulders. I felt a twinge of repulsion as I realized that it was the Uewatsu jacket, one of the symbols of their gang. Bear had one just like it. His, though, probably didn't smell like Luca. "They are probably blurry since my phone is so old, but it is better than nothing, right?"

I shrugged, surreptitiously sniffing the collar of his coat as I slipped my arms into the sleeves. I was having second thoughts about leaving, but it was hard to concentrate on them when that coat reminded me of long, slow kisses and whispered conversations beneath that sea of white-painted stars.

"We are going to have to walk pretty far to find a bus that will take us out of town," Luca went on, turning off the fridge now. "Remind me again why I gave that kid my truck?"

"Because you're a good man," I answered immediately, catching him by the lapel of his dark grey t-shirt as he hurried past again. I kissed him lightly on the lips, and his smile spread.

"You are making it very hard to stay focused, you know."

"Right back atcha." I teased, kissing him one more before I let him get back to his checking and rechecking.

I picked up our bags and pulled one onto my shoulder as he frowned down at the mattress. After a few seconds of indecision, he muttered something that sounded like "oh, hell," and pulled out the soft, brown, woolen blanket from beneath the checkered comforter and rolled it up. "It is cold out there" he told me, as he tucked it under his arm.

I almost suggested grabbing the comforter as well. From what I had gathered from Luca's half-formed plan, there was a very high probability that we would be spending one or more nights outside, sleeping beneath the real stars, with nothing to keep us warm but each other's body heat. While that idea was romantic as all get-out, I had to admit that the thought of sleeping, cold and exposed, on the sidewalk in the middle of another rough, violent city was not high on my list of "fun activities."

If we were lucky, I thought, maybe we would pass DeAndre on

our way out of town, and he would give us a tutorial on making nests out of newspapers.

"Okay, I think that is everything..." Luca looked around the apartment one last time. Unlike me, though, his eyes didn't linger over the incredible, one-of-a-kind artwork. Instead, they seemed to be quickly skimming over everything so that they could get back to me as soon as possible. "Ready?" he asked, once the scan was complete.

He didn't look nervous at all as he held out his big, rough, scarred hand to me. How could he not be sad to leave the apartment he had lived in for who knew how many years? How could he not want to find a way to roll up all those beautiful paintings and take them with us? How could it not affect him at all to think that he was leaving behind everyone and everything he had ever known to save a girl who had been no one to him up until two days ago?

I hesitated, caught between guilt and exhilaration at the thought of running away together like characters in a classic romance novel. Then I put my hand in his, summoned up all my courage, and said, "Ready."

Thirty-Five

The morning sun was warm as we stepped out onto the fire escape. I took comfort in the feeling of its soft rays on my hair, in spite of the gnawing feeling in the pit of my stomach. Something would go wrong, I could feel it. But for now, I decided to ignore that dark feeling and keep in the sunlight.

"It's a beautiful day for running away, huh?" I said to Luca as we began our long, slow, limping descent.

"We could not have asked for better," he replied, nodding in satisfaction. He paused on the eighth floor landing and drew in a lungful of the chilly autumn air. "And no rain until tonight, at least."

"You can *smell* rain coming?" It was one thing to smell the dampness in the air or the cool wetness on the concrete when it was coming down, but to catch the scent of rain that wouldn't reach us for twelve hours? That bordered on sorcery in my book.

"I told you, I am a tracker." Luca smiled at the look of disbelief on my face.

"No, you told me you were a 'scout.' I was under the impression that you searched for people and places, not that you predicted weather patterns with your nose!"

He laughed. We were on the sixth floor now, not bothering to be quiet as we passed the doors of people who were just waking up and preparing to leave for work. I could feel the pleasant buzz of busyness in the air again, and that, too, was comforting. The world hadn't seemed to notice yet that we were breaking with its plans and taking our fate into our own hands. It would surely only be a matter of time before it caught on, but for now, I was content to spend the morning in the sunshine, and in good company.

"I am not predicting the weather, I *know* it. I *know* it is going to rain tonight, around... seven thirty, at the earliest. We will have to be on a bus by then."

"What? How can you possibly know that?" I tried sniffing the air myself, and smelled nothing but the scent of rotting garbage wafting up to us from the dump a half mile away.

He tapped my nose affectionately and replied, "Practice. Years of practice."

"Can you teach me?"

"Sure, but not today. Today our schedule is already booked up."

"Oh, right." We stepped off the wrought iron staircase and onto the cracked grey sidewalk. I paused for a moment, pretending to look at the storefront next door as I gave Luca a chance to catch his breath. That leg of his would be a problem if we needed to move quickly, but for now, we had time to baby it a bit – even if he didn't know that was what we were doing. "Can you track anything else?" I asked, admiring a tarnished saxophone on display inside the pawn shop I had stopped in front of.

"Sure," he said, taking my hand and leading me on. "But it is not so much 'tracking' as it is 'being aware of my surroundings.' Like now, for instance. I can tell you that someone is watching us."

I jumped, startled, and scanned the street, but he laughed. "It is just that little girl over there, look." He pointed to a car sitting at the curb a few feet ahead of us. I could see through the windshield that there was, indeed, a little girl inside, watching us closely, as if she were trying to figure out what we were doing there. She couldn't have been more than three years old, with two big, bushy black pigtails sprouting from the top of her head.

"You scared me!" I told Luca, slapping at him with my free hand. "You know I'm already jumpy!"

He slipped his hand from mine and snaked his arm around my waist instead. Chuckling breathily into my hair, he kissed the top of my head again and said, "I'm sorry."

The butterflies in my stomach swirled as if they were caught in a tornado, and I felt my face flush. I guessed that meant he was forgiven. But I didn't tell *him* that. "And furthermore, you cheated! You saw her there, you didn't 'sense' anything!"

"Okay, okay," he said, pulling me closer. It was a bit hard to walk that way, especially as I had to be careful not to touch his wounded thigh with the bag dangling at my side, but I wasn't complaining. "Let's see what else I can tell you..."

I waved at the little girl as we passed her car. She raised her eyebrows in surprise, but didn't wave back. I tried not to be insulted by that.

"Okay, there will be a fruit stand around the next corner we come to."

"You live right there! You already know that!"

"True. But the fruit vendor has different fruit every day. Today, he has strawberries, mangoes, tangerines, apples, and... one lemon."

I grinned, not buying it. "Just the one lemon?"

He nodded, smugness personified. "But you don't want any of the apples. They are starting to rot."

I laughed out loud, sure that he was pulling my leg. As we turned the corner a minute later, though, the smile slid off my face as my mouth fell open in shock.

I stopped where I was on the sidewalk and gaped, unabashedly, at the fruit vendor's cart across the street from us. It was small, with just four boxes of fruit covering the tilted counter, but there was not one fruit there that Luca hadn't mentioned, including the overly soft apples. The only one missing was the lemon.

"Fruit for the lady?" called the Filipino man that stood beside the cart. He was bundled up against a much colder wind than we were experiencing, and his eyes peered out hopefully between the folded rim of his black toboggan hat and the upper layer of his black wool scarf. "We've got a big assortment this day! We've got for you some apples, some strawberries, some tangerines, and some beauty-filled mangoes all the way from my homeland in the Philippines!"

I looked up at Luca. He was smiling proudly, but he hadn't passed the test just yet.

"You don't... you wouldn't happen to have any lemons today, would you?" I called back, certain of the answer.

"Hmm... I am sorry, but no," the man shouted as a rusty grey sedan drove between us.

"Ha!" I said, victorious, but Luca's grin only widened. He shook his head slowly, and sure enough, the vendor spoke again.

"Ah! I forgot! I have here one lemon unsold from yesterday. Just one dollar. You buy?"

"We buy," Luca answered, as my mouth fell open again. He kissed me on the cheek, more smug than ever, and headed across the street for his prize.

"Witchcraft!" I said a few minutes later, as I rolled the lemon from hand to hand, enjoying the feel of the cool, bumpy skin of its peel against my palms as we strolled toward the center of town. "You're a witch! It's the only explanation!"

"Male witches are called wizards or warlocks," he corrected me, still grinning, "and that is really the only explanation?"

"Yes. Or, well, maybe that you're psychic."

"If I were psychic, don't you think I would have avoided this?"

He pointed at his bandaged ear, and then to his bandaged arm, then to his bandaged leg.

"Just because you're psychic doesn't necessarily mean you make good choices."

"Touché."

We had been walking for almost an hour. Now the streets were teeming with people either hurrying home from a night of drugging and debauchery, or hurrying to work, their eyes still puffy and red with sleep (or lack thereof). The busy buzz no longer felt pleasant, though, and I was beginning to feel uneasy.

We were not exactly inconspicuous among the throngs of rushing drug dealers, prostitutes, and nine-to-five blue collar workers, but Luca assured me that we were safe there between 1st Street and 12th.

It was the only section of Luthertown Heights that wasn't a territory of any of the seven gangs that ran the city, so in theory, no one would be bothered by its notorious White Girl strolling the sidewalks hand-in-hand with the Uewatsu's first lieutenant. More importantly, though, there would be no Uewatsu watchmen to report us to Bear, and no Sixes to narc on Lamont.

Safe or not, though, I could feel everyone's eyes on us as we passed a dilapidated strip mall containing one Dollar General store and two Cash Advance places. *You don't belong here*, the eyes told me, more so than they ever had before that day. But how could I tell them that I didn't belong anywhere?

Apparently my discomfort was contagious. The closer we got to the city center, the more light drained from Luca's face. As we neared 7th Street, where my apartment sat, empty and unoccupied now, he had completely turned to stone. His entire body was tense as his fiery eyes darted from corner to corner, face to face, building to building, searching for threats.

"Are you tracking something?" I asked quietly, with a nervous smile.

"We are being watched," he replied, in a raspy monotone.

My blood went cold. "Who?" I squeaked out, before my throat could seal itself up with panic.

I looked up at him, but instantly regretted it. With that hard, expressionless mask on his face and that stupid rope wrapped around his throat, he looked like the feral creature I had feared he could be the first time I saw him.

"I am not sure yet," he replied, and I swore I saw him sniff the air again, as if to catch the scent of the predator stalking us. "Just walk faster."

I didn't need telling twice.

Moving as quickly as I could without leaving him and his bum leg in my dust, I rushed down the sidewalk, away from my apartment building without even sparing it a glance. We passed three street signs, six apartment complexes, a motel, and another fruit vendor before we came to a crossroads.

"Right or left?" I panted, stopping at the intersection of 19th Street and 10th. The road to the east would lead us deeper into town, past the Y and eventually to the intercity bus station. To the west lay Miss Carmella's house and a lot more walking before we reached our destination.

Luca hesitated. Until now, he seemed to have had a solid route mapped out in his mind, but his Spidey Sense was apparently blocking out his other mental process for the time being.

"I... I am not sure," he said slowly. I wished he would at least frown – I had forgotten how much I hated the blank, closed-off expression he had once worn. It made him feel distant, as if all of a sudden we were miles and miles apart, even though we were standing right there next to each other.

"Right, maybe?" I suggested. We had been standing still for too long; I was getting antsy.

"That was my original..." Suddenly his eyes lit up and he grabbed me. I screamed as he whirled me around behind him, and he turned to face our stalkers as they finally revealed themselves.

"Well he doesn't *look* very dead, does he, brother?"

I fought hard to hold back a frightened whimper as Bear's malevolent voice rang out across the intersection. I clenched the back of Luca's jacket in my fists, wanting to squeeze my eyes shut, but knowing I shouldn't.

"Nope," replied another voice I didn't recognize. One of the other brother/warriors, I assumed.

"The Sixes were wrong to brag, then," Bear said coolly, strolling up the sidewalk from the same direction we had just come. He stopped a few feet from us, and bared his teeth at Luca in a wolfish grin. "And I guess we were wrong to kill their messenger."

The whimper escaped as I thought of Lamont. He clearly hadn't left town. But had he been the messenger? The image of his youthful, defiant face swam across my field of vision, and I fought back tears. *No,* I thought, *not him too...*

"Imagine my surprise when Dingo and I were going to your house to collect your body for a proper, Uewatsu burial and, lo and behold, my dead brother comes walking down the fire escape! And with my white bitch to boot!"

Luca had dropped the blanket he was carrying, and was reaching behind him, holding me protectively as he glared up at his half-brother.

"Did you finally give up your flower, little brother?" Bear mocked him, stepping closer to loom over us. "Did you tie her up like we taught you? Or is that still too scary for baby Slipknot?"

A low, rumbling growl was coursing through Luca's body now; I could feel it as I pressed myself against his back.

"Did you take his flower, little white bitch?" Bear leaned around Luca to leer at me. "Or are you saving yourself for me, like a good girl?"

I cursed myself for the shakiness in my legs, and the shiver of fear that started in my stomach and rose all the way up to my brain.

"Do not speak to her," Luca warned.

"Or what?" Bear laughed. It was a sick, repulsive sound. "Are you going to paint me to death?"

Luca snarled in response.

"It doesn't matter anyway, though," Bear continued, shifting his feet, completely at ease, "I told you already, she is mine."

"She does not belong to you," Luca growled. "She does not belong to anyone. Do not bring her into this."

Bear tilted his head, surveying Luca. There was a malicious smile on his tanned face, and a strange gleam in his dark eyes. His bare muscles bulged beneath the trademark Uewatsu vest, and I felt nauseous as I realized that that was what they wore when they were on the hunt.

"Do you really think that you can stop me, Slipknot?" he asked, looking sincerely interested in the answer.

Luca stared back at him in silence, his green eyes surely burning holes into his brother's face.

Then I remembered something.

Slowly, I released Luca's jacket and let my hands fall to my waist. A week ago, I hadn't had a chance to use my pepper spray to stop Bear and his pack from mauling me. But I had been carrying it in my pants pocket every day since, just in case.

"He asked you a question," prompted Dingo, a shorter, skinnier, dopier version of Bear with ears that rivaled Dumbo's.

"Stay out of this, Dingo," Bear snapped. "This is between me and Slipknot."

"There is nothing between us," said Luca. "We are leaving town. I am done with you."

I was surprised to see a flicker of hurt flit across Bear's face. "Oh, really? You are abandoning your own brothers *and* stealing my property?"

"She is not yours, Bear."

"We will see about that." As quick as a flash, Bear reached out, but this time, thank God, I was quicker.

We both knocked Luca aside as I pulled the uncapped tube of

mace from my pocket and squeezed the lever just as Bear's claws scraped across the front of my jacket.

He howled in pain, blinded by the spray of liquid fire, and Dingo leapt forward as he stumbled back. I was about to spray him too when Luca reappeared in front of me and cocked his arm back before punching Dingo in the face as hard as he could.

I could hear bones crack as Dingo went limp and fell to the ground, and I jumped as Luca grabbed my face with his hands, forcing me to look at him instead of his brother's concave skull on the ground at our feet.

"Are you okay?" he asked, his burning eyes searching my soul.

"I...yuh...yes!" I said, once I found my voice.

"Then let's go."

Bear had fallen to his knees by the time Luca bent over to pick up our blanket, and tears streamed down his rust-red face as he spat at us, "You will pay for this! Both of you! You have betrayed me for the last time, *brother!*"

"You are no brother to me," Luca said coldly as he stared down at him with contempt.

Then he took my hand, and we ran west.

"Oh, *hell* no, white girl! You ain't bringin' no dirty indjun inta *my* house!"

"Come on, Miss Carmella! He's hurt!" I grunted, supporting Luca over the doorstep and into Miss Carmella's narrow entry hall. Neither Bear nor Dingo had touched him, but our desperate fleeing from them had split open the stitches I had sewn into Luca's leg, and he was bleeding profusely. Miss Carmella's was the closest safe house I could think of, and she was the closest thing we had to a "friend" at the moment.

Maybe.

"What the hell do I care if he's hurt? I don't want no filthy animals stankin' up my house!"

"Miss Carmella, you know him!" I shouted over her, walking Luca into the dusty yellow kitchen before hurrying back to lock the door behind us.

"I sure as hell do *not* know any damned indjun! And I resent that implication!"

I pulled a face at her.

To be honest, Miss Carmella's was not my top choice of refuges. I felt guilty for not coming to clean her house the Saturday before (I hadn't even called to tell her why), and there had always been something about seeing her sitting there, day after day, taking up the whole three-person couch, that never failed to suck away my carefully constructed stores of hope.

But I had known that there was a spare key hidden under a rock just outside the front door, and I had hoped that her past connection with Luca would be enough to make her forget her prejudices.

"Tell her," I said to Luca, as I sat him down in a chair at the blonde oak kitchen table and rushed to the counter to snatch up a handful of paper towels.

Luca, at first, said nothing. He just watched me, looking pale and sweaty, with his green eyes glazing over. The running and the adrenaline and the blood loss had taken a great toll on him, and I needed to get him back into fighting shape if we wanted to have any chance of getting out of town in one piece.

"Luca?"

"At the cemetery," he said obediently, in that raspy monotone. "Fifteen years ago."

"Fifteen years ago! Boy, you think I'm gon' remember somethin' that happened fifteen fuckin' *years* ago?"

I stopped trying to roll up Luca's pant leg to gawp at her. "Miss –"

"Don't," Luca said gently, cutting me off. "It does not matter."

"No, it *does* matter!" I pushed a clump of sweaty hair out of my face with my arm and stood up, suddenly (perhaps overly) furious. "That was an important day, Miss Carmella. It meant a lot to Luca!"

"Don't you tell me..." She paused, and I watched her eyes widen amidst the flaps and folds of fatty tissue in her face. "Wait, did you call him Luca?"

"That's his name, yeah." I crossed my arms, still huffy, and Luca lightly stroked my side with his fingers, as if to calm the storm raging inside me.

"You're the boy whose momma died," she said slowly, recognition finally reaching her as she looked over at him. "She died the same day as my third husband, Harold."

"That is right, ma'am," Luca replied. "You, uh, you hugged me."

"And you cried..." she whispered, looking suddenly very close to tears herself. "'Poor little boy,' I thought, 'all alone out here with no momma to take care of him.'"

"Yes, ma'am."

"Then yo daddy came."

Luca was quiet for a moment. His eyes were troubled now, and mine went straight to the scar on his face, the one his father had given him as punishment for having feelings. "Yes, ma'am."

Miss Carmella was quiet for a moment too. Then, shaking her head as if to shake away what she must have seen, she said, "Well, you grew up just like him at any rate. You look like him too."

I was pretty sure I saw Luca cringe at that observation.

"But who am I to talk about looks? I'm three times the size I was back then. I bet you don't even recognize me."

"I would recognize you anywhere." The sincerity in Luca's voice made me reach out and caress his cheek. He gave me a sad smile.

"Whatever. Just... just do what you gotta do and leave, White Girl, I got shit to do."

"Yes, Miss Carmella," I answered, feeling a bit like crying myself now as I knelt back down to tend to Luca's wound.

I worked quickly and quietly, sopping up the blood with the paper towels before resealing the holes on either side of his thigh with the sewing kit we had brought with us. This time, I sewed the stitches smaller, tighter, and closer together, praying that they would hold if we had to run again.

Luca sat in silence the entire time, just watching me with that strange look on his face that I still couldn't decipher. I was relieved, though, to see that his eyes were no longer glazed, but shining, as he studied my face and hands.

"There," I said, pressing down on the sticky edges of an oversized bandage to seal it in place before tugging his pant leg back down over it. "All better. Did I hurt you?

He took my hands and pulled me to my feet, holding me between his legs as he tilted his head up and kissed me, right there in Miss Carmella's kitchen.

"No," he murmured, running his thumbs along my jawline as he cradled my face in his hands, "you did not hurt me."

Relieved and craving closeness, I wrapped my arms around his neck and leaned into him, resting my head on top of his soft, curly hair.

"What the hell are y'all two doin' in there, White Girl? Get away from him! Ain't you heard nothin' about him and his 'brothers'? They on the news every night!"

"You can't believe everything you see on t.v.," I sighed, not moving an inch. "And besides, he's not like the other Uewatsu. Luca's a good man."

Luca's arms tightened around my hips, holding me closer.

It was as that moment that I first began to wonder what would happen if Bear caught us a second time. He surely wouldn't waste any time shooting the breeze then – he would get right down to business, and we would all end up on Miss Carmella's news program that night.

"Uewatsu ain't 'men,'" spat Miss Carmella with disdain. "They animals. All of 'em. Even that boy there. I thought maybe he'd grow up to be better than them others, but he ain't. Are you?"

"Listen here, Miss – "

Luca stopped me, mid-rant, with a smile and a small shake of his head. I frowned, bursting with indignation, ready to really let Miss Carmella have it, but he wouldn't let me.

"Well, we had better be going now," he said, getting slowly, painfully to his feet. As he pulled himself up to his full, six foot two inch height, I felt small as I looked up into his face, worried.

Then he bent over and kissed me on the top of the head, and all my bad feelings faded.

"We should get you something to eat first," I told him, hurrying to dig a banana out of one of the bags we had tossed down on the floor when we came in. "You lost a lot of blood."

"We are imposing, Annabelle, no." He was smiling gently at me, and I almost cursed his placid politeness. I realized then that he was literally everything Miss Carmella accused him of *not* being – kind, refined, cultured, well-mannered, *human* – and I decided to follow his lead.

"You're right," I replied, finding it oddly difficult not to speak in a British accent as I drew myself up into a prim, perfect posture. "Miss Carmella, thank you for the use of your kitchen. Sorry to have disturbed you."

Miss Carmella griped something unintelligible, but she looked torn as she watched us sling our satchels across our chests and gather up our crumpled ball of blanket. We headed for the door, Luca trying his damndest not to limp and show weakness, but before we reached it, Miss Carmella let out a long-suffering sigh and said, "Well if you're already here, you might as well stay for lunch. I have a pizza delivered every day at noon, and you know damn well I ain't gettin' up to answer the door. And you stole my spare key, so..." she turned her glare to the television as she left her sentence open-ended, and I grinned up at Luca.

"You planned that!" I mouthed, delighted.

He gave me a wink as he tapped his nose, mouthing back, "I *sensed* it."

Thirty-Seven

The couch was the only piece of furniture in the living room, so Luca and I had to sit on the floor. The beige carpet was fluffy and soft, though, having been spared years of walking thanks to its sedentary owner, so it wasn't so bad. In fact, as Luca pulled me down to sit in his lap, wrapping his arms around me as I rested my head against his collarbone, I found it quite cozy.

"So, y'all are a 'thing,' huh?" Miss Carmella asked when a commercial break interrupted the cheesy soap opera she had been watching.

I opened my mouth, then closed it. I wasn't sure how to answer that. We were something, that was certain, but it had only been a couple days – we hadn't had time to define our shared interests yet, let alone our relationship.

"We are working on it," Luca answered for me. His voice rumbled through me as I leaned against his chest, and I felt tingly all over.

"Mmm, mmm, mmm..." replied Miss Carmella, shaking her round, wrapped head. She was wearing a flowery scarf over her head today, but bits and pieces of her natural hair were sticking out at odd angles, making it look like she was unraveling from the top down. "Girl, you dumber than I thought. Them injuns are trouble. Men in *general* are trouble."

"Some men, yes," I said, as my mind immediately went to Bear and his minions. "This man, no."

I could feel the smile on Luca's lips as he kissed my temple.

"That's what we all say..." Miss Carmella shot Luca a glance. "What happened after the cemetery that day, anyway? Child Services take you?"

"No. I went to live with my grandmother." Luca's words were heavy with sorrow, and I felt another twinge of guilt.

"At least you didn't go live with yo daddy... I saw what he did that day." She nodded at Luca's scar, and I sat up straight.

"Wait, you saw him cut Luca? Why didn't you do anything?"

"Annabelle, it is alright," said Luca soothingly, but I was not ready to be soothed, not by a long shot.

"So, what? You just watched that bastard slice a piece of his son's face off and you didn't do anything? You didn't call the police?"

"What the hell am I s'posed to do about it, White Girl? I ain't no doctor!"

"Yeah, and you ain't no decent human being, either!" I shouted, tossing Luca's arms aside and getting to my feet. I was incensed. Suddenly this was about a lot more than Luca and Miss Carmella, it was about a lot more than all three of us put together. "What did you do, then? Just watch? Just stand there while he took out the knife and cut Luca? Did you even think to scream or say 'Stop that! You're hurting him?'"

"Listen here, girl," Miss Carmella snapped, pulling herself and her massive stomach into a more upright and indignant position. "I wasn't about to get ganked by some indjun over – "

"Over another human being's life?" I was yelling now, getting louder and louder all the time, but I couldn't control myself. I couldn't quit picturing poor Luca, with his young, sweet, innocent face covered in tears, begging his father for permission to grieve, and getting his cheek slashed open in response. I couldn't stop picturing Marcus, lying bloody and glassy eyed and dead in my arms because no one had cared enough to teach a seven-year-old not to touch daddy's guns. And worst of all, I couldn't stop seeing all those lights on on my street, all those faces I knew were peering out from behind curtains, watching me get beaten and sexually assaulted in the street without even touching the dial pad on their phones.

"Annabelle." Luca was standing now, reaching for my hand, but I snatched it way.

"No!" I shouted. "No! I have to say this! Miss Carmella, you are exactly what is wrong with this whole freaking town. All of these terrible, painful, violent things happen on the streets every day, but does anyone do anything to stop it? No! They just stand there, watching, while little boys get stabbed and shot and bleed to death! They just hide inside their houses, letting the gangs run the streets because it would be too much of an effort to call the police! They just stare out of their windows, looking on while women get gang-raped on their way home from work, because it would be too damn much trouble to try to help her!" I was sobbing now, and both Luca and Miss Carmella looked stricken, but I didn't care. "Nobody in this whole fucking town wants to get involved in anything, even if it means saving someone's life. *That's* why Luthertown Heights is a cesspool of filth and slime – because nobody has the guts to care! And the people that *do* care are the ones who end up shot or stabbed or raped or dead. And it's all your fault, Miss Carmella. You and everyone else in this godforsaken place. I can't *wait* to get out of here. I hope you and everyone else rot in hell!"

I was out of breath by the time I finished, and Miss Carmella seemed to be too. Her mouth hung open, her bulbous lips gaping like a fish, and her brown eyes were wide with pure shock.

Then a single tear leaked out the side of one of those wide, brown eyes, and guilt hit me like a kick to the stomach. I wanted to take it back, all of it, but I was so confused, so angry, so conflicted, that I couldn't. So, without even a glance in Luca's direction, I ran off down the short hall to the bathroom, and locked myself inside.

What is wrong with me? I thought, as I sank down onto the fluffy pink lid of the toilet and buried my face in my hands. I was just as cruel as everyone else – maybe more so, because I had intentionally hurt Miss Carmella, I hadn't just been a passive observer.

But that was wrong too, right? It was wrong to save your own ass when someone else was in danger; it was wrong to turn a blind eye to another's plight just to keep yourself safe. If one or two people did that, maybe it wouldn't be a big deal, but an entire town of bystanders? That was a travesty.

I felt nauseous as the hate swelled up inside me again. I had never hated anyone in my life – not even Bear, not really, not yet, but I hated the people who had let me and countless others get hurt while they stood idly by. How could anything change for the better if no one ever *tried?* If no one ever *cared?*

"Annabelle, let me in."

"No." I sniffled, grabbing a tissue from the box on the sink and blowing my nose loudly. "I'm sorry, Luca. Tell Miss Carmella I'm sorry. I just... all those people... I just can't stand it."

"Open the door, girl, and tell me to my face."

I felt my mouth fall open in shock as Miss Carmella's voice replaced Luca's at the door. She hadn't stood up from her sofa in almost a decade, and now, suddenly, she was outside the door, waiting for me.

Leaping up, I threw open the white wood door and came face to face with a majestic creature the likes of which I had never expected to see. At her full (if not slumped) height, Miss Carmella was almost six feet tall, and though her limbs hung heavy about her, making the bare brown skin outside of her flowered smock look like a mass of lumpy boulders, she carried herself with strength and with a quiet, defiant sort of dignity.

"I... I..."

"Listen here, girl," she panted, as I watched a bead of sweat roll off her shining brow. "If you think I ain't never done nothin' worthwhile in my life, you a lot stupider than I gave you credit for. When I was nineteen I marched with Martin Luther King in Selma for equal rights for black people. When I was twenty-six, I had a baby who was born with Leukemia, and I fought every damn second of my life to save 'im, but I couldn't. When I was thirty-seven, I saved my second husband from a mugger by hittin' the creep with my purse. I took a bullet in my arm. And when I was fifty-eight I met that boy there." She pointed at Luca, who was standing behind her, looking solemn. "And I told him that if he ever needed anything, he could come to me, and I'd take care of 'im. He never came. But if you think I didn't scream when his daddy stabbed him in the face, or you think I didn't cry myself to sleep about it that night, or if you think I just don't give a damn about anythin' because I'm fat and slow and lazy and old and racist, then honey, *you're* the thing that's wrong here, not me."

As Miss Carmella came to a wheezy stop, I felt the tears well up in my eyes again. This time, though, they weren't tears of misery or of hopelessness, they were the tears of one who has just witnessed a miracle.

Too moved to speak, I flung myself at Miss Carmella and hugged her fiercely as yet another new light began to shine in the darkness of Luthertown Heights.

"Stupid white girls..." she sighed, but she patted me on the back anyway. I could feel her trembling from the effort of standing, and I clung to her even more tightly.

Over her shoulder, I saw Luca's eyes shining, and he grinned as he said, "Now you see why I put her on my wall."

"I was never angry at her, you know," Luca said, as we sat in the kitchen again a few minutes later, repacking our bags. Miss Carmella, with her trademark sass and "I don't give a damn" attitude, had told us to take all of the non-perishables in her cabinets with us when we left. "I don't eat any of that shit anyway," she had grumbled when we protested. Then she had gone to sit back down on the couch, crushing the spring-less springs beneath her as she let out another long-suffering sigh.

"I know," I told Luca, trying to stuff a can of pork 'n' beans inside one of his rolled-up sweatshirts. "You're never angry at anyone."

He raised an eyebrow.

"Anyway, I don't think I was really angry at her either," I said quickly, not ready to delve into that topic just yet. "At least, not *that* angry. It just sort of... got away from me there, for a minute."

"You fed the wrong wolf," he said wisely, referencing the quote I now knew he had gifted to me.

"Maybe." I shrugged. I sighed and plunked the can down on the table, giving up. "Sometimes I don't know which wolf is the good wolf, and which is the bad wolf anymore."

Luca didn't reply.

I had made my peace with Miss Carmella, but something was stirring inside me; some seed was taking root beneath the sorrow and the pain that I had been burying the past few days. I could feel it growing in jumps and jerks and convoluted lurches, but I didn't know what it was. Not yet. But whatever it was, it was restless.

"I think I yelled at her for the same reason I yelled at you that day when Bear... well, you know."

Luca's fiery eyes darted to mine.

"I was so... *mad,*" I said, shaking my head as I stared down at the fists I hadn't realized I was clenching. "There were people everywhere, in every apartment on that street. They had their lights on, I could see them. But no one did anything to stop Bear."

There was a strange intensity in Luca's gaze. I wasn't sure if he wanted me to stop talking, or if he wanted to reach out to grab me and hold me close.

"I screamed, Luca. I screamed really loud, but no one listened. No one *did* anything! I thought I was going to die." I looked down at my hands again, and forced them open. "And later that night, I thought, 'what if I did die?' Would they have felt guilty? Or is everyone in this town so numb to violence and killing and hate now that it wouldn't affect them at all?"

I sighed again as I thought about how hard I had worked to try to teach my ASC students to be strong and brave and compassionate. At the time, it had seemed so important, but now I was beginning to wonder if it had all just been a waste of energy. Perhaps nature always won out over nurture. That was another law of the jungle, wasn't it?

"I hope the next town we go to is –"

"I listened."

I lifted my eyes to Luca's. They were full of passion now, full of pain and suffering and a dozen other emotions I couldn't even begin to decode. "What?"

"I heard your screams," he said, not moving, not blinking, his entire body tense and taut. "I heard your screams and I listened. I ran halfway across town as fast as I could, praying to God I would get to you in time. When I got there and saw Bear on top of you, when I saw our brothers circling around you like hungry vultures, and your shirt ripped open, I wanted to scream myself. I wanted to scream and cry and lash out with all of my might and kill my brothers, all of them. I wanted to murder them with my bare hands, all because I had heard your screams, and I had listened.

"I heard you even before then, though, before you ever said a word. I heard you when you walked that little boy home from school. I heard you when you tried to convince DeAndre to go to the homeless shelter. I heard you when you walked home by yourself at night, wishing you had company, feeling like you were alone in this city. I listened because I was screaming too. I have been screaming since I was fourteen years old. But the only one who ever quieted those screams was you."

My lip trembled as he took a step closer and put his hand on my cheek, gently caressing my skin with his rough, calloused hand. "Maybe the people in those apartments heard you," he continued, his voice hoarse and crackling. "They probably did. But that does not matter. It does not matter how many people listened or thought or reacted. What matters is that one person did. And I have thanked God every minute since then that that one person was me."

"Luca, I —"

"So do not focus on the people who did not listen. Think about the person who did. Think about me. Because Annabelle, I will *always* listen. I will *always* act. I will *always* care about you. Fuck everyone else. You have me, and I will not stop until I become everything you need me to be, until I become the good man you say that I am. And I will never, ever stop listening."

For a long moment, my voice wouldn't work. I wanted to tell him that he didn't have to "become" anything, that he already was the man I wanted, and everything I could ever need. He was the brightness in the shadows of my mind, he was the one thing that had kept me believing in people even after all of the terrible things I had heard and seen and felt. He was right, I didn't need the whole city to care, I just needed him. He was enough, more than enough, and maybe, possibly, I was too.

But I couldn't say that. I couldn't form the words. I had a million thoughts to express, a million feelings to share, but I couldn't verbalize a single one.

He was staring at me, waiting for me to reply, with a look of such strangled passion on his face that I wanted to cry, to take him into my arms and hold him there forever.

Instead, though, I spoke the one phrase that my swirling, over-whelmed mind could come up with. The phrase that said every-thing while simultaneously not even coming close to expressing the full depths of my feelings.

"I love you," I whispered into the loaded silence between us.

Then he hurled me to the floor in a shower of glass as a hail of bullets came streaming in through the front door.

I really need to stop making declarations... I thought stupidly, as Luca crushed me to his chest, holding my head like a quarterback guarding a football as he shielded me from the debris. He had immediately flipped the kitchen table onto its side to give us a bit of cover, but I could hear the bullets slamming into it, getting closer and closer to us with each crackle of splintering wood.

"Fuckin' indjuns!" I heard Miss Carmella shout from the next room, and my spirits sank even lower.

Bear had found us. And he had brought an army.

That was it, it was over. We would never make it out of there alive, and if we did, he would never stop hounding us.

"What do we do?" I screamed at Luca, covering my ears. The house sounded like it was exploding. Bullets were colliding with every surface: the table, the refrigerator, the walls, the chairs; and there were so many of them! So many bullets coming from so many directions, it was impossible to escape them. The Uewatsu had to be using at least semi-automatic weapons to shoot that much that fast, and we had nothing to defend ourselves with.

Or so I thought.

"Stay down," Luca ordered, taking one hand off of me and sliding it into the satchel at his side. Squinting through the cloud of plaster dust and powder, I saw him pull out a shiny, silver and black Colt .45.

"What the hell?" I shouted over the din. "Where did you get that?"

"My father," he said grimly. Then he gently moved me aside and got to his knees.

"Wait, no, you can't!" I said, grabbing his sleeve before he could peek over the top of our bullet-riddled shield of splinters.

"I can," he replied, clicking the safety off. His face was a mask again: a terrible, blank, emotionless mask, and I knew that if he pulled that trigger, the Luca I knew would disappear beneath it forever.

"Luca, no! This isn't you! This isn't –"

Suddenly there was a bang so loud that I swore I could feel all my internal organs jump out of place. Gripping Luca's arm tightly, I chanced a glance around the table to see Miss Carmella on her feet again.

She was an impressive sight: a flower-smocked god standing atop a mountain, staring out over the kingdom she ruled as her thin, wispy silver hair blew wild and loose in the breeze blown by the incoming projectiles. She had been five foot eleven before, but she was ten feet tall now, ten feet of pure strength and solidity and fortitude, and her eyes glowed with righteous fury as she glared out the hole she had made in her front window with the twelve-gauge shotgun she was clutching in her plump, black hands.

The incoming bullets had stopped, and I could just picture the Uewatsu scrambling to figure out who was shooting at them, and with what cannon.

"Miss Carmella," I whispered, with something close to horror, but bordering on awe.

"Out the back," she muttered through clenched teeth, quietly, so our assailants wouldn't hear.

Luca leapt up and grabbed my hand. I got to my feet too, but I couldn't make them move.

"Come with us," I said to Miss Carmella.

She laughed. "Child, you know I ain't left this house in twelve years. I can't go wit'chu."

"But you can't –"

"Annabelle, we have to go." Luca was tugging on my arm now, trying to drag me down the hall toward the back door.

"We can't just leave her here!"

"Go on, White Girl." For the first time since I had met her, Miss Carmella was smiling. I felt my throat tighten as I saw how happy it made her look, how much younger, how much more vibrant and alive. "And thanks for cleanin' for me."

Luca jerked my arm harder, but I wouldn't budge. I could hear footsteps outside, and rustling. The Uewatsu were getting back into position.

"Take care 'a her, boy," Miss Carmella said, still smiling.

Then at least fifteen bullets pounded into her great, voluminous bosom.

"NOOOO!" I shrieked, trying to run to her, but Luca yanked me into the hallway. My legs were numb and I tripped over my own feet as we stumbled past the bathroom, past the office, past the bedroom Miss Carmella hadn't slept in in years, and would never see again, until finally we reached the back door.

Luca hurled it open and I followed him through it, sobbing so hard that I couldn't see as he dragged me out into the small, square, scraggly backyard. The long grass grabbed at my ankles as Luca limped toward the alley. He tripped over a Styrofoam take-out box and wrenched his bad leg, but he said nothing, focusing all of his energy on getting us as far away from that house as possible.

I was sure that there would be Uewatsu footmen waiting for us in the alley. I was sure that the last thing I ever saw would be the gaping hole in Miss Carmella's chest and that blank, lifeless mask on Luca's face, but I was wrong. There were no wolves lying in wait for us, no warriors hidden amongst the dumpsters and the piles of trash. There was only Luca and me and the sound of my wretched sobs as we raced toward the heart of the city.

Forty

It felt like we had been running for hours when we finally limped into the public library on 34th Street. My legs burned and my heart ached with much more than just physical strain as Luca led me into the handicap stall in the unisex restroom, and we sank down onto the grimy floor in one collective heap.

"We should be safe here, for a while," Luca panted, wiping the sweat from his face.

I laid my head on his chest without replying. The librarian on duty hadn't seemed perturbed by our disheveled-ness or our darting, panicked eyes. She had barely looked up from her desk when we crashed into the lobby and asked for the bathroom key (which she had also had no problem handing over). I was about eighty percent sure that she was calling the police at that very moment, but I was too exhausted and heartsick to care.

"Are you alright?"

No, I am not alright!, screamed the voice in my head. Everyone I knew was being killed off, one by one; dying brutal, ugly deaths because of me.

I shrugged my shoulders against him.

To my surprise, he didn't push me. He just wrapped his arms

around me as I remained in a leaning fetal position, and he sighed as he put his lips against my temple and left them there.

I don't know how long we stayed like that: two interlocking pieces of flotsam adrift in a sea of wordless grief. After a while, though, Luca's lips grazed my skin, and his low voice rumbled through me.

"I'm sorry," he said, ripping apart my already shredded guts with his heart-rending sincerity. "I am so sorry, Annabelle."

"It's not your fault," I whispered, inhaling the warm, sweaty scent of him from his collar as I squeezed my eyes shut. "It's my fault. All of it. None of this would have happened if it weren't for me."

"That is not true. Hey," he insisted, when I tried to shake my head in dissent. "This has been going on since long before you got here. It has been going on since before we were even born. We are just caught in the middle of it now."

I sniffled, considering his words. There *was* a ring of truth to them. But that didn't ease my guilty conscience.

"I was wrong about Miss Carmella," I said softly, as a tear slipped down my already damp face. "She *did* care. She was a hero. You knew that all along."

"I knew that that was what *I* saw in her," he replied, his lips still pressed against me. "But I never knew if that was the truth, or if I was just idolizing her because of how she had treated me at the cemetery that day. I had built her up in my head to be larger than life."

"And in the end, she really was." I sat up as another tear dripped down my cheek. Luca caught it on his finger and wiped away its track. "Luca, what are we going to do? We can't run forever, and we'll never make it out of town at this rate!"

He nodded, solemn. "And even if we do, we will be leaving behind too many casualties." He caught another one of my tears. "I don't know, Annabelle. I really don't."

I closed my eyes as what was left of my spirit broke. Well, that was it, then. If even Luca had given up, we really were doomed.

"Hey," he said softly, touching my cheek. "Look at me."

I opened my eyes to find his face just inches from mine.

"Listen, I might not know how we are going to do it yet, but I know that we will. I will not let you down. And I will not let anything else happen to you. I will not let anyone else hurt you. You have my word."

I gave him a sad smile. His words meant the world to me, and I wanted to believe them with all of my battered heart, but I knew for sure now that Fate was going to keep on taking what it wanted from me, what it wanted from us, what it wanted from Luthertown Heights, no matter how many promises Luca made.

I glanced down, unable to look into those beautiful, fierce, hopeful green eyes any longer, and I felt Luca's body stiffen.

"Annabelle, I am going to kill Bear."

My eyes darted right back to his face, and my stomach felt like it dropped out of my body completely. "What?"

"I am going to kill Bear," he said again, in a strange, stilted monotone, as if he were forcing himself to stay calm and not jump up and do it right then and there. "It is the only way to stop this."

"He's your brother!"

"He is a plague," Luca spat, finding it harder and harder to control himself. "*He* is what is wrong with this town. He is what is wrong with my life, with *your* life, with everything. He has broken your spirit, I can see it in your eyes. And he deserves to die for that alone."

"Luca, no, that's crazy!" I said, putting my hands on his shoulders as I knelt in front of him, just like I had in a much nicer bathroom the day before, under the sea and far away. "That's not who you are!"

"And *this* is not who you are!" he shot back, cupping my face in his calloused hands. "Do you know why I started keeping track of you? Why I started looking out for you?"

I shook my head no, remembering how many times I had asked him exactly that, and had received no answer.

"It was because I saw a light in your eyes," he said, his beleaguered voice on the verge of breaking. "I saw it the first day you went to work at the YMCA. You were so full of life and energy and hope – things that no one else in Luthertown Heights has even a trace of anymore. I expected it to go away after your first day of working with those kids and their horrible parents and terrible home lives, but it didn't even dim. Not after the first day, not after the first week, not after the first month – if anything, it only burned brighter!

"And I saw how kind you were to DeAndre and all the other people you passed on the streets, and how nice you were to that idiot kid Lamont who disrespected you every chance he got, and I saw how you walked that little boy home every night and made sure he was safe. You saw the good in everyone you met, no matter how good or bad they really were, and I saw the light in you. But now it is gone. Bear took it. And I will kill him for it."

For a moment, I was speechless. Was that how he had really felt about me all this time? When no one else in town seemed to care what I did or how I felt or even what my name was, Luca had seen something in me, something that had inspired him to reach out to me, to try to warm himself by the flame he thought he saw in me. All this time I had been admiring the fire in his deep emerald eyes, but now he was telling me that I had had my own fire all along, my own burning pyre of inner strength and passion, He was telling me that my own hope had inspired hope in him, and that was enough to reignite its smoldering embers and bring me back to life.

"Look again," I told him, trying to look past the pain in his eyes and into the soul beyond it.

He did as I said, piercing my soul with his own. I saw the briefest of smiles brighten his countenance before suddenly he pulled me in and pressed his lips to mine, kissing me fiercely, passionately, desperately, crushing me to him as if he wanted to absorb me into himself, to meld his skin to my skin, to solder my bones to his bones.

I kissed him back, just a deeply, just as feverishly, loving him with all my heart. He had saved me. He had taken those broken pieces of shell Bear had shattered and pieced them back together, sealing the cracks and making them vanish as if they were never even there. He was the reason to keep going, to keep fighting, to keep believing, and I knew then that I would never let my inner light go out again, not so long as I had him to fan the flames.

I pulled back, breathless, a few minutes later. Luca's eyes were still closed, and his face was flushed as he savored the moment, and I brushed a curl back from his forehead, wishing we had time to linger there. "Luca, we can't leave town."

"What?" His voice was hoarse with desire as his vivid eyes fluttered open.

"We can't leave town. We have to stay here. We have to fix what's broken somehow. That's the whole reason I came here in the first place: to make a difference, to change something for those kids at the ASC. I can't just leave them now."

"But... but that's not what..."

"If I just run away, those kids will find out, and they'll think that their only options are to either join a gang or spend their lives living in fear until they can find some way to escape their own hometown. I can't let them live like that, Luca, it's not right!"

"Okay, but –"

"I lost track of things for a while," I continued, almost to myself, as I stood up to pace. "After Marcus died, I couldn't think straight. It didn't even cross my mind to go back to check on those kids. But it should have! Then there was you and your apartment and all those beautiful things you said and you painted, and then there was your Elisi and Miss Carmella and..." I shook my head to stop my blabbering. "Anyway, I lost sight of my purpose. My purpose is to make this city better for those kids – or at least easier to survive. And I can't do that if I'm not here. Do you understand?"

Luca looked conflicted. "Yes..." he said slowly, carefully, "but I don't see how the two of us can change an entire city. Especially not with the Uewatsu and maybe the Sixes on our trail. What is your plan?"

I grinned, victorious. That thing that had been growing in my stomach had broken free of the pain and the grief that buried it, and it was now blossoming into a full-blown idea. "Tell me everything you know about every gang in Luthertown Heights."

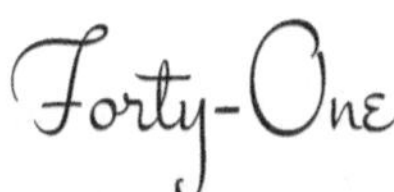

Forty-One

"I will start with the Uewatsu, because I have firsthand knowledge when it comes to them."

We had moved our meeting out of the bathroom and into the main library area, so that we could keep an eye out for threats (and so that we could give the bathroom key back to the librarian, in case anyone else needed to use it). We were now sitting at a table in the back corner, hidden behind several rows of thick metal bookshelves, all of which were weighted down with dusty, untouched volumes of Dickens, Tolstoy, and *World Book* encyclopedias.

I liked it much better out there. The scent of musty books and stale ink was comforting, and brought to mind all the time I had spent browsing books in my local library as a child. I wished we could stay there forever, or at least long enough for me to read a quick snippet of *Oliver Twist*, but there was no time. We were on a mission.

"Okay." I smoothed out a sheet of printer paper we had swiped from a basket on the copy machine near the restroom. "What is the Uewatsu's driving force? What do they want?"

Luca's huff of quiet laughter blew my hair as he handed me a pencil from his bag. We had plenty of space, but we were sitting side by side, with our folding chairs pushed close together so that our arms were always touching. We had tried sitting across from each other, but it just hadn't felt right.

"It sounds like you are writing a novel," Luca said. He seemed almost chipper now that the initial shock had worn off from my bizarre change of plans.

"The novel will come later," I teased. "Now, I need to understand what each gang wants, so we can come up with some sort of compromise to offer them."

His slight smile slipped from his face. He went pale as he gaped at me in disbelief. "*That* is your plan? Annabelle, that is suicide!"

"Well, no one can live forever, right?"

He was not amused.

"Okay, okay, it's just a broad goal," I said quickly, "calm down."

He pressed his lips together, the complete opposite of calm.

"Ugh, Luca, it's the only way!" I cried, before lowering my voice back to a whisper. "It's stupid, yeah, but you and I both know that the problem in this town is the gangs, and that's not going to go away. So we need to find a way to... to... placate them somehow. To keep them from fighting. So tell me what you know."

Luca let out a low growl, but I just sat there waiting patiently for him to begin. Finally, after what felt like five full minutes, he relented.

"Fine," he grumbled. "But let the record show that I hate this plan."

"The record will reflect that," I replied, giving him a kiss on the nose. His pallor went away as he blushed, and he let out a big, world-weary sigh as he began.

"I have already told you what the Uewatsu want: power. Bear wants to claim all of Luthertown Heights as his territory, because that is what our father wanted."

"So the Uewatsu have strong ties to family." I nodded, taking notes. "And they hate the Sixes the most, right? Why?"

"Because the Sixes are our biggest rivals. They are the only gang in town that has the numbers and the cunning to be a real threat to us. A few months ago, they pushed us out of our territory on 19th Street – an unforgivable offense in the eyes of an Uewatsu. Plus, the Sixes murdered our father."

I stopped writing and looked up at him. "Why?"

"Because he was a sick bastard." Luca shrugged. "He finally pushed the Sixes over the edge. He had killed several dozen of their men over a span of fifteen years, but that night, he did something even worse."

"What could be worse than that?" I whispered, afraid of the answer.

"He raped and killed the daughter of the gang leader, Shorty Biggs. Lucille was her name. She was thirteen years old. He told Bear afterward that he had been planning to bring her to the woods for my initiation, but his lust had gotten the better of him. A few hours later, he was dead. They cut off his head – the big one *and* the small one."

Luca's voice was empty as he spoke. He was completely dispassionate about the gruesome death of his biological father, his own blood, and it chilled mine.

"Jesus..."

Luca gave me a grim smile. "I don't think He had anything to do with it."

I sat in silence for a moment, biting my lip. Maybe this *was* a bad idea. With my wholesome, naive innocence, I had no way of fathoming the depths of these gangs' thirst for violence. And if I couldn't understand it, how could I stop it?

"The Sixes are like us," Luca went on, his face a mask now. "Like the Uewatsu, I mean. They are all family. That is why so many of them have six fingers on their right hand – it is genetic.

They pass the mantle of command from father to son, brother to cousin, always keeping it inside the family circle."

"But Lamont doesn't have six fingers on either hand, and they've been trying to initiate him for weeks."

"In some of them, the gene is recessive." He shrugged again. "Bear says that they are like apes that got caught somewhere along the evolutionary chain. Instead of evolving past their flawed mutations, they celebrate them. He says that they even mate with their own sisters to keep that particular trait alive."

I wrinkled my nose. I wasn't sure which was more disgusting: Bear's boorish insinuations, or the possibility that he could be right.

"And what do the Sixes want?" I prompted, deciding to just leave that topic where it lay.

"To kill the Uewatsu, mostly. And to maintain their turf. They want the Upper East Side of town, because that is where they were born, and that is where their relatives are buried, in a small graveyard behind the old sawmill."

"Hmmm..." I said, scribbling. That information could be useful. "And the other gangs?"

"The Creepers do not want anything, really, they are just ghouls." To my surprise, Luca shuddered. "I have seen them trying to conjure spirits at one of the other graveyards, the cemetery where my mother is buried. They used a squirrel as a living sacrifice."

"Poor squirrel!" I exclaimed, surprisingly hurt by this. "But who are they trying to conjure?"

He shrugged again. "That I do not know. What I *do* know is that while for the most part, they don't bother anyone else, they *can* be bought."

"What do you mean?"

"Well, once Bear offered them some Cherokee spirit sticks and a dead dog he had found on the side of the road in exchange for a few of their men helping us to trap one of the Sixes out and away from the group. They thought the sticks were full of ancient magic, so they accepted."

"Whoa..." My skin was officially crawling.

"And you heard how they were helping the Sixes the other night when I got hit. I am not sure how they bought them, but I am sure that it was not difficult."

"Creepers equal wishy-washy. Got it."

"The Crips are not usually a big problem either. They are all from out of town, so they do not really care what happens here in Luthertown Heights. Bear says they are like bees: they only really fight when they are threatened."

"Okay, that could be helpful too..."

"And the Dirty Dozen are the same for the most part. They are not fighters. They are more interested in getting drunk and talking about white supremacy and how every other skin color is an abomination."

"Those are the ones who look like ZZ Top, right? Those guys give me the creeps... One of them cornered me at the grocery store once and demanded that I give him a whole list of my ancestors so he could know if I was a quote-unquote 'pure-bred white.'"

"Are you?" Luca asked, grinning.

"How should I know?" I shrugged, and he laughed.

"Okay, okay. Let's see. Who is left? Oh, the *Caballos*, the Mexican gang. They are the new kids on the block. They will not be ready for a turf war for years. I think they sell fish near 17th Street, that neighborhood is almost exclusively immigrants."

"And what do they want?"

"I am not sure. Maybe just to belong somewhere."

I felt a bit sad as I wrote that one down. "Alright, one more... who are we missing... Oh! The girl gang that cuts off guys' – "

"The XXX Runners," Luca interrupted, shifting uncomfortably in his chair. I didn't have to finish the thought to make him squirm at the idea. "They are former prostitutes that got hurt or abused in the 'line of duty.' There are about ten of them, all women, and they only have one thing on their minds."

"Penises?"

"Penises." He grimaced. "Every month they cut off the member of another man who has done them harm, and they staple them all to a bulletin board in their headquarters on 6ᵗʰ Street. I saw it once." He looked green. "It was not pretty. Bear says they keep all the testicles they collect in a jar on a desk in the back, like marbles. I did not see that, though, thank God."

"Maybe we should send them after Bear..." I muttered, not at all opposed to that idea. "But wait... why were you at their headquarters?"

He shifted again, uncomfortable. "I was scouting with River. We were supposed to assess the level of threat they posed and report back. But we got caught. One of them – a very tall woman with a white wig and a sparkling black dress – lured River inside, and I had to go with him. They all swarmed on us one we were inside, and I thought we were done for."

"Or at least part of you, anyway..." I added, finding it both humorous and sickening at the same time.

"Yes. But then one of them, the leader, noticed the scar on my face. She had a scar on her face too, even bigger than mine. It split her entire face in half diagonally, from her eyebrow to her chin. She asked me if a man had given mine to me, and I told her yes. Then she let us go."

"Just like that?"

"Just like that." He exhaled heavily. "That was one of the tensest moments of my life."

"Thank goodness you got out of there alive," I said, stroking the scar in question with my fingertips.

"And in one piece..." he agreed, still squirming in his chair.

. . .

After studying my hastily scribbled crib sheet for a few minutes, I drew a small box on the back side of the paper and divided it into columns.

"Okay, this *might* be less work than I thought. I was thinking that we would have to work out some sort of deal with every gang, but I don't think that will be necessary. For example, the XXX Runners – " I wrote their name to the right of my dividing line. " – don't really bother anyone except for a specific group of men, who, if I have to be totally honest, almost, sort of, *kind of* have it coming to them anyway."

"Remind me never to wrong you..." Luca said. He kissed my temple, but he sounded wary all the same.

"The *Caballos* are the same. They stay within their own community, which is something we can work on later, assuming we survive this and it turns out that two people *can* change the world."

Luca was looking at me strangely, caught somewhere between exasperation and what looked like admiration, but I kept going.

"The Dirty Dozen are too drunk to do anything. The way I understand it is, they hate other races but don't go out of their way to instigate anything with them. Right?"

"Right." Luca nodded.

"So that leaves the Crips, the Creepers, the Sixes, and the Uewatsu. The Crips wouldn't be a problem either, but you said some of them were there when the Sixes ambushed you all the other night, so they must have some stake in this war."

"And we have to find out what it is?"

"Exactly."

"Annabelle, this is crazy," Luca said, in a weary voice that didn't match the emerald fire burning in his eyes. "We cannot bring four rival gangs together. We cannot form some sort of treaty, we are not –"

"A treaty!" I shouted, so excited that I jumped up out of my chair. Then, embarrassed but still exuberant, I sat back down, grabbed his face, and kissed him. "That's genius! A treaty!"

"Wait... what?" He was blushing from the kiss, and was shaking his head warily.

"We can get all four of the main gangs to sign a peace treaty! It'll be like a pact, where they all swear to stop fighting each other in exchange for... for something, I don't know yet. I'll figure it out. What do you think?"

"It will not work," he responded immediately.

"What? Why not?"

"Bear and the Uewatsu would never agree to it, no matter what we promised them."

"But *why?*"

"Because of my father. It would go against my father's wishes, against every single thing he wanted and believed in. And Bear would never cross my father, not even now that he is gone."

"But what is it that your father wanted? The whole city? That's insane! What ever made him want that in the first place?"

Luca heaved another heavy sigh, and I was appalled to see that mask sliding back over his features again. "The area that would eventually become Luthertown Heights originally belonged to the Cherokee before the quote-unquote 'white man' settled it and pushed them out in the 1800s. My father grew up on an Indian reservation not far from here. His grandparents had been forcibly placed there before he was born. He grew up being told that he was different, and that he did not deserve to live on land that had once rightfully belonged to the Cherokee people.

"When the reservation was razed in the 1970s to make room for some trashy casinos and hotels, the Cherokees moved back to Luthertown Heights, where the residents spat at them and called them savages.

"That is when my father decided to start the Uewatsu. 'If it is savages they want,' he said, 'then it is savages they will get.' Then he set out to take the power away from the people who had made him feel powerless, and to enslave the people who had enslaved his tribe decades before."

"Whoa..." I said softly, at a loss. Yep. No treaty was going to solve *that* problem... "But wait, you say *Bear* wants to carry on in your father's footsteps. What about the rest of the Uewatsu? Maybe they're more like you!"

He shook his head. "Not a single one of them would take a breath without getting Bear's permission first. It is a lost cause."

"There's no such thing as a lost cause!" I insisted, squeezing his hand. "Come on, think hard! Isn't there any way you know of that we could sway the other members of the gang? Can *you* convince them?"

"Me no..." he said slowly, as his mask folded into a frown. I watched as he sat up straighter in his chair, thinking hard, and jumped when his eyes flashed to mine. "But there *is* one person who might be able to get through to Bear. We have to hope it is a good day..."

I felt like a criminal on the lam as we raced back toward Waning Moon Elder Care. We darted from shadow to shadow, sidling alongside of buildings like cliff walkers, clinging to the bricks to keep from falling out into the great expanse of visibility that lay before us. We ran, we scuttled, we dashed, we scampered; we used every synonym for hurrying and sneaking ever invented, praying to God that Bear and his wolf pack wouldn't catch us out this time.

And somehow, amazingly, we made it to the nursing home with all of our limbs intact.

Even Luca's stitches were still holding strong when I sat him down in one of those poofy purple chairs and checked them before he even had a chance to say hello to his grandmother.

"What are you doing to my grandson?"

I jumped, knocking my head against Luca's chin as I leapt up from his lap. He grunted in pain and I massaged what would surely be a knot on the top of my head, but that didn't matter.

"You recognize him?" I asked, unable to believe our impossible stroke of unexpected luck.

"Of course I do," she replied, pulling herself up against her white pillows, indignant. "He is my grandson!" She looked like a regal queen now, with her long, flowing white hair and her clear, kind green eyes, and I loved her instantly.

"Elisi, we need your help," Luca interrupted, wasting no time on pleasantries and expressions of relief. "We need you to talk to Bear."

"Bear?" She frowned. "Oh, you mean Yonv?"

"Yonv?" I asked, thrown for a loop. Adrenaline was already flooding my brain – I could *not* deal with any more new information right now...

"Yonv is the Cherokee word for bear," Luca explained to me. "Bear thinks of Elisi as his own maternal grandmother, since his died when he was three, and she took care of him for years before he went to live with our father." To Immookalee he said, "Yes, Yonv. He is the leader of the Uewatsu now."

"Well I *know* that!"

"Okay, okay. We need you to talk to him. We need you to change his heart."

I cast Luca a sidelong glance. What a poetic thought. It wasn't Bear or anyone else's *minds* we had to change, it was their hearts. We had to make them care the way we did, and care about each other. *That* was the key to everything.

To my surprise, Immookalee shook her head sadly. "Luca, my sweet boy, that is a hopeless cause. Yonv is lost. You know that better than anyone. You cannot stop him. You cannot hold back the wind."

"We're not talking about holding back the wind," I interjected. "We're just talking about maybe changing its direction a little."

Luca's Elisi narrowed her eyes at me. There was an entire universe in those emerald green slits she called eyes, and I could not even begin to guess what she was thinking.

"Who are you?" she asked me, her tone bordering on an order.

"Annabelle Fitzpatrick. I'm Luca's... um... friend."

I glanced at Luca, but his face was blank again. Dammit!

Immookalee sat up straighter, regarding me with more interest than before. "Luca has never brought a friend to see me. You must be special."

"She is," Luca said firmly, but with none of his former sweetness. "And that is why we need your help. If we cannot get Bear to call off the Uewatsu and make a pact for peace in Luthertown Heights, he is going to hurt Annabelle. He already has. But this time it will be worse."

Luca's hand was clenched into a fist on his knee. I could see it shaking, trembling with tension as he tried hard to remain cool and collected while the flames of fury raged inside him. I put my hand over his, and his fingers unclenched slightly, allowing me to slip mine inside.

"I will speak to him."

We both turned to look at Immookalee. I felt my stomach twist as I saw that there were tears sparkling in her green eyes, so much like her grandson's. "I do not know what good it will do, but I will talk to him. What is it that you want me to say?"

Luca's own green eyes were alive again as he looked to me, the ringleader of this crazy, impossible scheme.

"Tell him... no, *ask* him to come to a meeting tomorrow night at Luthertown Park at 5:00 p.m. Tell him that the leaders of the other gangs will be there to negotiate a peace treaty, and ask him to leave his weapons at home. Tell him that it's for the sake of the town's children, and the innocent people who live in Luthertown Heights. They deserve to feel safe in their own homes, on their own streets. The violence *has* to stop."

Immookalee's eyes narrowed again, but her mouth stretched into a thin-lipped smile. "This girl has a fire in her, Luca," she said approvingly. "She shines like the sun."

I blushed and looked away, embarrassed, but Luca squeezed my hand. "That is what I told her," he said softly. Then he got to his feet. "And that is why you also have to tell Bear to leave her alone. If he really cannot rest until he has had her, then I will not rest until he is dead."

"Luca!" I said, startled by his low-voiced growl.

"You would kill your own brother, Luca?" Immookalee asked, tilting her head to the side, as if she were seeing him for the first time.

"For her, yes."

I didn't know whether to hug him or to cry.

"But not for yourself?"

It was Luca's turn to tilt his head. "What?"

"You will kill him for hurting your fiery friend, but not for making you live a life you hate? You are a caged animal, Luca, and your father used to own the key. Now Bear does. But you let him cage you and kick you and taunt you your whole life and let him live, but then you would cut him down for stealing her fire?"

"I... I..." I had never seen Luca look so uncomfortable. His mask had fallen to the floor, and he was barely holding himself together as the weight of his grandmother's words crashed over him. She wasn't telling him that it was wrong to kill his brother – she was saying he should have done it sooner. And for himself, not for me. He had needed saving too, he had just never noticed it before. He hadn't realized that *he* had been the one holding the key to his own cage all along – or that his Elisi (and I) understood that even when he didn't.

"I'd rather nobody killed anybody..." I said nervously, hoping to break the tension. "We'd rather find a way to resolve this all peacefully, without losing any more lives in the process. Right, Luca?"

Luca was staring at the ground, his eyes wide as millions of thoughts raced behind them. Slowly, though, he lifted them to me, and the storm inside them calmed. "Yes," he said.

I could feel Immookalee's eyes on us, but I couldn't look away from those smoldering emerald eyes. There was that strange look in them again; there was something important there that I needed to understand. But I couldn't quite put my finger on what it was.

"Get me the telephone from the front desk," said Immookalee.

Her voice was clear and decisive, and it broke through the fog forming in my brain. "Bear will recognize that number."

Luca squeezed my hand once, then raced off to do as she said.

"Luca is special too, you know," Immookalee whispered, once we were alone. The tears were back in her eyes, and there was a strong, vulnerable honesty there that tugged at my heart. "I may not remember much, but I remember that."

I smiled as I walked to her bedside, and squeezed the cold, frail, wrinkled hand that lay atop her blankets. "I know," I replied. "He's the most special person I have ever met."

Immookalee smiled her thin-lipped smile at me, and was just opening her mouth to say something else when suddenly a look of pure terror came over her. With wide, frightened eyes, she stared at something behind me, and pulled at me with her fragile hand.

"Look out!" she cried, tugging at my arm. "The monster! It is back!"

My heart fell as I realized that the Alzheimer's was overtaking her once more, and I turned to Luca with an expression of pure misery.

Only it wasn't Luca who was the monster this time.

I had just enough time to scream his name before the butt of Bear's pistol collided with the side of my skull, and darkness blotted out the sun.

I awoke some time later to a rocking motion, as if I were on board a ship sailing on rough water. A strange, unbearable nausea ebbed and flowed with the swinging of the ship, and I fought hard not to vomit as I tried to remember how to open my eyes.

My head was screaming in agony; it felt as if I had grown a second heart behind my right ear. The heart thudded and throbbed even faster than the waves of the ocean that were pulling at me, and I would have given anything for the world to hold still around and within me for just two seconds.

Squinting against the overly bright glow of the afternoon sun, I wrenched open my eyes and immediately felt even sicker. Pavement was whizzing by beneath me like a conveyor belt set to high speed. Trees and buildings blurred and swayed to either side, and the thick, strong, coppery scent of blood filled my nostrils like a mad butcher's perfume.

I closed my eyes, but that only made things worse now that I was fully conscious. I opened them again, and tried to lift up my hand to cover my mouth, but found that it was trapped – caught between my side and the taut, leather-bound chest that was now as familiar to me as the freckles on my own face.

"Luca..." I croaked, trying to lift my head. I yelped in pain as the second heart seemed to explode, and stars danced across my vision.

Luca was carrying me very awkwardly – with one arm beneath my legs and the other crushing me to his abdomen at an angle that was almost upside down – but when I spoke he lost his grip completely.

He dropped to the ground with me and broke my fall with his knees as his hands flew to my face, touching it, stroking it, caressing it.

"Annabelle, thank God!" he wheezed, his voice raw and winded. He helped me into a sitting position and caught me as I swayed. Even though we had stopped running, the world was still spinning around us, and it was all I could do to focus my eyes.

As soon as I did, though, I wished I hadn't.

"Luca!" I gasped in alarm. The entire left side of his face was covered in blood, which was still flowing freely from a thick, diagonal cut on his forehead. His bottom lip was bleeding too as he continued to feel my face like a blind man trying to commit my features to memory. His green eyes blazed beneath the blood and the gore, and suddenly I remembered what had happened, and what we were running from.

Bear had attacked me. He had found me in the nursing home and knocked me unconscious.

I dropped my gaze to my shirt front, swaying sickly again. Luca's borrowed shirt was still blurry, so I touched it with my fingers and whimpered when I felt the large, jagged tear down the middle, just over my breasts.

"He did not touch you," Luca said, as he pulled my borrowed jacket over the rip and zipped it up. "That happened when I pulled you away from him."

"O... oh..." I closed my eyes, more confused than before. Slowly, carefully this time, I tilted my head back to look up at him. "What happened?" Then a thought struck me and I clapped my hands over my mouth in horror. "Oh, God, did he hurt Immookalee?"

He put his palm against the side of my face, and I closed my eyes, grateful to have something solid to lean against. "No, Elisi is fine. Or she was when I left, anyway. But she had already forgotten me again. Most likely due to the stress."

"I'm sorry..." I whispered, apologizing for much more than just that. My mind may have been groggy and fogged with pain, but I was well aware that this was all my fault.

I felt him press his lips to my clammy forehead. "Do not be sorry," he murmured into my skin. Then he waited a beat and added, "I am just glad you are alright. I was not sure how far I could carry you with that hole in my leg."

"How far did we make it?" I asked, relishing the quiet stillness that had fallen over me as soon as he had leaned in.

"Not far enough. About halfway to the YMCA."

"Why are we going there?"

"To see someone about your head." He grazed what I was sure was an orange-sized lump on my skull, and I jumped. "Sorry! Sorry!" He hissed, sounding miserable. "Did I hurt you?"

"No," I lied, leaning back and opening my eyes once more. The city still spun, but those green eyes were fixed in place, holding me steady atop the ocean that was still threatening to wash me away. "How... how did we get away, though? How did you fight off Bear well enough to escape with... oh... oh, no." A new horror dawned on me, and I couldn't hold back the tide any longer.

I turned to the side just in time to keep from setting Luca adrift on a sea of sick, and the wet, splattering sound it made on the pavement only made me vomit more.

As I rid myself of the past year's worth of food in my stomach, punctuating each retch with a strangled cry at the blinding pain it caused in my head, Luca gathered up the hair hanging down over my face and held it tightly together at the nape of my neck. This made me want to break down completely, but unfortunately, there was no time.

"I'm sorry, Annabelle, but we have to go," Luca told me as my tank dried up. He sounded distraught. "They are close by, I can feel it."

I added a sob to my last gag and wrapped things up by wiping my mouth on the sleeve of the jacket that wasn't even mine. "Okay," I choked. "Let's go."

Luca looked to be on the verge of tears as he helped me to my feet, and his eyes never left my face. "I'm sorry," he repeated.

"Don't," I said, closing my eyes for a second to ward off an aftershock of nausea. "Not your fault."

He ran his fingers through my hair. "Do you think you can run? We only have a few blocks left, then we will be safe, I promise."

In reality, the only thing I knew I could do for sure was lay down and die right there on the sidewalk. What I said, though, was, "I can if you can."

He kissed me on the cheek, fiercely, as if he were struggling to contain himself. Then he took my hand, and we were off once more.

I had to stop three times on the way to the Y to puke, but by the time I saw that beautiful love note of a mural on the back door of my classroom, I actually felt a bit better. My stomach was officially empty, and the blood and adrenaline pumping through my veins had brought back some semblance of clarity to my brain. The throbbing in my head dulled as well, and now felt less like a racing heart and more like someone beating on a sheepskin drum a little ways off in the distance.

"We are here," panted Luca, unnecessarily, I thought.

I started to say "I know," when a second male voice answered from down by our knees.

"Well I can see that!" I heard a rustling as DeAndre, the hobo I had once counted as a friend, stood up from his newspaper nest. "Whatchu want me to do about it?"

"Luca, what –"

"Sanctuary."

I shook my head. Surely I was hallucinating. This was not Disney's *The Hunchback of Notre Dame*, and the filthy alley we were standing in was no one's idea of a church. I winced as my head spun a bit, but I was still able to see the surprised look that passed over DeAndre's face.

"What'd you say, boy?"

"You know what I said," Luca growled, squeezing my hand. "I give it up. You promised me."

"What the –"

Before I could finish being incredulous, DeAndre nodded as if this all made sense. He never took his wide, bloodshot eyes off of Luca as he said, "Okay. Follow me."

Forty-Four

"What the *hell?*" I was finally able to get the phrase out as we descended a long flight of narrow stairs leading down to some sort of subbasement area beneath the abandoned factory next door to the YMCA. We had entered the building through a short, squatty cargo door hidden behind the dumpster, not far from the wolf mural Luca had painted to inspire me to stay kind and positive after insulting our wizened old guide. I had never seen the door before – I would never have even guessed it was there. It seemed to have been put there specifically for clandestine purposes, and I would be lying if I said I wasn't intrigued.

The door – a folding metal panel like those on a garage – had been locked, but DeAndre had pulled up a chain from inside his three layers of dirty shirts and shown us a small, silver key. He had inserted it into the lock, and we had entered the building as quickly and as quietly as we were able. There was nothing inside but a vast expanse of slick concrete and emptiness, and it felt a bit like entering a crypt as DeAndre locked the door behind us. We had tiptoed past the rows of broken windows at the front of the main production area of the factory, where the empty tables had once held heavy, dangerous machinery of some sort, and arrived at a door in the back corner marked "STAIRS." Curiously, that door had also been locked, and DeAndre extracted a second small, silver key from his pants pocket to enter that one.

Down, down, down we went, down at least forty steps to the basement, which smelled like decay and was home to what sounded like a legion of chittering rats. DeAndre had pulled out a small, pen-sized flashlight when we had entered the stairwell, but I tried not to follow the beam of light, afraid of what monstrosities I might see if I did.

Instead, I clung tight to Luca's arm as we limped down onto the landing and listened as DeAndre fished out yet another key from yet another pocket, and opened yet another door.

When that metal door swung open, we were hit with the damp, earthy scent of limestone, wafted up to us by a chilly breeze. As we entered that stairwell, I noticed there was a light glowing below, and I wasn't sure whether to be relieved or fearful.

"We are almost there," Luca murmured to me, correctly interpreting my anxiety.

"Where is 'there?'" I whispered back, creating a chorus of hissing echoes that sounded like a coven of nervous snakes.

"Sanctuary," DeAndre answered, as he stepped off the bottom step and into some sort of cave.

Luca and I followed him, and I felt my jaw drop as we emerged into what appeared to be a brightly lit hospital facility, complete with cots, chairs, examining tables, and a cluster of stalagmites next to every bed.

"DeAndre used to be a doctor in the military," Luca told me. He looked pretty impressed himself. "He took care of soldiers who got injured in the line of duty."

"I've been all over the world," DeAndre said wearily, shaking his head. "Vietnam, Cuba, Iran, Afghanistan. But when I came back home to start my own practice, nobody wanted me around. There's not a lot of room for real doctors here in Luthertown Heights. No one can afford 'em, and they think you're uppity if you say you are one. I fell on hard times, drinkin' doin' drugs, doin' anything to try to make myself feel somethin', but nothin' made me feel like I did when I was in those trenches, helpin' those guys under enemy fire. Then, one day when I was out lookin' to score some heroin, I stumbled across this place – literally." He waved his arm around at the room we were in. "I fixed it up, I made it into a sanctuary where people can come if they've been hurt by a gang and don't want to go to a hospital. I haven't touched a single drug since that day."

"But there's a catch," said Luca, sounding somber.

"Right." DeAndre nodded. "To get in here, you have to renounce any ties you have to any gang – forever. I treat civilians now, not soldiers."

I turned to Luca, my eyes wide. "So that's what you meant outside! You gave up the Uewatsu!"

He nodded, his face unreadable.

"For me," I whispered, putting my hand on his chest, over his quick-thudding heart. I had already known he had renounced his gang, his family, his old life, but it had never seemed so official before. So final. So sad.

He put his hand over mine, but didn't speak.

"We should hurry up and take a look at that bump," DeAndre said, shattering the moment. "From the look of your pupils, I'd say you've got a concussion."

Reluctantly, I took my eyes off Luca and followed DeAndre over to a bed at the far end of the long, cold room. I was Doctor DeAndre's only patient; not a single blanket was disturbed on any of the dozen or so military-grade cots, and I wondered once more how much I should trust the man I had thought was a homeless, drug-addled drifter up until about ten minutes ago.

"This is why you didn't let me walk you to the shelter..." I said, marveling at an especially large rock formation near a metal desk we were approaching. It looked a little like a ghost oozing out of the wall and into the room. "You wanted to stay close to your hospital."

"Exactly." He gestured for me to have a seat on the bed, and he pulled over a folding chair from behind the desk. "I always worry someone will find out it's here."

"But how did *you* know about it, Luca?" I tried to turn my head back the way we had come, but DeAndre caught me by the chin and held me still.

"Let's save the questions for later, alright?" DeAndre had pulled that skinny little penlight out of his pocket again, and was shining it back and forth between my eyes. "Have you had any dizziness or nausea?"

"I thought we were saving the questions for later..."

"Yes, she has." Luca's voice appeared at my side and I immediately felt myself relax. "She vomited several times on the way here."

"Yes, I guessed as much..." DeAndre had put the flashlight away now, and was reaching out to touch the lump behind my ear. I tensed up, bracing myself for the explosion of pain, but I still jumped when his fingers made contact and let out a sound like a snorting Dachshund.

"Can you tell me your name?" DeAndre asked, as if he couldn't see the tears of white hot pain I was struggling to blink back.

"Annabelle Fitzpatrick," I grunted through gritted teeth as he kept probing my throbbing second heart. "But you know me as 'White Girl'."

"And what's your address?"

"Don't... have one... right now." I grimaced, clenching my hands into fists until Luca pried one open and slipped his fingers between mine, just as I had done with his at the nursing home. "But I *did* live at 340 7th Street, Apartment 2B."

"Okay, now who's the president?"

"It's 2017. I'd rather not say."

DeAndre chuckled. "Alright, you don't seem to be suffering

from any mental impairment at the moment, but you do have a grade three concussion. I'm going to get you some Tylenol for the pain, and an ice pack for the swelling, and you can sleep here tonight. But, as always, there's a catch."

"What's that?"

"Slipknot will have to wake you up every two hours on the dot, due to the swelling in your brain. But you'll most likely feel a lot better in the morning."

"Thank you," I said, still too shaken up to let relief wash over me just yet.

"You'll be safe here," he assured me. "I don't know what kind of mess you've gotten yourself into, White Girl, but you'll be safe here."

I smiled as he got up and headed for a locked cabinet across the room. Luca sat down gingerly on the bed beside me, perching like a worried bird about to take flight.

"Oh, and I'm comin' back with stitches for that head of yours, boy!" DeAndre called over his shoulder, and Luca sighed.

"Did you notice how different his speaking voice is when he's down here?" I asked Luca under my breath. "He's like a different person when he's in his 'doctor element!' I never would have guessed –"

"I did not kill Bear."

I stopped talking to stare blankly at him. "What?"

He shifted his legs, looking everywhere except at me. "I did not kill Bear. You seemed worried about that before. So I was just letting you know."

I should have felt relieved then, too, but there was something in his voice that made me feel guilty and nervous instead. "Okay..." I said slowly. "That's... good?"

He didn't answer. His face was hard and his jaw was clenched, and he looked as if he were being eaten alive by words he just couldn't bring himself to say out loud.

"What's the matter, Luca? What are you not telling me?"

He was quiet for a moment, then he let out a low growl of frustration and clenched his fists over his knees, just as I had clenched mine against the pain a few minutes before. "What I am not telling you is that it was all I could do to *keep* myself from killing him. My hands were around his throat, Annabelle, he was down to his last few breaths, but then I looked at you, lying there on the floor, pale and lifeless, and I thought about what you said before."

"What did I say?" I whispered, frightened by his intensity.

"You said I was not like him. You said I was a good man. You said... you said you loved me. No one has ever..." He growled again and banged a fist on his kneecap, making me jump. His eyes were wild, his impassive mask was cracked, and his fiery soul was all but spilling out as he turned to me and asked, "Would that still be true? If I killed my brother, my own flesh and blood? If I became the monster that my father wanted me to be, would you still think I was a good man? Would you still say you loved me then?"

I looked deep into his furious, desperate, blazing eyes and remembered the first moment we had met. I had thought he was a killer then, that he strangled his enemies with that frazzled, worn-out rope around his neck, but I had walked with him just the same. I had talked to him, I had shared with him, I had cared for him all the same. And I knew then that no matter what he did or who he chose to be, I would love him all the same too.

"Yes," I answered, without a doubt. "Yes, Luca, I would. Of course I would."

His eyes widened as if in disbelief, and the flames inside him seemed to settle down to a cozy roar instead of an all-out inferno. He was just parting his lips to speak again when DeAndre's face appeared between ours.

"Sorry to interrupt," he said, "but if I don't stitch you up soon, you're gonna lose all the blood in that hard, Indian head of yours." DeAndre didn't sound the least bit apologetic. In fact, he sounded almost giddy for the chance to patch up a patient again.

He handed me a bottle of extra-strength Tylenol tablets and a glass of water as he plopped a blue and white, plastic cooling gel pack onto my lap and nudged me aside. I scooted over to the very end of the bed as he took my place next to Luca.

"Who stitched up this ear?" he asked, peeking under the bandage as he began to blot away the blood around Luca's latest cut.

"I did," I replied, between gulps of water as I downed two tablets. I hoped they would act fast. My vision was pulsing along with my heart (the first one or the second, I couldn't tell anymore). "Are they bad?"

"No, they're great! Maybe once this is over, I can hire you as my apprentice."

"Her mother was a nurse," Luca informed him. He looked past DeAndre to smile proudly at me, and at last I felt that elusive sense of relief wash over me. Everything would be okay now. Luca and I were safe, and everything would be okay. I was sure of it.

Unfortunately, though, as I had well learned, you cannot fight Fate, and you cannot hold back the wind.

Forty-Five

As DeAndre patched up Luca (complimenting me several more
times on my "mighty fine" stitching skills), he told us more about
his sanctuary. It, like the factory building above it, had been abandoned for decades when he had stumbled across it – literally stumbling down the stairs and into the cavernous room. He had been
high on everything from crack to Nyquil, and at first glance he had
thought he had fallen down a well.

After doing some research at the library once he had sobered
up, he had discovered that half of the state of Kentucky had been
built upon subterranean offshoots of various cave systems, and
that the one beneath that building was one of the smallest caves
recorded by the National Caves Association. No one in Luthertown Heights knew it was there, save for perhaps whoever had
owned the now-empty factory thirty years ago, so DeAndre had
claimed it as his own.

He had stolen the cots, one by one, from the homeless shelter
he had refused to let me take him to (maybe that was why he didn't
let me take him there...) over a period of several months. He had
lifted the blankets from the laundry hamper at the "real" hospital,
and had picked up most of his tools and medicines there too. He

had however, paid for the locks for the doors himself, something he seemed to think canceled out all the other larceny he had just admitted to.

For ten years he had been running the sanctuary as a combination doctor's office and underground railroad, stitching people up before smuggling them out to neighboring towns, if that's what they wanted. The only rules were that they had to renounce any and every affiliation they might have to a gang, and swear never to reveal the location of the sanctuary. So far, he had treated thirty-eight patients, and not a single one had ratted on him.

"But how did you two meet, then?" I asked, glancing back and forth between DeAndre and Luca. Luca had settled back onto the pillows on the cot we had been sitting on, and I was sitting cross-legged on the one next to it, too wired to relax. Now that my swollen brain was clearing, there was so much I needed to know, so much I had to be caught up on.

"You wanna tell it, boy, or should I?"

DeAndre was smiling, but Luca looked glum. He shrugged, apparently taking up his vow of silence again, and I reached across the space between us to squeeze his hand.

"Alright, here's what happened." DeAndre cleared his throat, as if preparing for a long speech. "About five years ago, I was doin' my rounds – every night I visit a different area of the city, checkin' on folks, seein' if anyone needs any help. Well, that night, I found myself on 19th Street: prime Uewatsu territory."

I glanced a Luca. That seemed as if it should have been offensive somehow, but Luca only looked distant and world-weary.

"I met a girl on the street there, a little Cherokee girl, maybe eight years old. I asked her what her name was, but before she could answer me, someone had shoved a knife in my gut."

"Oh my God!"

"It was Bear," said Luca dully. "That girl was our cousin, Laila. She is a prostitute now."

"She's...what? She's only thirteen!" I sputtered, aghast.

"Fourteen now, but yes."

"That was good math, by the way," DeAndre told me, grinning proudly. "That's a great sign for your concussion."

"Um... thanks."

"Anyway, Bear left me in the street and took off with the girl. As he was leavin', Slipknot here was comin' up, and Bear told him to finish me off. I thought I was a goner. I'd heard about what you do with that rope around your neck."

Luca closed his eyes, as if to block out our conversation.

"But you know what he did?" DeAndre asked me.

I shook my swollen head no, even if I was already pretty sure I knew where this was going. Luca had been a hero to me from almost the very start. Tales of his goodness and humanity didn't surprise me the way they seemed to surprise other people.

"That bastard waited until his boss went around the corner, then he picked me up and threw me over his shoulder, and just started runnin' like he was freakin' Forrest Gump! He didn't stop until I told him to once we were near the sanctuary.

"I told him what was down here and he helped me down the stairs, and he sat with me while I sewed myself up." He lifted his multiple layers of grimy shirts to expose an even grimier belly covered in scars. He pointed to a particularly nasty one next to his belly button and said, "Toughest operation I ever did. But I wouldn't have lived to do it at all if it hadn't been for Slipknot. I tried to ask him why he'd saved me, but he wouldn't say.

"Once I was fixed up and settled down into a bed, he got up to leave. That's when I promised him that if he ever gave up the thug life and decided to go straight, he'd have shelter here. All he had to do was say the word 'sanctuary,' and everything he'd ever done or been would be wiped away, and I'd know he was ready to start fresh."

I frowned down at Luca. He was lying conspicuously still, with his entire body stiff and his eyes still closed, and suddenly I understood why he always seemed so conflicted. It wasn't just about choosing me over his family, it was about having to forget everything he knew and had done to become someone he wasn't even sure he knew how to be. He was starting over from scratch, from nothing, and he had no idea how it would end up, or if the new Luca would turn out to be any better than the old one.

"Welp, I'm gonna go back to my post for a few hours, so as not to raise suspicion." DeAndre got up and put his hand on my shoulder. "You two can stay here as long as you want. But remember: wake her up every two hours, boy. There's a clock on the wall across from you."

Luca nodded to show that he had heard him.

"And no hanky-panky down here!" DeAndre called as he reached the steps. "Those cots ain't made for that shit."

I bit back an embarrassed grin as I heard him leave, but it fell when I looked back to Luca.

Slowly and very gingerly, taking care not to jostle my aching head, I got up and joined Luca on his cot, perching on the edge like he had done earlier.

"That last part of DeAndre's story was wrong, you know," I said, softly stroking his blood-caked cheek with my fingers.

He leaned almost imperceptibly toward my hand as I continued to caress his scruffy beard stubble. "What do you mean?"

"You don't have to be a whole new person to be here. Who you were before was pretty great. I wouldn't want you to lose that."

He raised an eyebrow as he opened his eyes to gaze up at me. My stomach fluttered almost painfully at the trusting, vulnerable look he gave me, and I would have stopped everything and kissed him right then if I had trusted myself not to lose my equilibrium and vomit all over his face.

"You never *were* like the others, Luca. You saved people, you helped them, you cared about them. If you were like Bear or your dad, you would've killed DeAndre like he told you to. Same with that woman they tried to make you use for your initiation. Same with a lot of other people, probably. You never really were an Uewatsu, you were always *you*. And that 'you' is a pretty incredible person to be." I grinned again as I began to blush, feeling self-conscious as my speech teetered on the edge of cheesiness. "So don't think you have to change into someone else," I concluded. "Just keep being who you were inside all along. Because that's the man you were always meant to be."

To my surprise, his lips pressed together in a tight, thin line, and his body tensed up again. With eyes burning brighter than ever before, he took my stroking fingers and pressed them inside his own hand. "Sometimes I think you are too good for me," he said, his raspy voice tight. "You are too pure and trusting. You see things in me that no one else ever has. And I want to believe that you are right about me, and that I am the man that you think I am, but sometimes... sometimes, Annabelle, I still feel more like a beast than a human being. I do not understand how you can love me when no one else ever has."

"Because I see the light in you," I answered quietly, without hesitation. "Just like you saw the light in me."

He stared at me for a long time then, searching my eyes, mapping my freckles, memorizing my face. Then he pulled himself up and kissed me, first on my forehead, then on those freckled cheeks that he seemed to adore so much, then, finally, he pressed his lips to mine.

"I love you, Annabelle Fitzpatrick," he breathed into me, his lips grazing my lips as he spoke. "I will never understand you, but I love you with all of my heart."

Forty-Six

Although it was barely four-thirty in the afternoon, I fell asleep shortly after hearing Luca's declaration of love, partially because I was exhausted and in pain, and partially because I knew I would need energy for what I had planned for the next day. But mostly it was just because that moment had been so perfect that I wanted it to be the last thing to happen to me before I drifted off into a dream world that couldn't hold a candle to my real one.

I awoke several times, startled by the cot's creaking as it struggled to hold us both, but overall it was a good, dreamless sleep that erased all the terrible memories I had accrued that day, and left only the good ones. I slept with my head on Luca's chest, with my ear just over his slow, tranquil heart, and he had his arms wrapped around me. Every time I shifted, he kissed the top of my hair and murmured reassuring things to me, as if he were soothing a fussy infant. In my state of half-consciousness, I wasn't quite sure what he said, but it was comforting to know that he was watching over me.

"Sorry," he said into my ear eventually, "it is six-thirty. I have to wake you up for a bit."

"Five more minutes..." I groaned, burying my face in his t-shirt. It smelled like rust, sweat, and leather.

"Okay." I could hear the gentle smile in his voice.

"Nope, wrong answer!" I said, rolling over to look up at him. The room spun more slowly that time, and I took that as a sign that I was recovering. "You'd make a terrible nurse."

He chuckled. "Hey, it is not my fault that you look so peaceful when you are sleeping. Although I must say, I like it much better when your eyes are open." He leaned down and kissed the tip of my nose, and I blushed.

"Have you been watching me sleep this whole time? You must have been bored to death!"

"Not even remotely," he replied, still smiling. "How is your head?"

"A little sore." I shrugged, only lying a little that time. It really did feel a bit better, but now it felt more like a hot, gelatinous lump of flan stuck behind my ear; I couldn't feel it pulsing anymore, but I was very aware of the swelling.

"Here, I will hold the ice pack on it for you."

He activated the gel pack that I had abandoned on the neighboring cot, and I sighed in bliss as the cold bag met the boiling bump.

"That's nice," I breathed, closing my eyes again. "Maybe you *are* a good nurse after all."

"Not as good as you."

"Eh, now that you've had a professional doctor sew you up, you don't need me anymore."

"You know, to be honest," he lowered his voice conspiratorially, "I think your stitches are better than DeAndre's. And they hurt a hell of a lot less."

I laughed, winced at the pain that caused in my head, then laughed some more. "You're such a liar!"

"I am not!" he cried, offended. "I would never lie to you."

"I was kidding." I grinned, opening my eyes and reaching up to graze his chin with my fingers. "Even if I still think that maybe you're exaggerating to inflate my ego."

"Maybe I am," he said, taking my fingers in his free hand and pulling them to his lips to kiss them. "Or maybe your beauty just distracted me from the pain."

I snorted, and he raised an eyebrow. "Sorry, sorry," I said quickly, "it's just that no one has ever said these kinds of things to be me before. I feel like I'm in a romantic movie or something."

"This is real life," he assured me, smiling sweetly before kissing each of my fingers in turn, "and I meant every word I said."

My embarrassed laughter was fading into a warm, tingly feeling as he continued to watch me with those smoldering eyes, kissing my wrist now, lingering on the pulse point, where I was sure he could feel my heartbeat speed up with every touch of his lips.

Just as he was starting to make his way up my arm, making me yearn to disregard DeAndre's rules about hanky-panky in the sanctuary, we heard a thud from above, and we bolted upright.

The quick movement made my head spin sickly, but Luca wasted no time leaping out of bed and grabbing the gun from his bag on the floor.

"What do we do if it's not DeAndre?" I whispered, my throat tight with panic as I squeezed his free hand with both of mine. "We're trapped!"

What had once been a cozy (albeit chilly) safe haven had suddenly morphed into a windowless prison. I felt like the proverbial fish in a barrel as the thudding continued, finally reaching the door to the stairs.

I made it upright, but my legs were trembling as I stood behind Luca, peering around his left, leather-jacketed bicep as a key turned in the lock, and the door swung open.

The staircase was hidden from our view around a corner, so we could only wait in a state of dreadful anticipation as footsteps walked slowly down, one step, two steps, three steps, growing ever closer.

Luca's arm was steady as he lifted his pistol, but mine were both aquiver as I remembered the hole in Miss Carmella's chest, and the smaller, equally fatal one in Marcus'.

The concussion had released its hold on my mind, but I still couldn't think straight as the footsteps got closer and closer until finally they reached ground level.

I saw Luca's finger resting on the trigger right before I closed my eyes.

"Hey, bo – what the *hell?*"

I groaned as I let out the breath I had been holding and leaned my forehead against Luca's arm. It was just DeAndre.

"You can never be too careful these days," Luca responded.

"I thought you gave up on that stuff, Slipknot? You ain't supposed to shoot anybody anymore!"

"I didn't." Luca put the gun back under the cot and pulled me down to sit on it, putting his arm around my shoulders.

"Well, you could have!" DeAndre looked wildly indignant, a near caricature of himself, with his rough, wrinkled cheeks flushed and his short, salt and pepper hair standing on end. "And then you wouldn't get to eat any of this food I scraped up for you!"

My mouth began to water at the mere thought of food, and when he pitched a fat, brown McDonald's bag at us, I nearly swooned as the scent of cheeseburgers and salty fries hit my nostrils.

I hadn't eaten since that morning, but I hadn't realized just how ravenous I was until Luca opened the bag and handed me a McDouble.

"There must be fifteen dollars' worth of food here." Luca was frowning, I could hear it in his voice, but I was too busy trying not to moan with pleasure to check. The burger was cold, but the meat was thick and juicy, and the cheese might as well have been draped over the bun by God Himself. "DeAndre, you cannot afford this."

DeAndre heaved a heavy sigh. "Just eat, boy, and let me do the worryin'."

Luca still seemed dubious, so DeAndre sighed again and added, "Consider it a part of your treatment. You lost a lot of blood, you need to refuel. What kind of doctor would I be if I didn't provide you with the nutrients you need to be healthy?"

I snorted again, fairly certain that not a single nutrient had ever touched that burger.

That release of tension seemed to finally make up Luca's mind for him, and he thrust his hand back into the bag to pull out two more burgers. He tossed one to DeAndre, and unwrapped the second for himself, and I'll be damned if he didn't have to try not to let his eyes roll back in bliss too.

DeAndre sat down on the opposite bunk, facing us, and I felt another pleasant feeling wash over me. It was the closest I had come to having a family dinner in a long time, and I couldn't help but feel my fondness for our host double as I watched him stuff his mouth with cold french fries.

Then I remembered what happened to everyone else I grew fond of these days, and I immediately turned my thoughts to other things.

"So, DeAndre..." I said, swallowing the fourth and last bite of my cheeseburger, "You've had a home this whole time? Why didn't you tell me? I would have stopped pestering you about going to the shelter!"

DeAndre chuckled and handed me a box of fries. "I wouldn't exactly call *this,*" he nodded at the cold, damp walls, crawling with stalagmites, "a 'home.' And besides, it was nice to be fussed over."

I smiled as I blushed and looked down at my meal.

"And to be honest, you're one of the only people who acts like you know me when you see me on the streets. Most people just look on past, like I'm a pile of garbage. But you see me."

That sounded familiar. "But... if that's how you felt, why did you get so upset after you saw me with Luca the other day?" I thought back to the last real conversation I had had with DeAndre, where he had called me terrible names and called Luca even worse, and where he had accused me of letting the other Uewatsu rape me so I could be Luca's "girl." I felt whatever fondness I had been cultivating for him fade as my swollen brain reminded me that, even if he saved people for a living, he was no saint himself. "You said some pretty awful things to me."

Luca tensed up beside me. I hadn't seen him, but he had been there that day too. He had heard DeAndre tear me down, and he had heard me slap him for it. That's why he had painted the mural on the factory wall, to encourage me to feed the good inner wolf instead of the evil one. By the look in his eyes right now, though, he was about to feed the other.

DeAndre lowered his sandwich and scratched at his salt and pepper beard. "I shouldn't have said those things. Any of them." He glanced at Luca, as if he were afraid I had told him about the insults he'd thrown his way too. "I was just... angry... I guess. From the rumors I'd heard, you'd let yourself be dragged down to the same level as everyone else in this shitty ass town, and I took it hard. I wanted to believe that there was one pure person left in Luthertown Heights and I thought... well, I thought you'd let me down. I thought *he'd* pushed you to let me down." He nodded at Luca, who looked to be on the verge of snarling at him. "But I was wrong. And I'm sorry. To both of you. You're both decent folks and I should've remembered that. Is there anything I can do to make it up to you?"

Luca answered for me with a hard, dead-eyed stare that said clearly that DeAndre could take his apologies and go straight to Hell, but I had another idea.

"Maybe there *is* something..."

Luca tilted his head, frowning, without taking his eyes off the doctor.

DeAndre himself looked relieved, though, and said, "Tell me. Whatever I can do for you, I'll do."

"You know this whole town, right?" I asked, dropping the rest of my fries back into the bag and leaning forward. "You said you travel to a different section every night. So you must have connections with lots of people."

"I guess so..." he said slowly. He looked mildly intrigued, which was encouraging.

Feeling a faint flush of hope, I pulled the list I had made earlier out of my back pants pocket. It was scuffed and dirty and splotchy with blood now, but it was still legible as I unfolded it atop my lap. "Then do you think you could find a way to get a message to the leaders of these four gangs?"

I pointed at the chart I had drawn, and held the paper out to him. He wiped his greasy fingers on his grimy pants before he took it, and he frowned down at it with interest.

"The Crips, the Creepers, the Sixes, and the Uewatsu? Those last two are the hardest gangs in town."

"I know. That's why we have to convince them to stop fighting. They're tearing the city apart."

DeAndre ran a hand through his hair, noticeably less enthusiastic now that he had seen just what exactly he had offered me. "And you want me to... what? Get them all together for a chat?"

"More like a peace talk," I clarified. "We want to find a way to make each gang leader happy, so that they'll tone down the violence."

To my surprise, DeAndre laughed. "Honey, the only way any of those Uewatsu savages'll be happy is if everyone else is dead. Ask Slipknot here, he knows. They bred it into him. The same's probably true for the Sixes."

I glanced at Luca. His face was still stony, but his eyes were bright as he said in a stoic, raspy voice that gave me goosebumps, "There are two wolves inside us all. One is evil. One is good. Every moment of every day, they fight, trying to gain control. In the end, one will be stronger. Which one depends on which one you feed."

"What the hell does that mean?"

"It means that the Uewatsu and the Sixes and everyone else in

Luthertown Heights needs something else to sustain them besides violence and killing and lies. And we are going to feed it to them."

"And what, exactly, is on this menu of yours?"

That time, it was me who answered. "Trust. Understanding. Compassion. Equality. Hope."

DeAndre was quiet for a long time, staring at me as if I had suddenly grown a second head that was even crazier than the first. Then, miraculously, he sighed. "Alright," he said, as if in resignation. "I'm in. But you are one crazy-ass white girl."

I felt myself beaming back at him as I answered, "Apparently that's what people love about me."

Over the next hour and half, my tiny, half-formed idea had sprouted wings and taken off as a full-blown, surprisingly respectable plan. Now, as DeAndre left the hideaway once more to take to the streets, he wouldn't just be carrying messages to the gang leaders, he could be carrying a message to everyone he met along the way.

In just under twenty-four hours' time, all of Luthertown Heights' bravest, most hopeful citizens would be joining us as we met with the leaders of the Uewatsu, the Crips, the Creepers, and the Sixes in Luthertown Heights' biggest park. That park had recently played host to a turf war, but now it would serve as a neutral zone, where no weapons were allowed, and respect and tolerance would be encouraged.

"This is crazy," I said, blowing air out through my lips as I paced our windowless haven/dungeon. "This is crazy! What are we doing? But it has to work. It *has* to."

Luca didn't answer. I got the feeling that he didn't believe in our plan so much as he believed in me, but that was good enough in my book.

"Let's see... what are we offering the Creepers again?"

"Two of the three graveyards," Luca said, watching me pace.

"Right. But we have to remember to say that they can't bother any of the mourners. Write that down."

"We already wrote that down, Annabelle. We already wrote everything down." There was an exasperated smile in his voice as he said, "Come sit with me. You are going to wear a hole in the floor."

I did as he said and sat down next to him on our cot. "Sorry, I'm just nervous. I feel so helpless, just sitting here waiting for DeAndre to come back! What if something goes wrong?"

"DeAndre can take care of himself." Luca wrapped his arms around me and kissed my temple.

"Yeah, but this isn't just your average, everyday trip through the city! He'll be approaching every gang leader in town! Alone!"

"First of all, he will be approaching their contacts, not the leaders directly." He kissed me again. "And second of all, the Uewatsu are probably tearing up the streets looking for us. If we would have gone with him, we would have just made him a target. He is better off on his own."

I sighed, resting my cheek against his shoulder. "That's not very reassuring..."

"Annabelle, everything will be okay. You will see."

"You don't think I'm crazy?" My voice was much smaller and weaker than I had intended it to be, and I felt my cheeks redden.

Luca lifted my chin with his fingers, so that he could look me in the eye. He was smiling, his beautiful, green eyes aglow, and I was overcome with the conviction that nothing else mattered more in the entire world than the light in those eyes, and that I would not, could not, let it go out. Ever.

"Everything will be alright," he repeated in his low, hoarse voice. Then he kissed me, letting his lips linger on mine for a long, slow moment that I wished would last forever.

"I do have a question, though..." he said pulling back much too soon for my liking.

"Okay, what is it?"

"If everything gets cleared up in Luthertown Heights, are we still going to leave?"

I considered it for a minute, allowing some of the love dust to settle in my foggy brain. "I hadn't really thought that far ahead," I said finally. "I guess not. But I don't know. Like I said, I don't want to leave the kids... Why? What do you want to do?"

He ran his thumb across my left eyebrow, tickling my eyelashes as he continued down my cheek. "I want to be with you," he said, sounding so sincere that it made my heart swell in my chest. "But I am afraid that if we stay here, you will go back to your apartment and your job and your life, and I will have to go back to... whatever the hell it is that I decide to do with myself after this."

"Luca!" I said, sitting up straight to gape at him in shock. "How could you think something like that? After all we've been through!"

He gave me a melancholy smile. "This is wartime, Annabelle. Relationships formed during a war hardly ever last, even if both parties live. War is an exceptional time, when all of the rules change."

"What are you talking about?"

"Just think about it. If I had not walked you home that first night to keep you safe from Bear, you would never have spoken to me. You would have just been afraid of me like everyone else. We never would have talked, we never would have touched, we never would have kissed, we never would have fallen in love. Well, you wouldn't have, anyway. Not with me."

"What does that mean?"

"It means that I am pretty sure that I have been in love with you for months now, but I know you never would have given me a second glance if it had not been for this war. And you shouldn't have. I did not deserve it. I am not sure I do no–"

I cut him off by taking his warm, scarred face in my hands and kissing him hard, wanting him to stop talking, wanting to make his words ring less true. Was he right? Would I have spoken to him if he hadn't walked me home that night? Would we have ever really met? I knew that I had been intrigued by him from a distance, but at what point does intrigue become attraction? Does that attraction become love? Does that love become the one thing you live and breathe and hope and die for?

He kissed me back, just as forcefully, and I felt my panic give way to a certainty that blotted out all of the doubts he had just raised. "None of that matters now," I said breathlessly, wrapped in his arms as I stared up into his eyes. "None of that hypothetical stuff matters. We did meet, we were meant to meet, and what I feel now matters. I love you, Luca, and I'm not going anywhere. Not without you. Not ever again."

He stared back at me for a long time, like a thirsty man drinking in all the water he could before the well dried up. Then he kissed me again, slowly, carefully, thoughtfully this time, before murmuring, "That's all I need to know."

Forty-Eight

Even aside from Luca gently kissing me awake every two hours, I slept fitfully. The night seemed to drag on forever. No matter how many times I checked the clock on the wall, it was no closer to dawn, and we were no closer to the end of our journey.

On any other occasion, I would have relished an infinite night of lying beneath a blanket with Luca, but I had too much on my mind to savor the moment that time. Luca himself, though, appeared to be seeping peacefully beside me, his breaths long and slow, deep and reassuringly calm, and I wondered how he managed to wake up every two hours on the dot without the aid of an alarm clock.

With nothing else to do, I just lay there under the florescent lights, listening to him breathe, feeling the rise and fall of his muscular chest beneath mine, thinking about all the things that could go wrong tomorrow between gory dreams of little boys with paper crowns and bullet wounds the size of craters.

My plan had energized me before, but now, in the heart of the night, deep beneath the violent city above, I realized that I was risking the lives of everyone I knew, and many that I didn't. I would be a fool to trust that the gang leaders wouldn't bring their weapons – or backup. And I was a bigger fool already for encouraging DeAndre to let innocent citizens in on the danger.

Why had I done that? Why had I decided that hope lay with people I didn't remotely believe in anymore? The people who had let me get attacked and left for dead in the street? Was I insane to think that maybe there was something under the surface of those silhouettes that had watched idly from behind the shades of their apartment as the city ran rampant with crime outside?

I turned over, putting my back against Luca's chest as I clutched the frame of the bunk. I had been wrong about Miss Carmella, that's why I had changed my mind. I had been wrong about DeAndre too. Luca and I weren't the only people in the city who had souls. Deep down, other people wanted to do the right thing too – they just needed a reason to do it, and the motivation to take that risk. If I was right (and I hoped to God that I was), the citizens of Luthertown Heights wanted change as much as we did. They just needed someone to reignite the dying embers of hope they had inside them.

"You should be sleeping," Luca murmured in my ear, his voice slow and drowsy.

I pulled his hand up to my chest and held it there, over my heart. "So should you."

"As far as I know, I have been dreaming for the past three days. So I am pretty sure that I am already asleep."

I let out a breathy chuckle. "You sure talk a lot in your sleep, then."

"And *you* sure think a lot in yours. Your entire body is tense. It is like lying next to a statue."

"Sorry." I gave my limbs a shake and tried to relax.

"Do not be sorry," he replied, kissing the nape of my neck. "Do you want to talk about it?"

"No." I turned back over so that I could snuggle against his chest. "I just want to sleep."

"Okay." He rested his head on top of mine, and I sighed

deeply, inhaling the scent of him with my next breath. "But I am here if you need me."

"I know." A smile was still on my lips as I drifted off at last into a soothing, dreamless slumber.

By 10:00 a.m. the next morning, DeAndre still hadn't returned.

Luca assured me that he was fine, that he had probably just spent the night in his newspaper nest or in some other alley, so as not to draw attention to the sanctuary, but I wasn't buying it. My gut was churning with more than just last night's greasy burgers, and I knew something terrible had happened.

"I can't take it anymore, Luca. We have to get out of here and go check on him!"

I was pacing again, feeling like a caged animal trapped down there with no windows, no natural light, and absolutely no idea what was going on in the world above us. I felt claustrophobic, like the limestone walls were closing in on me, squeezing the life out of me as it got harder and harder to breathe.

"We can't," Luca replied, made miserable by my distress. "This is the only place we are safe."

"What good is being safe if I just sent someone else out there to die for me?" I shouted, finally coming to a stop as I mashed my fists into my forehead. Luca was right – if we left too long before the planned meeting at 5:00 p.m., there was a very good chance we would never make it there. But I had already seen so much death –

caused so much death from my own inattention – that I couldn't live with myself if DeAndre was hurt too.

Luca stood up and crossed the room on his long, limber legs, as quiet as the shadow he was when I first met him. He removed my fists from my forehead, and held my hands in his as he said solemnly, "We will leave at noon."

Fifty

I thought that maybe we would spend the next two hours making out or making love or making whispered declarations of passion; doing things we had never done before, and might never do again. I thought maybe we might pass the time by saying all of the things we might not get a chance to say if things didn't go the way we planned. But that all made it seem too final. It was too much like admitting we had already lost. I was no longer so sure of my plan, and I had never been sure that Luca and I would make it out of Luthertown Heights alive, but those were things I didn't want to think about. Not yet. Not ever, if I could help it.

So, we filled the time by going over our plan again, holding each other close, thinking of nothing but our peace talk strategies, and hoping, deep down, that DeAndre would show up with some good news before we set out to face the world again.

At 11:45, Luca's bag was packed and slung across his taut, muscular chest, and I was wearing a small, black, drawstring backpack I had found in the medicine cabinet and filled with first aid supplies and all the notes I had made. There was a scalpel in the pocket of my borrowed leather jacket that I prayed I wouldn't have to use, and Luca's gun was tucked into the back of his waistline, as if he were the one in a gangster movie now.

When the big hand hit twelve on the rusty silver clock in that damp, mildewy cave, we officially stopped being citizens, and became soldiers.

Hand in hand, we left the bunker for the battlefield.

The city was silent as we emerged from the catacombs beneath it. The air was damp with oncoming rain (the streets were already wet from last night's shower: Luca's prediction had been right), and the clouds above were hanging low and grey and heavy.

Not a single car engine hummed, not a single child yelled out across the concrete schoolyard at recess. Not a single daytime hooker flaunted her wares as she sauntered from corner to corner, enticing someone to stop her.

There were no lights on in the buildings we passed. There were no faces at the windows. There were no signs of life anywhere in sight, aside from Luca walking, tall and tense, at my side.

In the past few weeks, I had seen the streets of Luthertown Heights empty. But this was beyond empty. This was eerie. This was lifeless.

This was dead.

"Where is everyone?" I whispered. The silence pressing in on us made even the sound of my breathing seem deafening. It was as if the Apocalypse had come while we were in the bunker, and we had missed it.

"I have no idea," Luca replied. His raspy voice was even quieter than mine. His face was hardening, his worry lines smoothing out into that blank mask he wore to hide his insecurities, to hide himself, and I felt my own chest tighten with dread.

I had never felt as exposed and vulnerable as I did while we walked slowly toward Luthertown Park. We would be hours early, but we had nowhere else to go, and standing still in that barren wasteland for even a second was enough to drive even the calmest person insane with paranoia.

We passed the YMCA, where I had once taught the town's children not to fear their differences, but to have faith in their fellow humans. We passed the corner where I had thought DeAndre lived, alone and strung out, with no one to talk to but a silly white girl who kept trying to save him. We passed the liquor store where the old men used to stand around a barrel fire and shout hellos and wave to me. We passed a fruit stand where the vendor used to give me a free apple sometimes, because he knew I was a teacher.

I slowed as we passed Marcus' apartment building too, half-expecting to see his little round face beaming out at me from the second story window, assuring me that he was safe, and that I didn't have to worry.

My heart grew heavy as I realized that this could be the last time I saw any of these places, and that now, when my time there was running low, the only thing I could remember about the people I had met in Luthertown Heights was not that they had abandoned me, but that they had all, at one time or another, made me smile.

I closed my eyes and took a deep breath, saying a silent prayer as I squeezed Luca's hand in mine. I wasn't quite sure what I was praying for - Peace? Safety? Redemption? – but I wished for it with all of my swollen, battered heart.

The first raindrops began to pepper our faces when we were about fifteen minutes away from the park. The sky had darkened even more, making the street lamps come on, and plunging us into an unnatural twilight.

Luca and I had barely spoken a word as we had walked that last mile, hand in hand, but suddenly, as the tall oak trees of the park loomed large in the distance, it sounded as if he had begun to hum a tune.

Frowning, I turned to look at him. It was not in his nature to do something as lighthearted as hum – especially in the midst of a possible zombie apocalypse. But he was looking back at me with the same puzzled look I was giving him.

"What is that?" I whispered, spooked, as the humming grew louder. It was more like a murmuring now, like a television turned on at low volume behind a closed door.

"I don't know…" He had gone very pale. "Maybe we should turn back."

"We can't," I said, even though I wished very much that we could. "You can't hold back the wind, right?"

His jaw was clenched. The raindrops grew larger and the murmuring grew louder as we got closer to the park. The suspense was killing me; I could barely breathe through the lump of anxiety in my throat. Luca held my hand tighter and tighter, and I tensed up more and more until finally we turned the last corner, and the tension broke.

"Oh my God…"

As the grassy knolls of the sprawling park came into view, so did the answers to all of our questions. Huddled beneath the rusted streetlamps, strung out in wavy lines across the park's overgrown gravel walking paths, sitting under trees and on benches and swings, was the source of all the murmuring.

The entire town's population was gathered in Luthertown Park, all speaking in low, energetic voices as if they were waiting for something.

"They are waiting for you," Luca said, in a hushed, awestricken voice.

"They're waiting for *us*." I was blinking back tears as my heart overflowed with affection for the people I had been so afraid to believe in.

As we stood there, frozen, twenty yards from the gate, a voice called out, "They're here!," and all eyes turned toward us.

For a moment, the murmuring increased as the message was passed along. Then, like a cloud blotting out the sun, a hush fell over the crowd.

Trembling, I walked forward, my palm sweating against Luca's, and the sea of people parted to let us through. Everyone was watching us, each face wearing a different emotion. Some looked somber, solemn, even sad. Others looked curious, or even mildly excited by our presence. Still others, though, looked hopeful, and that was what kept me moving forward.

The fruit vendor who had given me the lemon smiled at me as I passed, and one of the old men from the liquor store waved at me. A few of the hookers winked, and a couple of the parents from my ASC class gave me curt, encouraging nods as they held their children to them – *my* children, the ones who would inherit the better world I was trying to create.

There was a wooden gazebo in the heart of the park. It was shaped like a hexagon, and had a roof full of holes. The crowd's path led us there, and I could see through the glittering drops of rain that there were three people sitting at the long, splintery picnic table inside, shrouded in shadow.

I hesitated at the foot of the gazebo, not sure what would happen when I crossed over the threshold. Luca, too, seemed reluctant to leave the safety of the huddled masses, and for a moment, we just stood there, irresolute.

Then, from out of the spotted darkness cast by the gazebo's broken roof, came a big, dark hand to take mine.

It had six fingers.

I had just enough time to be startled before I looked up into the face that went with it. It was just as dark as the hand – so black that it almost looked blue, like the sky at midnight. The face was attached to a bald head, and had a large nose and slightly protruding eyes, and a thick scar that curled its full upper lip. It was a face I had never seen before, but it was smiling at me, and I was flummoxed.

A second face appeared next to the first, this one more of a mocha brown, with a forehead covered by a folded blue bandanna. It, too, was smiling slightly, a crooked smile that seemed rusted with disuse, and it didn't seem bothered when a third face leaned in and said, "The spirits told us to come early."

This third face was black too, beneath a swath of white paint and intricate black and red makeup that made it look like a skeleton from *Dia de los muertos*.

That was when I finally figured out what was happening. DeAndre had done it: he had gotten our message to every gang, to every citizen in town...

And they had come.

Suddenly seized by some sort of insane brand of euphoria, I let go of Luca's hand and hugged the skeleton, eliciting a collective gasp from the crowd, followed by relieved-sounding chuckles as I hugged the other two gang leaders as well.

"I knew you had balls," said the six-fingered man as I let go of him, shivering with adrenaline and relief. "I just didn't know they were so big!"

Everyone laughed again (aside from Luca, who looked as if he were on the verge of a faint), and the three men led us inside, where we sat down at a cracked wooden table.

"You saved my men's lives," said the leader of the Sixes as he sat down across from Luca and me, wedged between the leader of the Crips on his right, and the leader of the Creepers to his left. "If you hadn't called in that exterminator to tent the place, we'd all be dead."

Luca shifted uncomfortably. This was not the best time to look like an Uewatsu – the only group absent from our peace summit.

"I... I'm glad everyone made it out safely," I choked, still finding it hard to breathe... and to believe that this conversation was actually happening. "But wait, how did you know it was me?"

"We didn't, until we got word that some crazy white girl was tryin' her damndest to keep the gangs from killin' each other. *And* she was doin' it in cahoots with a traitor Uewatsu. Who else could it 'a been?"

Luca's mask was fixed in place. He didn't react as all eyes turned to him.

"He *is* a traitor, right?" asked the Crips' leader. He sounded skeptical – and nervous. His right hand was fidgeting with something in his pocket, and I felt a knot form in my stomach at the realization that it was almost a given that no one at that table had honored our request that they leave their weapons at home.

Luca's jaw was clenched. He had reverted to his stoic, silent warrior mode, and I was on my own to answer questions.

"'Traitor' is kind of a negative word..." I said slowly, not liking the implications it carried. All three of the gang leaders leaned back, reaching for their pockets or their waistbands and I added quickly, "But he has severed all ties with the Uewatsu, yes! He wants to help us find a peaceful way to work out our differences."

"As an Uewatsu?" asked the Crip.

"As a human being," I replied firmly, remembering the speech I had given my ASC students about judging everyone as an individual.

The gang leaders seemed satisfied by that answer. "Okay," said the Sixes' leader, "so what's the plan?"

"Oh... uh... well, you see, I was thinking..." I started digging around in my pockets for the sheet of paper I had scribbled on. I felt flustered and nervous, and terrified that they would think I was searching myself for a weapon, but they all seemed calm and cool, since I was a fumbling white girl and not a big, bad Uewatsu. "Got it!" I said finally, holding up my folded notes as I pulled them from my backpack. My face was burning. "What I was thinking was that it might be a good idea to set up an established 'area' for each ga... er... group."

"So you're segregating us now?" The Sixes' leader sounded amused.

"No, no, no! Well... maybe." I sighed, chagrinned. "But not in a way that discourages intermingling. More like, in a way that gives everybody their own space, so there will be no reason to have to fight to keep your turf."

I glanced up to find that all three leaders were thinking it over. The Sixes' leader and the Crip looked intrigued. The Creeper, however, looked dubious.

"Man holds no domain over the living world," he said, in the mystical voice of a shyster fortune teller. "The land is not yours to give. If the spirits urge us to take a piece of land, we will take it."

"We're offering the Creepers the two main cemeteries and that empty field behind the morgue," I said flatly.

A surprised smile flitted across his painted face. Then, composing himself, the skeleton replied, "I think the spirits will find that satisfactory."

"Do the rest of you agree?"

The Six and the Crip glanced at each other, as if to confer. Then, realizing that they were of two separate creeds, they both turned back to me and shrugged.

"The land behind the morgue is full of potholes anyway," said the Crip, whose gang used to "own" that particular territory. "I think there's a sinkhole in the back corner."

The Creeper bolted upright and put his hands on the sides of his face like a teenaged girl at a boy band concert, and a small, white-painted subsection of the crowd around us squealed in excitement.

"So it's a deal, then?" I asked, taking out a clean sheet of paper and a pencil to draw up our makeshift contract.

"Deal," said the Creeper quickly, his eyes dancing as he thought about all the magical possibilities inherent in a sinkhole.

"Deal," said the others, shrugging again.

"Okay, great!" I beamed as I wrote it down. "But that means the Creepers also agree not to try to take any of the land from the other gangs, though, okay? You have to be content with what you have. And if someone wants to come to one of the cemeteries to visit their loved ones, you have to give them their space."

The Creeper found his followers in the audience, and like a contestant on *The Price is Right*, he waited for them to give him a sign. I glanced back to see them all nodding furiously (one of them was even jumping up and down), and he answered, "We're content, we're content."

"Perfect. Then sign here." I drew four crooked lines under the first condition in our contract, and he greedily took the pencil from me and signed his name.

He passed the pencil to the Six, who followed suit, then the Crip did the same. We left the fourth line empty for the Uewatsu leader, whom I was starting to hope would never show.

"Okay, now for the Crips. Does this say your name is..." I felt my stomach twist painfully. "Marcus?"

"Marco," he corrected, and my mixed visions of Marcus' punctured chest and smiling face faded a bit.

"Right, Marco." I cleared my throat to get my focus back, and Luca put his hand on my knee. I looked up to find myself still facing that stoic, silent profile, but his hand was warm and reassuring and supportive nonetheless, and it gave me back my strength.

"Marco, would you and the Crips be satisfied with keeping your current area around 37th Street?"

"I don't know, can you guarantee that the Sixes and the Uewatsu'll stop fightin' over it?"

He glanced at the Six, and I checked the paper for his name.

"Calvin? Do you think you can guarantee that the Sixes will leave that space to the Crips?"

Calvin Katz frowned, thinking it over. Unlike the Creeper

(who I'm pretty sure signed his name as "Lucifer666"), he didn't seek input from his fellow Sixes, reinforcing the idea that each and every one of these gangs had a different governing system, and a different set of values.

"I can guarantee that we'll stay off 37th Street..." he said slowly, "but only if you can guarantee that the Uewatsu don't get it either. We can't let them have more than us. And that land is on the border of our territory."

He looked expectantly up at Luca, who finally broke his silence. "I cannot speak for the Uewatsu," he said in a hoarse monotone. "I am not one of them."

"You *look* like one of them to me."

"Hey, let's stay focused here," I interrupted hastily, not liking Katz's accusatory tone. "If we can get the Uewatsu to agree to leave 37th Street to the Crips, can you promise the Sixes won't try to move in on that turf?"

Katz frowned deeply, his casual air of amusement long gone. "I guess," he said eventually. "But if the Uewatsu go there, the deal's off."

I looked to Marco, who seemed uncertain. "Marco?"

"All we want is that one block, man," he said, the words bursting out of him as if he had been struggling to hold them back for years. "Just dat one block. Dat's where the family is. We ain't got no beef wit nobody else, we just wanna survive! And we don't want these otha guys tryna work out *their* shit in *our* neighborhood! Or tryna make *us* fight for *their* causes! We ain't bad people, man! We just tryna live!"

Katz, for the first time, looked uncomfortable. Many times I had wondered what the Sixes had offered the Crips to get them to join in their fight against the Uewatsu three nights before, but now I wondered if maybe it hadn't been an offer they had given, but a threat.

"We can't make no promises like that," said Katz, almost apologetically.

"Then no deal." Marco stood up to leave.

I stood up too, and grabbed his wrist. "No! Wait, please! This is important. We have to figure this out. Calvin, come on, we need you to agree to this."

Marco was staring at my hand like it was a snake that was hissing at him, and Katz was staring at the table, looking conflicted.

"I can't do that..."

"Yes, you can! What Marco and the Crips want is the same thing you and the Sixes want – it's what we *all* want: to feel safe in our neighborhoods with our own families and friends! That's why we're all here!"

I gestured around at the crowd, standing there, huddled in the rain, hoping for change, and Katz let out a heavy sigh.

"Fine, dammit, fine. The Crips can have 37th Street. No one gives a fuck about that place anyway."

I gave Marco a victorious smile, and he finally looked up from my hand to ogle at me in amazement.

I sat back down and scribbled out the second term in our agreement. All three leaders signed, but Katz kept the pencil when he had finished.

"But what do *we* get outta all this? The Sixes own half this town, and we're not gonna let you give it to someone else."

"'Own' is a strong word, don't you think?" We all jumped. My blood went cold as a low, seductive voice called out from the crowd.

We all frantically searched the faces around us, trying to find the source before it had time to strike us first. There was a collective gasp as suddenly six lines formed in the crowd. Six paths appeared, like six spokes to a wagon wheel, with us sitting exposed in the center, completely defenseless, as six hungry, smiling werewolves prowled toward us like the prey we were.

I didn't recognize five of the wolves, but the sixth one, the one whose path led right to me and Luca, wasn't a wolf at all.

It was a bear.

He limped as he walked, and his smug face was puffy with bruises and crusted with blood. His head was held high as his long hair blew back in the wind, exposing two purple handprints around his throat.

I felt the hands that made them close around my own wrists as Luca and I stood up. He pushed me behind him, blocking me with his body as his former tribe advanced, all decked out in their uniforms of war.

"I see you started without us," Bear said, stopping a few feet from the entrance to the gazebo. The rest of his pack followed suit, and the other gang leaders were on their feet, weapons in hand. We had led them into an ambush, and I had no idea how to save them now.

"You should've waited," he went on, licking his lips as he grinned at me. "I've got the solution to everything."

"Fuck off, you deerhumper," Katz muttered, and a shiver of foreboding went through the crowd of innocent townspeople.

"Don't you want to know my solution?" Bear asked me, keeping his eyes on my face, and my face only, as I peered around Luca's bicep.

"We do not want to hear anything from you," Luca growled. "Go home, Bear. Let us work this out in peace."

"But that's why I am here! I know the path to peace, Little Brother. And it starts by giving the land back to its native people."

"You can't have it," I said, wishing my voice didn't sound so tiny. "We've been dividing up the town fairly. You can have part of it, but Luthertown Heights as a whole belongs to everyone."

"Are you sure you don't want to reconsider?" He took a few steps loser, and my human shield turned to stone. "You could be the queen of this town, White Girl. And I will be the king." His eyes moved down to my chest as he licked his lips again, and a warning growl rose from Luca's throat.

"This town has no king," I said, my voice a bit stronger now, belying the cringing fear rippling beneath it at the memory of the terrible things Bear had done – and still wanted to do – to me. "We're splitting it up, fair and square. You can't scare us into giving you anything."

"I thought maybe you would say that. That is why I have a plan B."

My stomach clenched as he snapped his fingers, and two more Uewatsu emerged from the crowd and dragged a man up the aisle, stopping at the foot of the gazebo. They forced the ragged man to his knees, and there was a glint of metal as one Uewatsu held a machete to his throat, and the other forced his head back.

I clapped my hands over my mouth to cover my scream as DeAndre stared up at me, his face pale and his eyes full of fear.

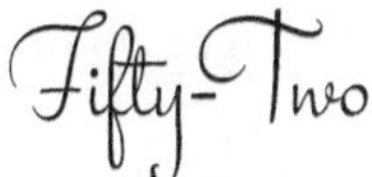

"Let him go." Luca's voice was hard and clipped. It was an order, not a request.

DeAndre's Adam's apple bobbed as he swallowed, wincing against the sharp edge of the machete blade resting against his skin.

"I will." Bear gave me a sick, wicked grin, taunting me. "But only if I get what I want."

I saw movement out of the corner of my eye, and felt my tortured spirit sink as several people on the outskirts of the crowd began to scatter. They wanted unity in their city, sure, but they didn't want to play witness to a murder for it, and I didn't blame them.

Still, though, I was seized by a desperate sort of panic as I realized we were losing the crowd. We were losing whatever support we had had amongst the townspeople, and soon my not-so-brilliant plan would crumble, and we would lose the city itself to that gruesome band of jackals.

"What do you want?" Calvin Katz demanded. I hadn't heard him move, but he had come around the picnic table and was now standing at my side. Marco and Lucifer666 followed suit, and the five of us stood together, shoulder to shoulder, to face the beast and the horrified crowd.

"I told you, I want Luthertown Heights for the Uewatsu. It is our land. The Cherokee tribe used to live on it two hundred years ago, before the white people stole it from us and sent us to live on that reservation. Our father fought and died to get it back for us. It is our birthright."

"So you're going to kill everyone else who lives on it, or send them away like the white people sent away your ancestors?" I said, stepping out from behind Luca to face him head on. My legs were trembling beneath me and the lump on my skull pulsed with the same panic that was flooding through my heart, but I stood tall as I demanded, "Where's the justice in that?"

I heard a few mutters of "yeah!" and "that's right!" from the crowd and felt a surge of hope. Maybe we weren't losing them after all. Maybe they were made of stronger stuff than I gave them credit for.

Maybe we all were.

"Justice is for movies and superheroes," Bear chuffed, mocking me with another toothy grin. "There is no such thing as justice in Luthertown Heights."

"There is today," said a voice to my right.

I flinched as Katz raised a pistol at my side and flipped back the safety. The barrel was aimed right between Bear's eyes.

"Wait, no!" I said, reaching up to grab his wrist, trying to force his arm back down. "That's not what we're about!"

"That might not be what *you're* about," said Marco, the Crips leader, cocking his own Glock, "but we ain't about to let this asshole kick us around anymore."

"Stop, put the guns down! We—"

"Let 'em do it." DeAndre's voice came out as a guttural croak. "It's the only way to stop 'im."

"No! Everybody stop, please!" I shouted, as the crowd took a collective step back. "We're trying to start fresh here! We're trying to solve our differences peacefully!"

Bear let out a long, low laugh. "Poor, poor White Girl," he said between chuckles, not fazed in the slightest by all the guns pointed at him. "You are so naïve. You think you can come in here and 'save' us all? You think you can stop this war all by yourself?"

"She is not by herself," said Luca, his words strong and hoarse and full of conviction. "Look around you, brother. These people want freedom, not your tyranny."

A muttering arose in the crowd, and the mass of bodies shimmered in the rain as dozens of people nodded in agreement.

"Let DeAndre go and we will find a compromise," Luca continued.

Bear stepped forward. He ran his hand over the veteran's stubbly skull, feigning thoughtfulness. "Alright..." he said slowly, as DeAndre closed his eyes. "I have a counter offer."

My gut turned to lead. This was not going to be good.

"The Uewatsu will settle for our original territory, from 7th Street to 19th Street. The Sixes and these other worms can have the rest. We will stay on our turf, never to be heard from again... under one condition."

His eyes locked on mine, and he flashed the perverted smile I now knew so well.

"No." Luca was shaking his head. "No. No, no deal."

"What does he want?" asked Lucifer the Creeper, lost.

"He knows." Bear grinned maliciously, nodding at Luca. "Don't you, little brother?"

Luca tried to shove me behind him, but I planted my feet. I was terrified, more afraid than I had ever been in my life, but I couldn't let him get to me, not again.

And anyway, I wondered, with an odd sort of hysterical detachment, did one idealistic white girl's life really amount to that much in comparison to the greater good?

"He wants the girl," DeAndre choked around the blade.

"That's all he wants. That's what he told the rest of 'em –" he cut off with a hiss as one of his captors pressed the machete more firmly into his neck, and a dribble of bright red blood slipped down into the collar of his many layers of sweatshirts.

"The trash heap is right," Bear announced, as if he were on stage now. "You give me the girl and I will let him go. I will let you *all* go. The Uewatsu will disappear. Your precious city will be safe."

"No," said Luca. His face was paler than I had ever seen it. His scar stood out like a smear of violet paint on his cheek, and his fiery emerald eyes were filled with fear.

"What do you want her for?" asked Katz, as if he were considering his offer and needed more information before he came to a decision.

"What the fuck do you *think* he wants her for?" Luca snarled, losing his grip on that calm, stoic mask he wore.

"Stop, everybody, just... just stop." My voice rang out, brittle and high-pitched, in the damp autumn air.

"See? She *wants* to come," Bear said, leering at me. "She wants to be a martyr for this shithole town, and all of its shithole people." He paused to throw me a wink. "And, if you ask me, I think she also wants a taste of my big, hard –"

What happened then, I will never fully understand.

Just as Bear was reaching for his crotch to make me an obscene gesture, a fist came out of the sea of innocent bystanders and clocked him in the jaw.

Before he could react, six more hands had grabbed him, and were pulling him, kicking and screaming, into the undulating crowd.

More hands reached out to take hold of the foot soldiers who were holding DeAndre, and the machete fell to the sidewalk with a clatter as they were dragged away too.

Luca rushed forward to pull DeAndre into the safety of the

gazebo, and we all watched as the once-silent crowd came to life, crying out for vengeance, roaring with power.

"THIS IS *OUR* TOWN!" bellowed a voice I didn't recognize, as the Uewatsu were wrested into submission and dragged toward the swing set on the other side of the park.

"OUR TOWN! OUR TOWN!" The others took up the chant, and I was filled with a frightening mixture of pride and dismay as the people finally reacted, and finally took back their city.

"NO MORE! NO MORE!" The chant changed as twelve Uewatsu in total were rounded up and pressed together under the confines of a rusted, eight- by fifteen-foot jungle gym dome.

I moved closer to Luca, not sure whether to follow the charge or run away, and he put his arm around me, looking just as conflicted as I felt.

A part of me was sure they would kill the Uewatsu, and a smaller part of me almost hoped they would, because I knew DeAndre was right: that it was the only way to really, truly stop Bear. A bigger part of me, though, was afraid of what the crowd would do now that it had morphed into something more akin to a lynch mob.

The townspeople had risen up to rescue me – little, insignificant, unremarkable white girl Annabelle Fitzpatrick – and I would forever be grateful for that. It was all I had wanted since that night when Bear attacked me the first time – I wanted them to defend me, to help me, to be there when I needed them. I had wanted them to *care*, and they did now, they did it fiercely. But I couldn't bear it if twelve people's lives were lost so that I could live in the city's warm embrace.

Without a word, I darted out of the gazebo and into the throbbing crowd. I shoved my way past men I knew, women I didn't, and children who never should have been there, all shouting "NO MORE! NO MORE! NO MORE!," whipped into a frenzy by their righteous rage. I could hear Luca's voice amidst the din, calling out my name, but I didn't stop. I couldn't. I kept catching glances of the Uewatsu tribe members, crammed under the jungle gym like animals trapped in a cage, their eyes wide and wild as the crowd pelted them with insults and chants and threats. I had always thought of them as wolves, as jackals, as fierce, rabid dogs, ever since the night they had attacked me, but they weren't. For better or worse, they were human beings, just like the rest of us, and they deserved justice too.

"Stop," I panted, when I finally made it through the crowd and emerged into a small ring of emptiness around the jungle gym, clutching a stitch in my side as my swollen brain swam in my skull.

I had spoken quietly, but my voice had reached the ringleaders nonetheless. A hush fell over the lynch mob once more, broken only by the sound of thudding feet as Luca found his way to my side.

"What are you doing?" he rasped. "Are you trying to get yourself killed?"

"We can't do this," I replied, pointing at the cage full of frightened men. "They're not animals. *We're* not animals." I raised my voice so everyone could hear me. "This isn't right."

"They want to kill you!" someone shouted.

"Yeah! They wanna kill all of us!"

"They deserve to die!"

"No, they deserve to go to prison!" I shouted back, clenching my fists. "This isn't the Wild West, we shouldn't be taking the law into our own hands! And we sure as hell shouldn't be killing people to stop them from killing *other* people! That just leads to a cycle of death. Is that what you want? An eye for an eye? A head for a head?"

The crowd shifted uncomfortably.

"I used to do housekeeping for Miss Carmella Washington," I said, plucking up my courage as my heart began to spill out in words. "I think a lot of you knew her. She used to talk about how she met Martin Luther King, Jr. once. She told me it was like meeting Jesus and Elvis and Luther Vandross all rolled into one."

A few people laughed nervously.

"Luca painted a picture of him on the wall of his apartment." I took his hand. "He put a speech bubble over his head that said 'I have a dream.' But that's not my favorite quote from him. My favorite one says this: 'Darkness cannot drive out darkness; only light can do that. Hate cannot drive out hate; only *love* can do that.'"

There was more shuffling in the crowd, more nodding, more repentant-sounding muttering.

"We can't end the violence in Luthertown Heights by committing more acts of violence. We have to find a different way. A better way. A more peaceful way. That's why I set all this up in the first place – to try to find some new strategy for solving our problems and bringing this community together. Maybe this wasn't the right way to go about it, I don't know. But I had to do *something*. Somebody did! I don't want to die in this town, and I don't want to be afraid to live in it either. I'm sure the same goes for all of you guys too. And for them." I nodded at the Uewatsu captives. "I want the kids in this town to grow up believing that people are good at heart, not that they should have to carry a knife in their pocket when they walk to school. I want them to see people as *people*, not as colors or enemies or gang members. I want them to feel safe and loved and hopeful and free! Isn't that why you all came to this park today? To be free?"

I was on the verge of tears when I finished my speech, and Luca squeezed my sweaty hand as the crowd rose up and shouted, "FREEDOM!"

This was the moment I had dreamt of, the one I doubted would ever come. The whole city was chanting, cheering for me, letting my hopeful message give them wings so they could fly out and over the mess their predecessors had made of that town. They were safe now, they were whole, and it was all because I had never stopped trying to change the world for the sake of those kids at the ASC.

A few people disentangled themselves from the crowd and moved to the jungle gym. The Uewatsu cringed under the dome of their iron cage, but then a woman I didn't know with hair that hung down to her knees held out her hand.

I began to cry as one of the skittish Uewatsu took it, hesitantly, cautiously, and allowed her to help him out through one of the large, diamond-shaped holes in the metal structure.

More people held out their hands, more of the Uewatsu took them, and one by one, they were all released from their cage, except for the one who had started it all.

Bear was sitting, cross-legged in the wet dirt, squinting slightly in the heavy drizzle. His face was calm, placid – a mask, much like Luca's. He wasn't calculating or scheming or devising another clever plan to take over the city or cut off my "tittaays," he was just sitting there, defeated.

"What do we do with him?" someone asked from the crowd, sounding as if he were a dead rat she had found in a trap in her attic.

"Send him to jail?" someone suggested.

The free Uewatsu members were watching their leader with worried expressions. They, too, were traitors now: they had betrayed him as soon as they had accepted the proffered olive branch from the crowd.

Bear's black eyes slid up to mine. I expected to feel the familiar jolt of fear as his gaze locked on mine. I expected to remember the way his rough, grabbing hands had felt as they clawed at me, or the panic that had overtaken me at the thought that I would never escape his wrath.

I felt none of those things, though. As I stared right back into the empty, soulless depths of his eyes, I felt only one thing: pity.

There was a collective "shhh!" as I slowly moved toward the jungle gym. I felt Luca's reluctant hand clench into a fist around mine, wanting to hold me back, but knowing that he couldn't, not now. This was what I had been striving for. The city wasn't the only thing that needed peace. I did too.

When I reached the iron cage, I stuck my hand through the bars.

Bear's eyes narrowed slightly as he searched my face for sincerity, just as Luca had four days and a hundred years ago. The rain made a dull sizzling sound as it spattered against my leather jacket and his cowhide vest; it was the only sound in the entire seven-acre park.

Finally, just as I was beginning to doubt my own courage and sanity, Bear's big, rough hand closed around mine.

A few people clapped nervously as he got to his feet and climbed out through the hole. The others just watched, stuck between amazement and foreboding as the head werewolf drew himself up to his full height in front of me, his thick, barrel-like chest just inches from mine.

"I underestimated you, White Girl," he said, no longer trying to seduce me with his velvety voice.

"Does... does this mean it's over?" asked one of the men from the liquor store.

"It is over." Bear nodded, his eyes still locked onto mine. "The Uewatsu will stop our killing. We will take the land you give us."

I couldn't believe it.

I could not even fathom that Bear, my mortal enemy, the antithesis of everything good and right and innocent, was agreeing to our contract.

A shocked, semi-grin spread across my face as I looked up at him. "You won't regret this," I told him, praying he would keep his promise.

Finally, his eyes left mine and moved to Luca's. I was holding both of their hands now, linking them back together, forming a bridge over the rift I had caused between them.

For one brief, beautiful moment, I thought I had fixed everything. Not only had I saved the town, but maybe, just maybe, I had salvaged Luca's relationship with his family too.

Then I saw that old, familiar smile return to Bear's face, and I knew I had been fooling myself all along.

"I just hope you can forgive me, little brother," he said, in the slickest, slimiest, most shamelessly arrogant voice he could muster.

Then he pulled out a knife from behind his back and stabbed me in the chest.

I was too stunned to scream, so the crowd did it for me as Bear withdrew the long, bloody silver blade and I dropped to my knees.

I could feel the wetness of the grass seeping through my jeans as a hoarse yell followed me down. I clapped my shaking hands over the hole just above my left breast, and I felt dizzy as I saw that my fingers were instantly drenched with blood.

For a second, my vision was fuzzy with shock. I could see nothing but a blurred expanse of grey-brown earth before my eyes. Then Luca's face appeared, inches from mine, his eyes more green than I had ever seen them, and his once-copper skin the color of dirty mop water.

He took my face in his hands, those bright, panicked eyes boring into mine, then he looked down at my blood-soaked sweatshirt and coat.

I wanted to ask him how bad it was, and if I was dying, but I was afraid to know the answers. The crowd wasn't screaming anymore, it was running, rushing, scattering. This was it. It was over. My big plan had seemed so promising just a few seconds ago, but now everything I had been working to fix was lost. All of it.

Luca's eyes flashed back to mine, and they were full of rage.

Before I could stop him, he leapt to his feet with a primal, savage roar, and he sprang at his brother, catching him off guard. Bear tumbled to the ground, sending his dagger flying, and I was repulsed by the sound of his laughter as Luca pummeled him with his fists.

In the meantime, the world began to spin around me. I was finding it harder and harder to draw breath. Each inhale was ragged, and each exhale came with a wet, squelchy sputter.

Luca was growling and spitting like an animal as he clawed at his brother, ripping him to shreds with his bare hands, exacting a revenge that would surely mean nothing to me in a few moments.

I started to cry as I found that my breath was barely coming at all now. I tried to call out to Luca but only managed to cough up a mouthful of blood. There was a searing pain across my chest that was nothing compared to the sharp, crushing pressure inside of it. Black specks began to appear at the edges of my vision, and I struggled to stay conscious, to stay upright, so that I could take one last look at the mess I had made.

"Are you finally going to kill me, little brother?" Bear taunted though busted lips, after spitting out a few teeth at his side.

"Yes, I am," Luca growled back. He was livid, more beast than man, as he ripped off the rope from around his neck and wrapped it around his brother's. As I watched helplessly, he was becoming what the Uewatsu had wanted him to be all along.

A monster.

"Stop!" I tried to scream, not wanting him to prove the rumors right, not wanting him to give in to the darkness within himself, within all of us, but nothing came out but more blood. I tried again.

"*STOP!*" That time the voice was louder, but it wasn't mine.

I heard the thunder of running feet as a figure raced past me, his sneakers squeaking against the wet grass. "Stop, man! Let go!"

Blinking hard to combat the ever-thickening veil of blackness, I felt my blood-glazed mouth fall open as I realized who it was.

Lamont.

My most reluctant student, the pupil I wasn't sure I would ever get through to, the boy Luca had given our only means of transportation to save, was trying to pull the two bigger men apart. Tears were flooding his face as he shouted, "This ain't right! This ain't what she wants!"

Bear shoved upward and caught him in the gut with a kick that sent him sprawling across the lawn. As he fell, a silver pistol flew out of his back pocket, the same one he had aimed at Luca last night. It landed a few feet in front of me.

Lamont didn't notice. Without missing a beat, he fought his way back into the scuffle, in which Bear had gained the upper hand. He had somehow flipped himself over and was now kneeling on Luca's stomach as he held a second pistol to his head.

"I told you she was mine," he grinned, spitting blood, just like me. "You should have just given her to me when I told you to. But instead you let me down. You let everyone down. Again. You are nothing, little brother. You are trash. Always have been. You are a disgrace to the family name. That is why Father always hated you."

Lamont was trying his damndest to pull Bear off of Luca, but his skinny arms were no match for the massive wall of muscle that was Yonv.

"He tried to make you into a man, but you will never be one. You are not even man enough to kill the guy who tried to do your bitch! You are worthless, little Luca. You know it, I know it, and *she* knows it. And that will be the last thing on your mind when you leave this world, right along with her."

There was a click as he flicked back the safety on his gun. Luca turned his head and his wide, green eyes met mine one last time.

Then the gunshot rang out across the park.

Lamont let out a curse and leapt away as Bear tipped to the side and fell like a stone to the ground.

I could barely see the hole in his temple as my vision blurred and I dropped the gun, letting it fall back into the grass where I had found it.

My fingers felt slick and numb as the heavy weapon left them, and I swayed, crashing down, face-first, into that same wet grass.

It had taken all my remaining strength to crawl those two feet to that gun, and it had taken everything I had to pull that trigger and save the man who had given up his whole world for me.

"Annabelle? Annabelle!" His voice was raspy, hoarse, panicked, as he rolled me over and scooped me up into his arms. "No, no, no," he whispered as he saw the leaking slit in my chest, and heard my ragged, labored breathing. "No, no, no," he repeated, clutching me tightly to him with one hand, caressing my forehead and stroking my hair with the other. "Annabelle, no..."

My lung had collapsed, I was sure of that now. Just like Marcus'. I couldn't draw any air, I couldn't push any out. I was suffocating under the weight of my own bodily fluids. I was going to die in Luca's arms, just as Marcus had died in mine.

"Stay with me, Annabelle, stay with me," Luca said through gritted teeth. All I could see now were his eyes, those beautiful, iridescent, emerald green irises, burning in the darkness, burning for *me*. My own eyes rolled back in my head of their own accord and he shook me, hard.

"No!" he choked. "No! Annabelle, please! Don't leave me. I need you! You promised me!"

I couldn't feel my body anymore. I couldn't catch my breath. I couldn't speak. All I could think about was how much I wanted to tell him that I loved him, and how much I wanted to beg him not to ever give in and let the world make him hard and jaded and hopeless like everyone else.

But I couldn't.

I made one last sputtering, gurgling sound, and he pressed his forehead to mine, pleading with me to hold on.

Then the darkness overtook me, and for the first time in fifteen long, hard, devastating years, Luca cried.

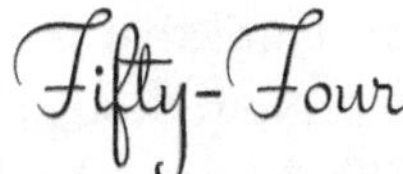

"Miss Annabelle! Miss Annabelle! Look what I made for you!"

I smiled and held out my hands as Marcus ran toward me. He had made me a paper necklace to go with my paper crown, and he giggled with delight as I put it around my neck, taping it together behind the collar of my leather jacket.

"Another masterpiece!" I declared, making a big show of marveling over the crayon-colored jewels on the thick, lopsided circle of construction paper.

We were sitting in the basin of the swimming pool in the waterpark, on a faded comforter I had brought from Luca's apartment. There were sheets of paper strewn across the concrete, all covered in Marcus' adorable attempts to recreate the Sistine Chapel-esque artistry beneath us. As cute as his wobbly tree trunks and chubby birds were, though, Marcus' Crayola creations couldn't hold a candle to Luca's.

Still smiling, I traced one of the pink orchids with my finger, stroking its stem lovingly as it looped up and around a branch the way that only wild orchids do. The colors seemed richer that day, more vivid, almost as if they were buzzing, pulsating with life.

"Did I tell you that I know the artist who painted all this?" I asked Marcus, as he placed a second paper hat on his head – this one more like the papal mitre.

Marcus nodded. "You said he's the one who painted the door outside the Y for you. You said you used to love him."

"Used to?" I frowned. Until that moment, the day had been bright, beautiful and sunny. Now, though, a soft shadow fell across my lap as a small cloud drifted past in the sky overhead.

"Yeah. You said you broke your promise. So you must not love him anymore."

The calm, tranquil feeling I had been relishing began to curdle as the shadow over me grew darker, and the one inside my mind grew thicker.

"What did you say?"

"I *said*..."

But that wasn't right either, was it?

I had never told Marcus anything about Luca. And he had never, in the entire time I had known him, said anything.

Except once.

There was a crackle of thunder as the clouds multiplied and covered the sky, blotting out the sun and plunging us into an eerie, early twilight.

With shaky hands, I reached up to touch the paper crown on my head.

"What's wrong, Miss Annabelle? You don't like it?"

My eyes darted back to Marcus. His own brown eyes were wide and innocent, staring out of his round, pudgy face, but there was a flower of blood on his sky blue polo that bloomed before my eyes, and began to spread.

"No..." I whispered. "No, not... not again..."

My memory was threatening to return; reality was struggling to set in, but I refused to accept it.

"Leave it on," said Marcus cheerfully, pointing to the hat that I now knew had been crumpled on the street two weeks ago. "You're my queen."

"Come here." I was starting to feel a pressure in my chest, and I pressed him to it, using his little round body like a warm compress to try to ward off the pain.

"What are you doin', Miss Annabelle?" He was giggling again as he hugged me back, his little hands barely meeting each other as he reached around my torso.

"You know that I love you, right?" I choked, as tears began to fall from my stinging eyes. I wasn't sure what was happening, but I knew I didn't have much time. "And you know that I'm sorry, right Marcus?"

He laughed that silly, infectious little laugh he always laughed, and I held him even tighter. "I know *that*, Miss Annabelle," he replied, as if I were being foolish.

"You do?" I sniffled, knocking off his papal hat as I rested my cheek against his short, wiry hair.

"*Everyone* knows that, Miss Annabelle." He sighed. "But I'm not sure I love you back anymore."

"What?" I held him out from me at arm's length, searching his face. "Why?"

As I watched, his big brown eyes turned green, and filled with the familiar, inscrutable flames of passion I had once wanted to lose myself in forever. "Because you broke your promise."

"What promise?"

"You said you would never leave." His voice seemed distant now, and rougher. Older. "You said you would never leave, but your body has been lying here in this bed for three days and your mind has gone somewhere far away."

"What the... what?"

Marcus' face was lightening, changing, fading, melting into an amorphous mass of shapes and colors and feelings that didn't make sense. My chest was aching, burning, and my limbs felt heavy as my head swam with pain.

"Wake up!" said the raspy voice that was no longer Marcus', but Luca's. "Wake up, Annabelle, I am begging you! Just please, please, open your –"

With a strangled gasp, I opened my eyes, staring up into Luca's face as I rejoined the living.

Fifty-Five

"I thought I had lost you," Luca murmured into my hair. I felt the familiar (if not faint for now) flutter in my stomach as his lips moved against my temple and he inhaled deeply, as if he were savoring the scent of *me* for a change.

My cheeks were slick with tears, but I was no longer sure whose they were as his tears mingled with mine and he stroked my face with his calloused fingers.

"How long was I out?" I winced at the effort it cost me to speak, but I was glad to feel the pain just the same. The pain meant I was awake. The pain meant I was alive.

"Three days. An eternity."

"That's right... you told me that. Or maybe Marcus did..."

Luca lifted his head to peer down at me. "You could hear me?"

"A little. I think. Toward the end. What did you say? What did I miss?"

He let out a soft, breathy chuckle. "I have been talking to you for almost seventy two hours straight," he said sheepishly.

My chest swelled for a different reason then, as I realized how much effort it must have taken him and his scarred larynx to keep talking for so long – and to keep his faith in me when he had already lost so many other people he cared about. "Oh. So I missed a lot then!"

He leaned his cheek into my palm as I reached up to touch his tousled curls. "You caught the most important part," he said, smiling, "the part that brought you back to me."

My head was heavy and my neck felt too weak to support it, but I lifted it up anyway, and pressed my lips to his.

"I love you," I whispered, as I lay back down, still stroking his hair, his face, his beard stubble. "I wanted to tell you that at the park, but I couldn't."

A tear slid down his tanned, scarred face, and his smile looked a bit pained, as if he were feeling so much that it hurt him. "You didn't have to tell me," he said, his voice breaking slightly. "I know you love me. And I know I love you. I did not even know what love was before you, but you taught me. You made me better. You taught me to care about people, and to believe in people... and in myself. You made me feel like maybe, possibly, I can be the type of man who deserves the love you give me. That is what I wanted to tell *you* at the park. Actually, that is what I have been telling you over and over for the past three days."

I tried to blink back a new rush of tears, but one slipped out anyway. Luca caught it on his thumb and wiped it away. I smiled as I said, "I think your last words were better than mine."

To my surprise, he let out a low, joyful laugh. "Well, I have had a few days to practice."

"I'm sorry I kept you waiting so long." He was stroking *my* face now, his long fingers skimming across my freckles as I closed my eyes. "And I'm sorry for... for what I did."

My mind was still a bit hazy, but that didn't stop the memory of the hole in Bear's temple from springing up, crisp and clear as the picture on an HD TV screen, behind my closed eyelids. The happiness I had been feeling just now, the gratefulness for Luca and for being alive, was suddenly blotted out by the crushing weight of guilt. The darkness had been almost blinding then, as I had struggled in vain to suck air into my deflated lung, but I had seen the dark, red-ringed hole. I had seen the fragments of skull and the spray of blood and brain matter come out the other side. And I had seen the look of pure, unadulterated shock on Bear's face as he realized, in that one fraction of a second, that he wasn't as untouchable as he had thought. He was no werewolf. He was a mortal creature after all.

I had spent six months preaching the values of compassion, and I had condemned any and all physical violence up to what might have been my very last breath, but I was a hypocrite. I had killed someone. I had taken a life. I was just as deplorable as Bear and the others like him.

"Do *not* apologize," said Luca firmly, squeezing my hand on top of my white cotton blanket. "Not for that. Never for that."

"But I *am* sorry," I replied miserably, too ashamed to open my eyes. "I spent the last three days telling you not to kill your brother, and telling the kids at the Y that killing is wrong, and convincing the townspeople that murdering someone is never the right thing to do, but then what do I do? I turn right around and –"

"Save my life." Luca's voice was softer now, and as guilty as I still felt, I couldn't resist the urge to open my eyes and catch a glimpse of the face that went with it.

His green eyes were warm and deep and full of fondness, and there was a slight smile on his face that made me remember exactly why I had pulled that trigger. I realized then that if I had the chance to do it all over, I would pull it again. I would do anything and everything I possibly could to keep that sweet, shy smile on his face, to keep that fire burning in his emerald eyes, and that was one thing I could never be ashamed of.

"What are you thinking?" He asked, when I hadn't spoken in several long, pensive moments.

I felt a faint twinge of a blush color my cheeks as I debated whether to tell him the truth or not. "I was thinking... Honestly, I was just thinking that no matter what happens to Luthertown

Heights now, no matter what happens in the whole entire world, I don't care. The only thing I can't live without is you."

Luca's eyes grew misty again as he leaned down to kiss my forehead. "You will never have to," he murmured, moving his lips against my skin. "I will never leave your side again as long as I live."

I was just tilting my head back to kiss him when I heard a knock at the door.

As if waking from another, much sweeter dream, I looked away from Luca and noticed my surroundings for the first time. I was in a small hospital room at St. Joseph's (I assumed) with a stained ceiling made of white-painted particle board and what looked like several rolls of white masking tape holding the tiles together.

Luca sat in a plastic chair beside my narrow bed, reaching under and over the metal bars on the side to hold me as I lay beneath a white crocheted blanket, much like the one his grandmother had worn at Waning Moon.

My curious eyes eventually made their way to the visitor at the open door, but before they got there, they took in a card table at the foot of my bed that was overflowing with flowers and packages and balloons. The flowers were scraggly and the cards looked homemade, and the balloons all said "Happy Birthday!" but that made me love them even more as I struggled into a more upright position to look at them, and to welcome my guest.

"Lamont!" I exclaimed, ignoring the pain in my chest as I did so. There was a pain in my upper torso as well, a sharp one, but I would look into that later.

"Hey, Miss Annabelle," answered Lamont, not moving. He was peeking around the doorjamb, toeing it with his sneaker as he bowed his head shyly.

"Lamont has been here every day since you were brought in," Luca told me, helping me prop myself up against my pillow.

"I came twice yesterday," he said, looking a bit embarrassed. "I had to leave and come back cuz there was a basketball tryout at school, and my pops said I could go. I thought you... well, I thought that's what you woulda wanted."

What I wanted was to cry... or to hug him with all of my might. "Of course that's what I want! How did you do? Did you make the team?"

"I won't find out 'til next Friday, but..." A smile brightened his melancholy face. "Coach said I've got a natural talent as a center. He said I could be the next Shaq."

"I knew it!" I beamed, clapping my hands. "Come in, come in! Tell me all about it."

"Well, I don't know, I was just..." He took one step into the room.

"What, you can visit me when I'm asleep but not when I'm awake?" I teased.

Lamont glanced at Luca, blushing beneath his healing bruises and cuts, and the latter took the hint.

With a big stretch, Luca got to his feet and announced, "I think I will go get a drink of water. I will be back in a minute, okay?"

My overworked heart ached at the thought of being without him for even a single second, but I nodded anyway, and he kissed me lightly on the lips before heading for the door. He patted Lamont on the shoulder as he passed him – a companionable, almost brotherly gesture – and I couldn't help but wonder what sort of conversation and understanding had passed between them as they had stood vigil at my bedside together.

Once Luca was gone, Lamont entered the room, and pulled a handful of flowers from behind his back. They were marigolds (suspiciously similar to the wild marigolds that grew in the vacant lot near the hospital) and I could smell their musky scent as Lamont approached.

"I know you already got a bunch of flowers," he said. That arrogant swagger he had once had was still miles away. "But I thought you might like these. They reminded me of a basketball."

"They're beautiful," I said, smiling as I took them and held them gently to my chest. "Thank you, Lamont."

He gave me a curt nod and looked around, as if getting up the nerve to say something. "Those flowers are from Janelle and her mamma." He made a sweeping gesture toward a garden of daisies, jonquils, and weeds on the table. "There's some from Patrice too, and Chyna. And that hobo dude, DeAndre. I think his might just be grass, though... And those balloons are from the guys from the liquor store. I think they got 'em for free cuz one of 'em's grand-daughter was havin' a party last week. The cards are from every-body in town. There's probably like fifty of 'em. I can help you read 'em later, if you want."

I was feeling a little choked up again, and he noticed. As quick as a flash, he raced to the bedside table and whipped out a tissue from a small cardboard box and handed it to me.

"Thank you," I said again, more touched than ever. "I'm sorry, I just didn't realize so many people... well, that so many people cared."

"Everybody cares," he replied, taking Luca's place in the chair at my bedside. "You're like the town hero."

That stuck a weird chord with me, and I shook my head. No, I was no hero. My plan had failed, and I had done the one thing I was begging everyone else not to do.

"You are," he insisted. "The gangs split up their turf, like you said, and there haven't been any murders at all for the past two nights."

"What? Are you serious?"

He nodded vehemently. "Even the Uewatsu agreed to stick around 19th Street. With their leader gone, the fight seems to've gone out of 'em. They have a new leader... some guy named Copper Moon or some shit like dat, but from what I hear, he ain't so bad."

He seemed heartened by this news, but I was stuck on another point. "Lamont, I want to apologize to you." My smile was gone now as I reached out to touch his wrist.

"To me? For what?"

"For what I did to Bear... and for putting you in that position. I hate that it happened, and I hate that it went against everything I was trying to teach you. It wasn't right."

"It wasn't right for dat fool to try to take out you and Luca either!" he exclaimed, as if my apology offended him. I felt something inside me swell with wonderment as I realized that he had just called Luca by his real name. Who was this kid? "And it wasn't right for him to try to ruin the good thing you were tryna do for the town! And it sure as *hell* wasn't right for him to stab you when all you was doin' was tryna help! You had no choice, Miss Annabelle, I know that. You didn't shoot 'im cuz you *wanted* to, you shot 'im cuz you had no other way to stop him. So don't you worry about settin' a bad example for me. I know right from wrong now. Thanks to you."

I got a bit weepy once more, and he whipped out another tissue in the blink of an eye.

"You're the bravest chick I know, Miss Annabelle," he said, with something that sounded like pride.

"You're pretty brave yourself." I sniffled, finding my smile again. "When everyone else ran away at the park, you jumped in to try to help. *You're* the hero, if you ask me."

"Aww, come on..." He was blushing now. "But anyway, the other people weren't all runnin' away. Most of 'em were runnin' to get help. The ambulance got there in five minutes, faster'n any ambulance *eva* moved in this town."

"Really?" I couldn't believe it. Would people ever stop surprising me?

"Yup. As soon as you passed out, the EMTs were there. They said your lung had collapsed, and this dude had to cut a hole in your side, between your ribs, to let air in and out. He did it right there on the grass, in the rain. It was sick." He grew a bit pale and his eyes glazed over as he remembered what must have been a grisly scene. "I thought you were dead. Luca was cryin' somethin' awful. I was too. Everybody was.

"I came right to the hospital, and you were in surgery for somethin' like eight hours. Dude was a mess. Luca, I mean. Then he wouldn't leave your room, not even for a minute, because he didn't want you to be alone when you woke up. The doctor kept sayin' 'if' you woke up, but he said 'when.' They'd barely been able to sew your parts back together, and the knife nicked the side of your heart, but he knew you'd live. He said you promised him."

Lamont couldn't seem to stop talking now that he had started, and I was hanging on every word.

"I offered to sit with you while he went to the bathroom. At first he said no, but then he musta really had to go. So I sat here and reminded you about that promise you made 'im, whatever it was, like he'd been doin', and just... well... kept you company, I guess."

Luca appeared in the doorway as Lamont was trailing off, and I felt as if my newly repaired heart would burst at the sight of both of them.

"Come here," I said to Lamont, as I pulled him into a hug. My chest and side screamed in searing agony in response, but I didn't care. "I am so lucky to have you," I told him, weeping openly now. I lifted my eyes to Luca's face as I added, "Both of you. You're both good men. The best. Don't you ever forget that, okay?"

Lamont nodded into my shoulder, and I could feel the wetness on his face as he wrapped his lanky, adolescent arms around me. Luca watched, standing tall and proud and content in the doorway, smiling as the flames danced in those beautiful emerald eyes.

"You made us that way," he said, in that scratchy, raspy voice that I loved. ""Don't *you* ever forget *that*."

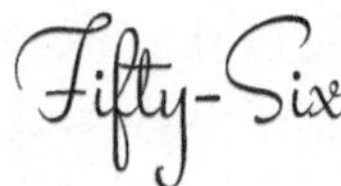

After all that had happened and all that we had tried to do to escape it, in the end, Luca and I decided to stay in Luthertown Heights.

I spent a few more days in the ICU, then I moved into Luca's apartment, where I spent my days admiring the garden of flowers he had painted for me as he nursed me back to health.

Lamont returned Luca's truck, and they both used it to move my bed frame into what was now "our place," so we no longer had to sleep on the floor. We filled the one-room apartment with furniture and flowers and my handwritten get well cards from the city; we burned that old rope from around Luca's neck and hung a new dreamcatcher from the hook it had once been tied to; and we made what had once been an empty, haunted place into a home.

Once I started to feel better, Luca spent the day teaching me how to paint (I was getting pretty good at those leaves, if I did say so myself), and we spent the nights wrapped up in each other, lost in love beneath the blanket of acrylic stars shining down on us from the ceiling above.

I had never known such happiness. Everything seemed so

perfect, so *right*, inside that apartment. Outside, though, was another story.

Although the four main gangs, for the most part, had respected the terms of the agreement we had drawn up in Luthertown Park that day, their truce hadn't lasted long. About a week after I left the hospital, one of the Creepers had caught a member of the Crips peering into their new sinkhole behind the morgue, and they had shoved him in.

This triggered a brief but bloody scuffle that lasted four days and left two Crips and one Creeper dead before the old men from the liquor store performed a drunken citizen's arrest and took the leaders of both gangs to the police station in the next town over.

More violence followed, but things were different this time. Yes, there were still murders and rapes and other cruel, vicious crimes, but the city was changing, slowly but surely. Luthertown Heights' residents no longer put up with these things; they no longer just considered themselves to be helpless bystanders, with no power to do anything but watch as the streets ran red with blood. They had a new strength now, and a new belief that they deserved something better than senseless squalor – and a determination that they were going to get it.

To put this new sense of duty into practice, they had formed a new community outreach program that someone had lovingly titled the "Safe Streets Initiative." On the first Monday of every month, the entire city was invited to meet at the YMCA gym to discuss crime and other issues over store-bought cookies and lemonade. They had wanted me to lead the group, but I had declined. I was flattered, but my crusading days were behind me for the time being. I much preferred to go back to keeping my students entertained after school and to live a calm, quiet life with the man I loved.

So, DeAndre had taken charge, and had proven, so far, to be a very good leader. For the first time in over a decade, he felt useful and vibrant again, and the city's citizens loved listening to the eloquent, intelligent thoughts and ideas he had been keeping to himself all that time. By the end of the committee's first meeting, he had organized a plan to petition the state for more and better police presence in Luthertown Heights and organized a drive to bring in donations to give Miss Carmella the best, most beautiful tombstone money could buy. He had even started book clubs for teens and single moms to give them a better sense of community.

So, even if they would probably never be perfect, things weren't so bad in Luthertown Heights as I made my way to the YMCA for the first time in six long, blissful weeks. The sun was shining as Luca and I walked, hand in hand, down the bustling streets, and I smiled as I waved to the guys at the liquor store and the daytime hookers on 6th.

"Hey there, Annabelle!" they called to me, grinning as they said the name I thought they would never learn.

"You are like a celebrity," Luca teased, nudging me with his elbow as we reached our destination.

I laughed, blushing, as I took in the painting of me he had made on the back door of the building before he had even really known me. It filled my heart with gladness and hope to see that it hadn't changed a bit in my absence, and Luca stooped to kiss my cheek as I reached out to touch it fondly.

"That is my favorite one," he told me, a smile in his raspy voice.

"Mine too," I agreed, grinning as I tilted my head back to kiss him on the lips.

"I think my new one might be a close second, though..."

"Your new one?"

His copper cheeks reddened as he turned the handle on the door and pulled it open. Gently, he put his hand on the small of my back and led me inside, where he flicked on the light, and I gasped.

Where my once dull, once grey, once lifeless classroom had once been, there was an entire art gallery of shapes and color and life, all cheering at me from every wall. There were children playing on swingsets, turtles and rabbits racing down winding dirt paths, ladybugs the size of dogs, dogs the size of horses, and flowers of every shape, color, and size imaginable. It was a child's dreams come to life: it was pure energy, pure excitement, pure joy, brought to life with bright yellows, bright blues, and warm oranges, reds, and greens. It was amazing, it was a happy childhood personified.

But there was one thing that stood out to me above all the rest.

As Luca turned to pull the door closed behind us, I saw a round, grinning face staring back at me. He was so happy, so full of little boy joy that I couldn't help but smile right back at him.

And, best of all, he was wearing his paper crown.

"You painted Marcus," I said, hugging Luca as I marveled at it, teary-eyed. "It's beautiful. It looks just like him!"

"I painted him on the back of the door," he said, wrapping his arm around my shoulders and kissing the top of my hair, "because I had painted you on the other side. Now you will be together always. Two parts of the same whole. Just like you and me."

I tried to stop the tears from spilling over. I tried to stop from beaming up at Luca. I tried to stop my heart from overflowing with love for that man and that boy and that town, but sometimes you just can't hold back the wind...

I hope you enjoyed reading these books as much as I enjoyed
writing them!

As you probably know, reviews from readers like you can mean the
difference between success and obscurity for authors like me. If
you have a moment, please consider sharing your thoughts about
this book on Amazon or your other favorite book review websites.
This would not only help me as a writer, but it would help other
readers in their search for their next book as well.

If you'd like to learn more about me and my books (or join my
mailing list and get updates, exclusive offers, and free content), visit
www.jessicascottromano.com.

Thank you for reading!

About the Author

Born in Louisville, Kentucky, Jessica Scott Romano has been writing since she was three years old. After reading far too many books about grand adventures in faraway places, she was inspired to go on a few of her own.

She now lives in Italy with her husband and two cats, where she spends her days writing, traveling, and sampling every delicious dish the country has to offer.

You can find Jessica online at www.jessicascottromano.com.

To learn more about her adventures in Italy, you can also visit her blog at www.anamericaninitaly.com.